FINE BLUE STEELE

A Daggers & Steele Mystery

ALEX P. BERG

BATDOG PRESS
KNOXVILLE, TN

Batdog Press
www.batdogpress.com

Publisher's Note: This is a work of fiction. Names, characters, places, and incidents portrayed in this novel are a product of the author's imagination.

Cover Art: Damon Za
Book Layout: ©2013 BookDesignTemplates.com

Fine Blue Steele/ Alex P. Berg — 1st ed.
ISBN 978-1-942274-13-1

1

I awoke to a gentle, syncopated knocking, coming from the direction of my front door.

Moaning in protest, I cracked an eyelid, only to be greeted by a field of white. For an instant I feared I'd passed into the spirit realm—at least until I felt the tickle of down against my nose. I shifted my head against the pillow and tried the other eye.

Wan light drifted through the slits in my window shutters, illuminating the confines of my bedchamber. A half-dozen meticulously-placed piles of dirty clothes dotted my floor like rumpled anthills, and my trusty antique dresser, covered in loose leaves of paper, empty mugs, and spare change, shot me a dusty smile from its half-open bottom drawer.

I groaned out a response, something along the lines of 'Geroffa mer fernt sherps,' but whoever was at the door either didn't hear me or didn't quite grasp the gist of my command. The knocking continued.

"Go away!" I shouted. "Whatever you're selling, I don't want any. And that goes doubly if you're proselytizers."

The knocker was unimpressed by the ferocity of my response. The knocking transformed into angry, heavy thumping that rattled my door in its frame. A familiar deep, gravelly voice accompanied the thumps and carried throughout my apartment.

"Open up, Daggers. We know you're in there."

I pried myself from my mattress's lumpy embrace, threw on a robe, headed to the front of my apartment, and yanked open the door.

Folton Quinto stood just outside the frame, filling the majority of my field of view. He wore a deep purple duster over his wide, muscular frame, making him look like the world's largest and meanest plum. Not that he looked particularly aggressive at the moment. In fact, he sported a wide grin on his face, one that showcased his collection of mismatched teeth. Something told me the big, grey-skinned lug wasn't too upset about waking me from my peaceful slumber.

"Nice coat," I said. "Where'd you pick it up? A five and dime? Or did you dye it yourself using expired box wine?"

Quinto opened his mouth to respond, but he wasn't quick enough.

"You're one to talk." My partner, detective Shay Steele, slipped around Quinto's side and positioned herself at the door frame's edge. "Have you seen yourself in a mirror, Jake? I mean...what is that? *Velour?*"

I spared a glance at my robe, which true to Steele's suspicions was, in fact, velour. And pink. And noticeably shorter than I would've hoped.

"I, uh...think this must be one of Nicole's old robes," I said. "I didn't exactly look closely when I threw it on."

Steele herself sported a sharp teal blazer with sleeves that left her forearms half uncovered, and a puffy yellow scarf wrapped itself around her neck. She'd chosen to pair the fashion-forward ensemble with a pair of dark denim jeans and a set of low-heeled lambskin leather boots that reached to mid-calf.

She lifted an eyebrow at me as she tucked a loose strand of hair behind one of her pointed elf ears. "Your ex-wife? Didn't you separate, what...three or four years ago?"

"Something like that." I wrapped the robe tighter around my body, suddenly feeling exposed.

"And you still haven't gotten rid of it?" she asked. "Or returned it to her? Or at the very least picked it up off your floor?"

"Don't give me that," I said. "I've been busy. Swamped with case work. You know how it is."

Shay snickered, her azure eyes twinkling with mirth. She shook her head in disbelief, which set her chocolate brown hair to bouncing—hair held in a jaw clip at the back of her head and that, if I wasn't mistaken, had been recently curled. Hence, the bounce.

"Yeah," chuckled Quinto. "You've been *so* busy working, we couldn't even find you at the precinct. We figured you must've collapsed on the way there under the weight of all that responsibility. Imagine our surprise to find you here."

I frowned. "Is there a reason the two of you are here at the crack of dawn?"

"It's seven thirty," corrected Steele.

"As I said. The crack of dawn. Or at least at certain times of year...in certain portions of the world."

"You're a smart guy," said Quinto, the grin still on his face. "I'll give you one guess."

"Someone croaked?" I said.

Quinto elbowed Steele. "Told you he'd figure it out."

I turned my eyes to Shay. "Implying you *didn't* think I'd figure that out?"

"I'm going to invoke my right against self-incrimination," said Steele with a smile.

I shivered as some of the chill hallway air crept under my robe and in the direction of my tender bits. I jerked my head toward the interior of my apartment. "Well, no need for the two of you to stand out there forever. Might as well come in while I make myself presentable."

"Or at least attempt to," said Quinto as he barged past me.

Shay gave me a curious look, but after a hint of hesitation, she too entered. As I closed the front door, I tried to ferret out the motives behind her glance, but in my foggy, wee-hours-of-the-morning-induced state, the best I could think of was that she might be offering me an opportunity to clean up—and in all likelihood, I should've. The clutter plaguing my bedroom had emigrated to other parts of my flat, as well, though the infestation wasn't quite as bad.

At least I knew the smell inside was pleasant. I'd been attuned to that ever since evicting the cats that had populated my apartment before I'd moved in. Their stink took an entire year to displace, and so now I always made sure to have a healthy supply of candles and fragrant oils on hand.

I shooed Quinto and Shay in the direction of the blue-corduroy covered loveseat and lounge chair combination in my living room. "Make yourselves comfortable. I'd offer you two coffee, but I know neither of you are drinkers."

"You have coffee on hand?" asked Quinto.

"I should," I said as I returned to my bedroom. "At least I did."

The walls muffled Quinto's snort, as well as his response of "Maybe sometime last year..."

"I heard that," I called.

I checked my closet to see if I'd hung any of my clothes, but after coming face to face with a barren garment rack and the bare wall behind it, I delved into the nearest wrinkled pile in search of a clean shirt and a functional pair of pants.

"Nice place, Daggers," said Shay, her voice muted. "Needs a few finishing touches, but overall it's not bad. You'll, uh...have to give me the tour sometime."

I froze, up to my elbows in cotton and twill. *Of course!* I wanted to slap myself.

Shay had never set foot in my apartment before! Given the way our relationship had been progressing, one of us was certain to visit the other's place sooner or later—I know I'd fantasized about it on more than one occasion—but I couldn't imagine either of us thought the experience would include me, mumbling, bleary-eyed, and with my two hundred and ten pounds of bulk stuffed into an undersized pink bathrobe. Certainly if Shay had, she was far kinkier than she let on.

I sighed. Shay and I had started to spend much more time together, including a fair amount of time alone. At dinner. On walks. Chatting over coffee—or tea, in Shay's case. And we'd exorcised the dreaded dating demons. Neither of us was afraid of the 'd' word anymore, even if we didn't use it particularly often. But that didn't mean our relationship was evolving anywhere near as quickly as I'd hoped it would.

For all the growth between me and Shay, a couple of walls still loomed between us. One of those was physical. We'd shared a few benign hugs, and Shay had even pecked me on the cheek once or twice, but that was the extent of our amorous activities.

Much of the fault in that area was mine. I'd never really made any moves, but how could I when I couldn't even convince myself she found me attractive? After all, why would she? Nearly ten years her senior, weathered and beaten, with touches of premature grey starting to fleck my umber-colored hair? And in the few moments where I mustered the courage to do anything, it always seemed as if there was someone hanging over our shoulders with a disapproving frown, most notably the Captain—who still didn't know about the extent of Steele's psychic powers, much less our budding romance.

The Captain, and everyone else around the office, comprised the bulk of the second wall. I liked Shay, and I was fairly sure she liked me back—even if neither of us had gone so far as to voice such brash thoughts out loud—but should our relationship become too one-sided, or if we were to embark on an affair that quickly turned into a raging dumpster fire, what would happen to our careers? As a divorced father of one, I couldn't jeopardize my employment for financial reasons, but it went beyond that. Shay and I now ran with the same circle of friends—Quinto, Rodgers, and Cairny, to name a few. What would happen to those friendships should something blossom between Shay and me only for it to wither and die shortly thereafter?

I'd have to ask Quinto how he and our resident coroner Cairny were dealing with the same issues, but for the time being, I tried to switch my caravan of thought to the other member of our crew.

"So where's our fair-haired co-detective?" I called as I extracted a pair of tan slacks from the pile of clothes before me.

"Rodgers?" came Quinto's voice from around the corner. "Not sure. He hadn't arrived at the office when we left."

"Probably because he's at home, sleeping, like most other reasonable humanoids are doing," I said.

"You know he has two little kids, right?" said Quinto. "He may be at home still, but I guarantee you he's not sleeping."

I grumbled as I disrobed—literally—and stepped into the pants. "So fill me in on today's case. What do we know?"

"Not much," said Steele. "A body was found in the Delta district. Male, mid thirties. Well...not a body, really. The guy was alive but bled out before police arrived on the scene. Witnesses reported yelling and confusion, but we don't know a whole lot more than that."

I donned a shirt miraculously free of both stains and unappealing earthy fragrances before joining my partner and Quinto in the living room.

The walking brick wall took up at least two-thirds of the love seat, his duster clashing horribly with the upholstery.

"You ready?" he asked.

"Almost." I snagged my worn leather jacket from a brass rack in the corner of the room and shrugged into it. I patted the interior coat pocket and felt a hard eighteen-inch piece of steel battle back against my rough touch.

"How's Daisy?" asked Steele.

"Hale and hearty as always," I said.

Shay rolled her eyes. She'd repeatedly informed me my make-believe relationship with my nightstick was not, in fact, adorable but rather irritating and, for lack of a better word, *creepy*. So far, I'd successfully ignored her. My anthropomorphization of Daisy was one of the few things that made me uniquely *me*, and no amount of Shay's influence would ever change that...*would it?*

I blinked and jerked my thumb toward the door. "Come on. Let's head out before the stiff gets any stiffer than he already is."

2

Before heading out to the crime scene, we stopped at a breakfast cart near my place. There, I purchased a cinnamon chip scone and had the owner fill a thermos I'd snagged from my apartment with piping hot coffee. Black, of course.

As we waited for the chefpreneur to make change for my silver eagle, a chill wind whipped up the street, carrying with it hints of the night's cleansing rains. It prickled the skin at the nape of my neck, but I resisted the urge to grumble. It was a well known fact the gods held little sympathy for whiners, especially those who forgot their gloves at home. I wondered if I should go back for them, but if Steele could survive the day with half her forearms exposed to the elements, then surely I could get by under my well-loved coat's caress. Plus, I'd purchased enough coffee to poach a dozen eggs in.

After I'd scarfed my breakfast and collected my pick-me-up, we hoofed it to the 5th Street Precinct and headed to the Delta district, which was situated north of the station despite the fact that the river Earl's delta lay to the southeast.

While I've never held the city's planners in high regard, even they weren't stupid enough to overlook the obvious geographical discrepancy. Rather, the 'Delta' designation was a popular nickname. A corruption of the district's most prominent feature—the joint Department of Emigration and Immigration and Transit Authority building, or DEITA. Given the city's widespread illiteracy problems, I suppose people could be forgiven for mistaking the uppercase 'I' for a lowercase 'l'.

While the DEITA building first and foremost served as a transportation center—dozens of boats arrived and set sail from its docks every day—its poor reputation came primarily from the DEI's side of things. Every immigrant arriving in New Welwic by boat, either coming down the Earl or up through the Wel Sea, was by law forced to stop at the DEITA station for processing, and given the speed of government employees, this often resulted in lines that stretched for hours, zigzagging back and forth through runs constructed of thick iron bars more suited to herding cattle than humanoids.

Pragmatic reasons existed for the processing, of course. DEI agents checked immigrants for visible health problems and mental disorders, as well as making sure they had some level of cash on hand to make sure they weren't likely to become part of the 'public charge.' And, most importantly, every human, elf, dwarf, goblin, ogre, or what have you was fingerprinted and supplied a with a shiny new identification card, free of charge, thanks to the fine folks over at Taxation and Revenue.

The neighborhoods surrounding the DEITA building were collectively known as the Delta district, and the businesses there catered to the diverse needs of the immigrants setting foot off the boats and barges.

Basically, there were lots of churches and bars.

I stifled a yawn as we reached a crowd of gawkers at what I assumed must be the crime scene. To my right loomed a tall, ostentatious structure that harbored a canopy of leafy green shrubbery on its roof, and to my left, separated from the tall building by an alley, was a shuttered bar with a faded sign overhead that read 'Lucky Baldwin's.' Apparently, Baldwin had needed a little less luck and a little more business acumen.

A young, clean cut beat cop extricated himself from the throng and approached us, a smile plastered across his face.

"Detectives. Daggers. Steele. Quinto. How are you this morning?"

"I'll be fine once I polish off this." I hefted my thermos. "How about you, Phillips? You seem surprisingly chipper."

Phillips beamed at the mention of his name. I'd struggled with it at first, but after the sixth or seventh time he'd helped us wrangle a crime scene, the moniker had finally stuck. Now I only had about another hundred or so beat cops to go.

"I get excited whenever we find a body," said Phillips. "I know I shouldn't say that, but it's true."

Phillips fancied himself a detective in training, but I had my doubts about him. He wasn't the most observant chap, but on the bright side, he was smart enough to make sure nobody touched anything until the cavalry arrived.

"It's all part of the gig," said Quinto. "Don't worry. You'd be surprised by the things that excite Daggers."

I raised an eyebrow. "Remind me. Back at my place...what closets of mine were you snooping in, exactly?"

Steele extinguished our lively banter with a flick of her hand. "Why don't you bring us up to date, Phillips?"

"It's easier if I show you, detectives," he said. "Follow me."

Phillips enacted his best Quinto impersonation and shouldered his way through the crowd, maneuvering us past a ring of bluecoats keeping onlookers at bay. Inside their circle, a man lay facedown in the dirt, a sticky, half-dried mass of blood pooled around his head. A trio of individuals in tan fatigues sat against the walls on either side of the alley, two on one side and one on the other.

"So, here's what we know," said Phillips. "A few people reported hearing yelling near this alley in the early morning hours. The next thing anybody knows, this guy was lying dead here in the dirt. Our only witnesses on the scene are the three service members you see here. That over there is Sergeant Tim Holmes."

I followed Phillips' finger to the GI left of the alley, a guy with light brown hair, an army-issue buzz cut, and a nose that bent noticeably to the side. He sat on the ground with his knees up and his arms resting atop them, but even seated I could tell he was tall—perhaps my height—and his muscles bulged under a shirt that probably could've stood to be a size larger.

Phillips continued. "Over on that side are Private Drake Delvesdeep and PFC Kelly Chavez."

I glanced at them, too. Both sat in similar positions as Sergeant Holmes, with their arms over their knees. Drake, who sported short black hair to go along with a matching beard, hung his head and stared at the ground, while Kelly, who styled her hair in a bob, held her head high and clenched her jaw. Kelly spotted me looking at her and whispered something to Drake, who lifted his head and glanced at us in return. In addition to his thick beard, Private Delvesdeep had a wide nose. Given that, his relatively short stature, and his name, I guessed he possessed some dwarven lineage.

Something finally clicked in my mind. "Wait...they have women in the army now?"

Steele shrugged. "Yeah."

"Since when?" I asked.

"I don't know," she said. "Six months ago? The legislation passed late last year."

"Quinto, did you know about this?" I asked.

The big guy scratched his head in thought.

"Just say yes," I said. "Make me feel less ignorant."

"Ok," said Quinto. "Sure."

What an ambiguous answer. Sure, he did know? Or sure, he agreed with me? Either way, I let it slide as I knelt by the body. "What else do you know, Phillips?"

"Not much," said the eager beaver beat cop. "The army crew contends the dead guy—well, he was alive at the time, but you know what I mean—accosted them in the alley and bled out shortly thereafter. We didn't touch the body, and we've expended most of our efforts making sure none of our witnesses wandered off."

I passed my eyes over the stiff. He wore a pair of moth-eaten pants and a threadbare coat that hung limply over his large frame. His hair was long and matted, both from a clear lack of personal hygiene as well as from the dried blood that now infused it. I couldn't make out much of his face, partly as it was pressed into the dirt but also because it was hidden behind a bushy beard that ran from his cheeks all the way down to mid neck.

Shay knelt beside me. "Looks like blunt force trauma to the back of the head."

I nodded my agreement. A portion of the guy's skull a couple fingers wide caved in awkwardly. Coagulated blood and tangled hair marred the wound, but I thought I caught a glimpse of white within it. Skull fragments, I guessed.

"Probably a transient," said Quinto, stuffing his hands in his pockets. "Not too surprising, given the area."

Despite the DEI's best efforts, some immigrants who arrived through the port failed to find work. Many of them made it no farther than a few blocks from the DE-ITA station's exit before taking up panhandling bowls.

"Give me a hand, Quinto," I said. "Let's turn him over."

I grunted as we flipped the dude, and after a cursory examination of his pockets, I came to the conclusion that the effort had been wasted. I found absolutely nothing on him. No cash. No identification. Not even so much as a ball of lint. Apparently the guy had pawned it all in exchange for a better spot in line at the soup kitchen. I did notice a few scrapes and cuts on his hands and face, though the mud that caked him hid any possible bruising.

I stood and dusted my hands on my pants. "Alright. Well, I don't think we're going to get a whole lot more from this corpse until Cairny gets her hands on him. Why don't we split up and interview the witnesses, one on one? I'll take Sergeant Timmy over there. Steele, you take Kelly, and Quinto, take Drake. Make sure to pay attention so we can compare notes afterwards. Sound good?"

Quinto and Steele nodded, and we all got to work.

3

The army sergeant picked himself off the ground as I approached, grimacing as he did so. I glanced at the chevrons on his shirtsleeve to convince myself I'd picked the right guy, but as I did so, I noticed a few other things as well.

A number of blood splatters pockmarked his shirt, as well a cluster of larger stains on his shoulder that resembled a handprint. Another swipe of dried blood crusted his shirtsleeve—possibly from a cut above his eye. I noticed the gash more from its puffiness than the cut itself, which was largely hidden by the man's bushy eyebrows. A nice bruise also sprouted underneath his eye.

"You Sergeant Holmes?" I asked.

He nodded and cracked his neck. "Yeah, that's right. Buck sergeant Timothy Holmes. 3rd infantry division, 1st battalion, 2nd squadron."

I waved a hand as I produced a spiral-bound notepad from one of my interior coat pockets. "Don't bother. All that army jargon is going to go over my head. Your name is enough. So I understand you and Drake and Kelly over there...what are they? Your troop mates? Squad mates?"

"Squad," said Tim.

"Right. I understand you and your squad had a run-in with this guy last night." I used the pencil I'd liberated from the notepad's spiral to point at the stiff. "Why don't you tell me exactly what happened? And start at the beginning please."

Tim rubbed his shoulder. "Right. Well, me and Drake and uh...Kelly, we had some leave time, so we went out for drinks."

"Hold on," I said. "Quick question. Are you guys situated at the local base? What's it called? New Welwic Main?" I pictured it in my head. It couldn't be more than a fifteen or twenty minute walk from the Delta district.

Tim nodded. "Yeah. That's right. And we are. Anyway, we didn't plan on staying out all night, but our outing turned into a bit of a bar crawl."

"Where did you go?" I asked.

Tim rattled off some names. I noted them in my pad, then nodded for him to continue.

"Right," said Tim. "So at the end of the night, we finally start to head home. We're all pretty drunk at this point, and we stop by this alley here."

The alcohol fumes rolling off the guy's tongue were a testament to his narrative. I suspected the muscular sergeant was *still* drunk, but witnessing a man's death had sobered him up somewhat.

"What time was this?" I asked.

"I really couldn't tell you," said Tim. "Before sunrise. Maybe five? Five–thirty?"

I made another note. "Ok. Keep going."

"Well, I went into the alley to relieve myself—"

"No need for euphemisms," I said. "You won't offend me. I'm a homicide cop, you know."

Tim looked at me blankly. I suddenly felt like between his exhaustion, drunkenness, shock, and overall army bone-headedness, I might be pushing my luck with my iterative interrogation strategy.

"How about I hold my tongue and let you finish?" I said.

Tim nodded and continued. "Sure. So I go into this alley to pee. Which I do. But everything's slick from the rain, and when I turn to go back to the street, I slip and fall, hitting my face."

Tim gestured to the bruise under his eye. I lifted an eyebrow, but true to my word, I didn't interrupt.

"Like I said, I was pretty drunk," said Tim. "Anyway, Drake and Kelly must've heard me fall, because they came in after me. They helped me up. And as they're doing that, we hear a yell. Real shrill. And loud, too. And then the next thing we know, this guy—" He pointed at the stiff. "—comes barreling out of the dark toward us. He's screaming bloody murder, but it's all nonsense. Gibberish. And he's stumbling. He almost falls over, but he grabs me for support." Tim pointed to the bloodstain on his shoulder. "And that's when I felt it. The wetness on my shirt. It was blood. His blood. I couldn't see it at first because it was so dark. But I guessed there must've been a lot of it, and I was right.

"We tried to help the guy, but he didn't want anything to do with us. Just wanted to get out of there, I guess. But he couldn't walk very well. He stumbles again and bounces off the wall. Takes a few more lurching steps and falls down, right there at the mouth of the alley. Drake and I checked on him, and he still had a pulse, but he'd gone unconscious and was bleeding badly. Someone at that bar over there—" He pointed across the street. "—sent a runner for help, I think. But by the time anyone got here, the guy was dead."

I tapped my pencil against my note pad as I thought. "You have any idea who the guy is?"

Tim shook his head. "None."

"Did he have anything on him when he died?"

"I didn't rifle through his pockets if that's what you're asking," said Tim. "The only times I touched him were to try to keep him from falling over and to check his pulse."

"And you say he came from somewhere up the alley?"

Tim nodded.

I replaced my notepad and pencil in my interior coat pocket, then extracted the thermos protruding from the pocket at my side. I unscrewed the cap, poured myself some joe, and took a sip. Still hot, but no longer scalding.

Tim gave me a narrow-eyed sort of look. "Well? Are we done here? Can I go?"

"Not yet," I said. "I need to talk things over with my fellow detectives."

"I don't think you understand," he said. "Command will not be pleased with my absence. I was supposed to be back by oh-eight hundred."

I ignored his plea and took another sip of coffee before gesturing at his face. "That, uh...must've been some fall. Are there rocks in that alley or something?"

Tim's eyes narrowed further. "What are you trying to say?"

"Just wondering if you might want to revisit that part of your story."

Tim's tight-lipped snarl said he didn't.

"Very well," I said. "Hang tight, then, Sergeant. I'll be back."

4

I had to wait a few moments for Steele and Quinto to finish questioning their charges, so I filled the time by pouring more coffee down my gullet, but only one cup. Any more than that and I might soon be the one in the alley relieving myself, and I wouldn't want to 'slip and fall' in a puddle.

I glanced at Shay as she continued to interview PFC Chavez. The curl job my partner had inflicted on her hair had given it some much needed body, and the teal jacket she wore did a fair job of doing the same for her waist and hips.

Beautiful Shay might've been, but curvaceous she was not. It still amazed me how much her influence alone had changed my tastes in women. I'd always found my eyes straying to the parts of ladies that stuck out the most. Even as far back as grade school, I'd joked to my instructors that I'd rather score a pair of D's than A's any day. And although my love for the greatest of female organs would never fade, Shay had at least shifted my perspective. The elegance and grace of her long, lean form were second to none—although for work-related reasons, I still felt she'd be prudent to add some extra muscle to her frame.

I thought I caught a glimpse of Phillips staring at me as I stared at my partner, so I forced my eyes from Shay's slender backside over to the female army recruit. She wasn't anywhere near as attractive as my partner, but thankfully my peepers weren't put to waste. As I inspected her fatigues, I noticed a few telltale signs that had previously escaped my attention. With the new knowledge in hand, I glanced at Drake and made a few more mental notes.

Eventually, Steele and Quinto returned.

"Took you two long enough," I said.

"Apparently we're more thorough than you," said Steele.

"Not a chance," I said. "I'm just abnormally efficient in processing information."

Quinto grunted. "Unless said information is in regard to the color, size, and shape of a bathrobe that you throw on to answer the door."

Shay snickered.

"Give it a rest," I said. "I was half-asleep. So, give me the run down. What did Kelly and Drake have to say?"

"Well," said Steele as she crossed her arms, "Kelly's story goes something like this. She and Drake went out for drinks last night at the suggestion of Sergeant Holmes, who thought it might be a good team building exercise."

"Squad," I said. "But go on."

"What's the difference?" asked Steele.

"I have no idea," I said. "But Tim does. You could talk to him if you want the details. I don't recommend it, though. He's not super friendly."

Shay raised an eyebrow. "Right. Anyway, Kelly says they all had too much to drink and stayed out way too late. At the end of the night, they started to head back to their base and stopped at this alley because Sergeant Holmes had to pee. Holmes went into the alley, and she and Drake waited here at the mouth. Then they heard a thump and went to investigate. Apparently, Tim had fallen. They helped him up, but as they did so, a crazy guy—" She pointed at the corpse. "—ran out of the dark yelling and screaming. They tried to get him to slow down and make sense, but he bounced around like a pixie in a pickle jar before eventually collapsing in the mud. They tried to resuscitate him, but without success."

I nodded to Quinto. "And what did your guy say?"

"The same thing, basically," he said.

I snorted. "Well, at least they were smart enough to get their story straight before talking to us."

"I take it you don't believe them?" said Steele.

"Are you kidding?" I said. "Have a look at Sergeant Timmy over there. He has a gash above his eye that requires medical attention, and that bruise on his cheek is going to look spectacular in a few hours. In addition to that, he moved as if he got put through a meat grinder. Now, you tell me. A big, strong guy like that...you think he suffered those injuries from a fall?"

"Not unless he fell off the roof of this thing." Quinto jerked his thumb at the tall, leaf-topped building at our backs.

"Exactly," I said. "Steele, you're observant. Did you notice anything about Kelly? Was there anything she didn't mention?"

"You want the emotional or the physical?" she asked.

"Um...why not both?" I said.

"She's pissed," said Steele. "Part of it is her personality, I think. She seems like a no-nonsense kind of gal—which she'd have to be as one of the army's first female recruits. But there's something else there, too. A resentment. And pain—but of the emotional variety."

I recalled Steele's first day on the job. Her attitude, her hard exterior, her fiery demeanor. As the precinct's first female homicide detective, she'd carried a similar burden on her shoulders as PFC Chavez. I could only imagine the pressure she felt. Proving one's own worth was hard enough, let alone trying to carry a flag for an entire race or gender at the same time. Hopefully, Quinto, Rodgers, Cairny, and I had lightened the load for her somewhat through our evolving friendships.

Steele continued. "On the physical side of things, she has a couple tears in her fatigues. One on the side of her shirt, another on the inner thigh of her pants, which she was trying her best to hide. And she's missing a couple buttons."

That's what I'd been looking for, though I'd only noticed the buttons and the tear in her shirt. "Now, I don't know a ton about the army, but I do know they're sticklers for proper dress. I can't imagine they'd stand for sloppiness of that nature. Quinto, what can you tell me about Drake?"

Quinto shrugged. "He's quiet. Reserved. Didn't seem particularly comfortable talking to me."

"I was looking for more physical cues," I said.

Shay answered for him. "He's bruised, too. Hard to see under his beard, but it's there. And his hands are swollen."

"Right," I said. "Now take another look at our formerly-breathing vagrant friend on the ground here. Remember what you said about how he died?"

"By blunt force trauma," said Steele.

"You see where I'm going with this?" I asked.

Steele nodded. "Yeah. I was more of less coming to the same conclusion myself."

I eyed Quinto. He looked back at me blankly, then at Steele, who gave him a double eyebrow raise.

The big guy eyed my thermos, which stuck out of my coat pocket, and frowned. "Her, I've come to expect this out of, but you, Daggers? What in the world did your guy use to brew your drink?"

"Just coffee beans, to my knowledge," I said. "But that's enough. It's a miracle drug, I swear. Want some?"

"No thanks," he said. "I'll settle for an explanation of whatever it is you two are thinking."

"Alright," I said. "Let's assume much of what of what our three GIs said was true. But what if, instead of Tim heading into that alley to pee, it was Kelly who had to go instead. Or perhaps they all had to go, but Tim and Drake went first and Kelly second."

"Which brings us to the dead man," said Steele. "I think we're all in agreement he was a vagrant. Chances are he lived in this alley, or at least spent last night here. Then he sees Kelly wander in. Alone. She drops her pants, and his baser instincts take over. He tries to cop a feel, or perhaps worse. I'm guessing the latter, based on the tears in Kelly's clothes. But Kelly fights back, and she screams, bringing Tim and Drake running."

"Exactly," I said. "Her two buddies figure they'll teach the bum a lesson, so they start to wail on the guy. But he's big, and they're drunk, and he fights back. The sexually deviant hobo gets a few good licks in on Tim before the tide starts to turn. And now Tim and Drake are *really* pissed, and they go to town on the guy. Deliver an epic beating. A little *too* epic."

Quinto rubbed his chin. "And the guys dies. Yeah, it's plausible for sure. But it's just a theory. We'll need solid evidence if we want to put a case together."

"Well it sounds as if there were other witnesses," said Steele. "They may not have seen what happened, but they may have heard something. And there's the issue of a murder weapon..."

I nodded. "Yeah. Cairny might be able to prove otherwise, but it does look like they beaned the guy with something." I drummed my fingers on my chin. "Maybe we should check the alley? If there's a weapon, it could still be there."

Steele and Quinto voiced their agreement, and we wandered into the dimly lit muck.

5

Back in the halcyon days of my youth, the city embarked on a fairly serious campaign to rid New Welwic of homelessness. Tens if not hundreds of thousands of crowns were raised through new taxes and private donations to help solve the problem, but in the grand wisdom of political groupthink, it was decided that said monies wouldn't be used to fund meal centers, half-way houses, and vocational facilities where the homeless could learn skills that would help them feed and house themselves. Instead, the crowns were spent in the hire of teams of roving mercenaries who would impound the homeless, load them onto carts, and drive them into the countryside where they'd be unceremoniously dumped.

The plan had only a couple minor problems. The first was that the homeless, despite their excessive quantities of hair and dubious aromas, were a crafty folk. They realized they had appendages attached to their hips, known as legs, that would allow them to walk back to the city. The second problem was that the city hall-sanctioned thugs roaming the streets realized their pay would cease as soon as the hobo infestation cleared, so they began to drop off the impounded bums closer and closer to the city to ensure their continued employment.

Of course, the city eventually caught word of the scam, so they cancelled the program altogether, which only made things worse because the majority of the mercenaries then joined the ranks of the homeless.

I wrinkled my nose as I walked into the alley, greeted by the ever-too-familiar aroma of stale urine. It was at times like these I wished the city's efforts to eradicate the homeless had succeeded, but then again, if our nation's finest couldn't even be counted on not to relieve themselves against lonely brick walls, what did it matter?

I heard a rustling, and a couple street people at the far end of the alley made themselves scarce, darting into a cross street. I grunted. We might have to round them up later. One of them might've seen or heard something of significance.

At my side, Shay dropped to one knee to inspect a wall. A mask of impassiveness shadowed her face, which was no small feat given her sense of smell was notably better than mine.

"I don't think you're going to find the murder weapon embedded in that abandoned bar's exterior grout," I said.

Steele ignored my jab. "Seeing as we're dealing with red brick, I'll forgive you for not noticing, but there are blood splatters here."

I leaned forward to get a better look, but I honestly couldn't make out a thing. I did notice a patch of dirt at my feet that seemed darker than those surrounding it, though. "I'll have to take your word for it."

Shay leaned over to a scuff mark on the wall and gave it a rub with her thumb. I walked over to a collection of trashcans, where I found Quinto standing, staring at them, with his hands on his hips.

I clapped the big guy on the back. "Ah, the joys of police work. Am I right, old friend?"

"Yeah," rumbled Quinto. "Nothing gives me more joy than sifting through piles of stinking refuse in search of bloody instruments of death."

I grabbed a can and tipped it over, spilling its guts all over the alley floor.

"Hey, Steele," I called. "You going to come over and help?"

"Sorry," she said, her voice oddly melodious. "I'm busy with these scuff marks at the moment. Besides, my elite observational abilities would be wasted digging through trash."

I couldn't see her face as she had it pressed against the wall, but I was sure she sported a malicious grin.

Quinto snorted and adopted a similar smile as he dumped another can's contents on the ground. "I think she means our skills, on the other hand, are ideally suited to rifling through garbage."

"Hey, I can live with that," I said. "It means I have job security. There's always a demand for guys like me. Guys willing to get dirty in the line of duty."

I dug Daisy out of the interior of my coat and gingerly used her to poke through the trash, making sure to keep my fingers clear of the gross rubbish.

Quinto shook his head. "Have you ever looked up 'hypocrite' in the dictionary?"

"There aren't any pictures, if that's what you're getting at," I said. "I learned that early on in life while looking up 'gullible.'"

The big lug nodded at my nightstick. "How's Daisy feel about being used in such denigrating fashion?"

"She knew what she was getting into when I liberated her from that construction site all those years back," I said. "Besides, it's not the worst thing she's been subjected to."

"*Creepy*," said Steele in a high, undulating voice.

Right. I shut my yapper and kept sifting. Amidst the refuse, I found plenty of the usual: old newspapers, spoiled food, a few tattered rags that might've once been clothes, crumpled flyers for local bars and peep joints, and a rat that was very much alive and unhappy about its current housing situation. But there were also some oddities: the cracked remnants of a ceramic vase, a bent metal plate that looked as if it had served one too many tours of duty, and a fair amount of ashes, either from wood or charcoal. The latter wasn't particularly odd, except for the fact that the spent fuel emitted an interesting aroma. A floral one, and not unpleasant. Considering the alternative, I didn't complain.

Quinto finished sifting though his share of the garbage, and despite his mockery, I'd noticed he'd primarily used his feet. *Who's the hypocrite now, big guy?*

"Find anything?" I asked.

"Not really," he said. "You?"

I shook my head. "Not unless you count the remains of this vase, and I don't think Tim or Drake asked their assailant for a break, dug around in the trash for an urn, smacked the hobo over the head with it, and then stashed the scraps."

"Probably couldn't have killed anyone with it anyway," said Steele as she wandered over.

"You done with your inspection?" I asked.

"Just finished," she said.

"How convenient."

Shay flashed that malicious grin I was sure she'd been wearing before. She shrugged in response.

"So did you glean anything from your endeavors that us plebeians couldn't have?" I asked.

"The blood I showed you is recent, no doubt about it," said Steele. "The spray pattern indicates someone was hit, not that someone fell. And while I did find scuff marks on the brick, I didn't see any that could've been left due to an impact with Sergeant Holmes' face."

"So, basically," I said, "you confirmed our suspicions."

"Someone needed to," she said.

"Quinto's confusion not withstanding, I felt they were rather obvious."

"Says the man with trash juice on his shoes." Shay's eyes twinkled.

I grumbled and took another look around me. The hobos at the end of the alley had smartly chosen not to return. At the cross street where they'd disappeared, smoke puffed from a chimney in the back of a building. Above me, high on the second floor of the ostentatious building with the leafy topping, a few windows stood open to the elements.

I turned toward the mouth of the alley and called out. "Phillips! Hey, Phillips!"

The clean cut young chap popped his head in and ran over. "Yes, sir, Detective. Any leads?"

It wasn't any of his business, but I could understand his curiosity. "Not so much. You said there were witnesses from the bar across the street? That heard fighting?"

"That's right," said Phillips. "I think they're still here, chatting with Gorman or Poundstone."

"Good. And what about these two buildings?" I indicated them with my thumb.

"Um...I think this big one's a church," said Phillips. "And the one that backs into the alley...a bar, maybe?"

"You're a paragon of knowledge, Phillips," I said.

The kid looked at me blankly. "Um...what sir?"

"Never mind," I said. "Quinto, why don't you go see what you can wring out of those barflies? Steele, you're with me, as always. Let's flex our vocal muscles and see what else we can learn about the events of last night."

6

Steele and I pushed our way through the wide double doors gracing the front of the church. As they closed behind us, I stopped, craned my neck to the sky, and stared.

"Well," I said. "I did *not* expect that."

Apparently, my initial characterization of the church as having shrubbery growing on its roof was grossly inaccurate. The shrubbery *was* the roof. Centenarian trees sprouted from the floor of the church, stretching their boughs up, up, up toward the sky. Dense clusters of leaves, some of them orange and yellow but many still green despite the oncoming cold, blocked our view of the sun and spilled over the church's exterior walls.

Heavy vines, also thick with leaves, wrapped themselves around the tree trunks and boughs. They wandered across cables that had been hung from the top branches of the trees and crept onto the thick, unfinished wood columns lining the sides of the common area, adding a muted brushstroke of bluish-green to the space.

The floor was of packed dirt rather than tile or stone, and although a cluster of two dozen rough, wooden benches surrounded an open area on the far side of the church, the majority of the building's interior was pockmarked with much smaller gathering spaces—circles of brick, recessed into the earth, where people might sit and dangle their legs. If only they'd had a fire pit in the center, I could've envisioned myself rubbing shoulders with Shay at one, drinking a beer and toasting marshmallows.

"This place seems right up your alley," I said to Steele.

She gave me a furrowed brow sort of look. "I'm no more religiously inclined than you are, Daggers."

"Yeah, but this place is so open," I said. "So airy and natural. So very...*elven.*"

Shay's look deviated not one whit. "I grew up in a small apartment in midtown. The nearest park was four blocks away."

"So you're telling me you don't feel any connection to the trees?"

"We had a bonsai in our living room," said Shay. "I liked it. It was cute."

A stone path meandered around the church interior, eventually making its way to the cluster of benches at the backside, though it did so with no sense of haste whatsoever. I strolled across it as I continued to gaze upon the interior. A number of worshipers sat at the organically distributed stone circles, though upon further inspection, many of them appeared to be curled in balls, sleeping. More hobos, based on their attire. Churches always attracted them in droves, but given this particular chapel's lack of a solid roof, I wasn't sure I understood the appeal.

Before we'd made it halfway along the path, a couple of men materialized from a doorway set in the wall not far from the benches and approached us. I pegged the first of the pair as in his mid-fifties. Wavy, salt-and-pepper hair swept across his temple and over his ears, pairing nicely with the pale grey frock that reached to the tops of his shoes. He walked with a slight limp, but his cornflower blue eyes seemed as bright and healthy as those of a man twenty years younger.

Behind the older gentleman followed a tall and thin adolescent. *Exceptionally* tall. I'd wager he had me beat by at least a foot. His long arms hung at his sides, capped with hands the size of frying pans, and his sandal-clad feet would've fit comfortably in clown shoes. Angry, red acne dotted his face. Between that, his gangly build, and an outdated bowl cut, I gathered he probably wasn't beating young ladies off with a stick.

"Good morning, pilgrims," said the elder statesman as he neared, "and welcome to the warm embrace of the divine. May the strength of nature course through your veins and fill you with the spirit of the everlasting."

Oh boy. Here we go...

I waved a dismissive hand at the pastor. "I'm sorry, but we're not here for your insights into life, death, and the grand purpose of the cosmos."

"Oh?" The man lifted a brow. "Do you need a place to rest your weary heads? Or a hot meal, perchance?"

Ah. Food. That would explain the hobos.

"No, thank you," said Steele with more grace than I could've mustered. "We're here for information, actually.

I'm Detective Steele, and this is Detective Daggers. We're with the NWPD."

"I see." The man clasped his hands and dropped them to his lap. "Well, I'm Pastor Bellamy. Julian Bellamy. What brings you to the Church of the Divine Rebirth?"

"Church of the Divine Rebirth?" I asked.

I regretted the question as soon as it left my lips. Bellamy launched into a well-rehearsed spiel.

"The Divine Rebirth is an idea as old as civilization, as old as nature, as old as time itself. We followers of the Divine Rebirth believe in a cyclicality in all things. Wealth and poverty. Bounty and famine. Wetness and drought. But most importantly, we believe in the cyclicality of life and death.

"You see, detectives, we all possess within us an essential core of our being—a spirit, if you will—that existed before our birth, that has always existed, and will always exist. It is the spark of life, and every living being, every plant, insect, or animal, sentient or not, carries within it this divine spark. And upon our deaths, this spark will travel through the divine cycle and give new life in what we call the gift of creation. That is why we celebrate and revere every life, from that of our fellow downtrodden man to that of the noble trees and every creature that makes them their home."

Bellamy punctuated his speech with a grand sweep of his arms, as if to encompass the entirety of his church. Throughout the discourse, the supremely tall youth stood at Bellamy's back, his head bowed and his lips sealed.

I surprised myself by not only staying awake through the impromptu sermon, but staying alert. Must've been the coffee.

I pointed at the beanpole. "What's up with Slim?"

Bellamy blinked. "Oh. This is Chester. He's my assistant."

Chester bobbed his head.

"Does he talk?" I asked.

"He is physically able, but he chooses not to," said Bellamy. "He took a vow of silence a little over a year ago."

"Is that a thing in your religion?" I asked.

"Yes," said Bellamy.

Stupidly, I waited for an explanation, but by some miracle, none came.

"So," said Bellamy. "What can I do for you, detectives?"

I pointed to the far side of the building, past the benches where Julian and Chester had emerged. "We noticed some windows high on your church, backing up to the alley. Tell me, Pastor, what do you have on that side of the building?"

"Kitchens and meeting spaces on the first floor, primarily," said Bellamy. "Living and work quarters on the upper levels."

"So you live here?" I asked.

"Yes," he said. "Why?"

"We're investigating a disturbance that occurred late last night in the alley," said Shay. "A few other witnesses reported hearing yelling. We were wondering if perhaps you heard anything more concrete, given your proximity."

The pastor nodded. "Ah. Yes. That. It woke me up. Before the break of dawn. I'd say...five thirty or so."

"And what did you hear?" I asked.

Bellamy rubbed his smooth cheeks. "Well. There was an argument. Between a man and a woman. And yelling, both male and female. Oh, and fighting."

I gave my partner a tilted head and raised eyebrow combo, as if to say Bellamy's story matched our suspicions. She'd clearly hoped for more.

"Can you be more specific?" asked Shay. "Did you hear any names, or make out any phrases?"

Bellamy shook his head. "I'm afraid not. With the chill in the air, I keep the windows closed overnight, and they do a fair job of muffling sound—which is a good thing, to be honest, because we have more than our fair share of boisterous partiers roaming the streets in these parts. Eventually I did rise and head to the windows to investigate, but by that point, whoever had been involved in the altercation had moved to the end of the alley."

"And what about you, Slim?" I asked. "You hear anything?"

Chester—who now that I thought about it, must've been a half-giant of some sort—gave me a blank stare before looking to Bellamy for guidance.

"Go on," said Bellamy. "Answer the detective's questions, Chester."

The tall youth looked at me expectantly.

I scratched my head. "Um...do you have a system for communication? Hand signals or something?"

"We ask yes or no question, and he nods or shakes his head."

"Clever," I said. "Ok, then, Chester. Did you hear the yelling last night, too?"

He nodded.

"Did you overheard anything specific?" asked Steele. "Anything Pastor Bellamy didn't?"

He paused briefly, his eyebrows wrinkled, then shook his head.

"Well, that was...brief." I'd meant to say pointless, but Shay had given me one of those 'be nice' looks. I glanced at her. "So, now what?"

"You could try the restaurant next door," offered Bellamy. "It's possible someone there heard something I didn't."

"At five thirty in the morning?" I said.

"They serve breakfast, lunch, and dinner, seven days a week," he said. "Someone should've been there."

"Thank you, pastor," said Shay. "We'll check it out."

We turned to go.

"Wait," said Bellamy. "Pardon my curiosity, but...what exactly happened out there?"

I paused and looked back at the guy. "A transient got beaten to death."

His face fell. "You're kidding."

"You're right," I said. "The other bums actually threw a birthday party for him, but he suffered a heart-attack when the stripper burst through the cake."

Steele smacked me in the arm, and Bellamy looked at me sternly. "Are you always so glib in the face of death?"

"Comes with the territory," I said. "You get immune to it after a while."

I also wanted to ask why Bellamy seemed so crestfallen over the death of a downtrodden transient, given his belief in the 'Divine Rebirth' or whatnot, but I'd learned my lesson the first time—which was to not feed the priest any straight lines he might interpret as requests for theological discourse. I had enough on my plate at the moment, and my coffee's intellect-perking magic could only be stretched so far.

7

S hay and I exited the church and walked over to the restaurant in question, a shabby, mottled brick building with a weather-beaten sign above it labeling it the Delta Deli. A smaller sign hung underneath, with the words '& Brew Pub' in a different type. A chimney puffed smoke out from the back, the same chimney I'd spotted from the confines of the alley.

"A ratty joint that serves sandwiches and beer?" said Shay as she gazed at the sign. "This place might be tailor made for you, Daggers."

"Hey, don't tempt me," I said. "That scone I devoured is already a distant memory."

I pulled the door open for my partner, and a shopkeeper's bell mounted in the frame jingled. Inside the restaurant, two score seats, evenly distributed between tables and booths, languished, empty. A lone patron—a guy with a shaggy crop of light brown hair and glasses—occupied the last booth on the left, an elbow propped on the table and his face pressed into his hand.

I couldn't tell if the guy was despondent, drunk, or dead.

A dry, musty smell worked its way into my nostrils, giving me the impression the place would benefit greatly from a good sweeping and a day with its windows spread open. A rickety, wooden hostess stand at my right went ignored by any possible employees. I squinted as I peered into the back of the establishment in the direction of the kitchen, but the owners hadn't bothered to light any lamps—or even purchase them. I couldn't be sure which, given the gloom.

Steele reached out and rapped her index finger twice against the tip of a call bell on the edge of the hostess stand. A few seconds passed with no response. I tipped my head in Shay's direction, but before she could ring the bell again, I spotted movement in the back. A hand grasped the edge of a bead curtain that separated the dining room from the kitchen, sweeping it to the side, and into the darkness stepped an individual wearing khakis and a puffy jacket.

His visage materialized as he stepped into the light, but he might've been better served staying in the gloom. Long, black hair spilled around the sides of his oval-shaped face and over his pointed orc ears, laying flat over grayish green skin that shimmered with a waxy sheen. A wide nose dominated his face, and a cleft in his upper lip hinted at yellow teeth underneath.

He stopped behind the hostess stand. "You, uh...want table?"

Shay took the decision out of my hands. "No thanks. We're actually detectives with the NWPD. We're investigating a death that occurred in the alley behind this building early this morning. Are you in charge here?"

The orc's eyes narrowed, and he glanced at the door before looking back at us. "Sort of."

"What does that mean?" I asked.

"Me dayshift manager," he said. "Not owner."

"Have you got a name, dayshift manager?" I asked.

"Wheyiane Dekkar."

I blinked. "Say what now?"

The orc slowed his speech. "Wheyiane. Dekkar."

"*Wayne?*" I said.

"Close enough," he said.

"So do you mind if we ask you some questions?" asked Shay.

Wayne shrugged. "Sure. Me guess."

"What time do you guys open?" she asked.

"Six."

"Was anyone here earlier?" said Shay. "Say, about five thirty?"

"Not sure," said Wayne. "Cook maybe. Why?"

I stuffed my hands in my pockets—or at least I tried to. I'd forgotten about the thermos full of coffee. "Did you miss the part about us investigating a death in the alley?"

"Oh. Right," said the orc. "Me forget."

"We're hoping someone nearby might've overheard something that could help us better understand what happened outside," said Shay. "Perhaps you could check with your chef...?"

"Yeah. Me check."

Wayne disappeared behind the bead curtain, only to reappear a few moments later. "He coming. Just sec."

I crossed my arms and sucked on my lips as we waited. I thought about going after the rest of my coffee, but I figured it would be bad form to do so inside the restaurant, especially considering how sparse their clientele appeared to be.

"So," I said, tapping my foot, "you guys shift much product in the morning hours?"

The orc gave me another squint eyed glance, but then he seemed to figure out what I meant. "Business ok."

"How exactly does a breakfast deli work, anyway?" I asked.

"Easy," said Wayne. "Same sandwich. Put egg on it. Serve with potatoes."

The door chime rang behind us, and a pair of dwarves with waist-length beards and knee-high work boots stomped in. They moseyed around to the edge of the hostess stand, which was almost taller than they were. They glanced at Shay and me and then at each other before shifting their gaze to Wayne.

"Table?" offered the orc with raised eyebrows.

"Um, no," said the dwarf in front. "Take out order. For Truevein. And Brewmantle."

The second dwarf stared at me curiously. I offered a cheesy smile in return.

Wayne held up a finger, I think for Shay's and my benefit. "Just sec."

He disappeared again behind the curtain, this time to return with a small paper bag, its top folded over. He handed it to the dwarves. They muttered their thanks and left.

I blinked. *Breakfast take out? From this place?* Perhaps it made sense. Clearly, the restaurant wasn't raking in the dough from its dine-in business.

A rain shower of a thousand tiny beads brought me to attention. A green-skinned goblin emerged from the back, a chef's apron hanging haphazardly across his front.

"Ah," said Wayne. "Here go. This Bok. He cook."

The goblin forced a smile, showing off his double rows of pointed teeth. Something dark stained his fingertips, possibly ash from a cooking fire, but somehow it hadn't marred his apron. The latter shone a pristine white.

"You like chicken, Bok?" I asked.

The goblin stared at me in confusion.

"Don't mind him," said Steele. "That's his idea of a joke. I'm Detective Steele, and you've already met Detective Daggers. Do you mind if we ask you a few questions?"

The goblin turned to Wayne and uttered a series of pops, clicks, and grunts, gesturing with his hands as he did so. Wayne responded in kind before addressing us.

"Bok only speak Goblin tongue. It ok. Me translocate."

"Translate," I said.

"What?" said Wayne.

I sighed and turned to Steele. "Seriously? It's not even nine in the morning and already we've found two witnesses who either can't or won't speak."

Shay patted me on the shoulder. "Why don't you let me handle this?"

I held out my hand.

"Wheyiane," said Steele, "can you ask Bok here if he was in the kitchen by five thirty?"

Wayne translated, and Bok nodded.

"Ask him if he heard anything transpire in the alley," said Steele. "If he heard any yelling or arguing."

Wayne and Bok held a conversation. Then Wayne spoke.

"He say you right. He hear yelling. Two, three people. Woman, he think. He not pay much attention."

"Why not?" asked Shay.

Another discussion. Another response from Wayne. "He say we not pay him enough."

I snorted. This Bok character was starting to grow on me.

"So I'm guessing he didn't go out to investigate?" said Steele.

Wayne and Bok talked.

"Bok give same answer," said Wayne.

"Does Bok have anything else to add that he thinks might be pertinent to our investigation?" asked Shay.

Wayne asked. Bok shrugged.

Shay sighed. "Very well. Let him know that if he thinks of anything, he can come talk to us at the 5th Street Precinct. Or, better yet, you take his message and bring it to us, for obvious linguistic reasons. Daggers, you ready to go?"

"Always." I propped open the door and let the jingle of the bell wash over me. "Ladies first."

8

Shay and I exited the restaurant and ducked into the alley, headed in the direction of the crime scene.

"I'm impressed, Daggers," said Shay, as the Deli's shadow enveloped us. "I was sure you'd walk out of that place with grub in hand."

I smiled. "I know you're yanking my chain, but believe it or not, I haven't totally ruled them out yet."

"*Really?*" she said.

"Really."

Steele smirked. "So what transgression at a restaurant would be so egregious that it would actually make you consider eating elsewhere? Besides, of course, the obvious, like piles of trash that prevent you from walking through the front door, rumors of deadly flesh-eating bacteria growing in the kitchen, or a menu featuring unfamiliar horrors along the likes of cilantro and papaya?"

I smiled and shook my head. Despite growth on both of our parts, Shay's and my culinary tastes still remained worlds apart. I liked my food simple, subdued, and familiar—and preferably served between two slices of bread. Or, as Shay would say, *booorr-ing*. She preferred her mouth to run the gamut of culinary extremes in every meal. She wanted to taste the sweet and the salty, have her lips pucker from acidity and the sides of her tongue tingle from bitterness. To feel the heat of hot peppers on her lips and cool them with a fruity cocktail or use the spice to cut through a bite of something unctuous and savory.

We'd made strides towards understanding each other's tastes, of course. We traded off on lunch choices, and even when we went out together in the evenings, we tried our best to ensure the other's culinary desires were met. Shay had found a number of enticing gastropubs and high-quality nosheries, just as I'd culled from my repertoire virtually all eateries that served their meals on butcher paper.

But as it did with Shay, the dining experience greatly impacted my overall satisfaction with the meal—just in a different way.

"I'm not sure you'll ever understand my love affair with dives," I said as I avoided a puddle of—I hoped—rain.

"Try me," said Shay with a smile.

And she meant it. Her openness to new ideas was one of the many things I loved about her—not because I was the same way, but because it gave me hope that I could eventually convince her of the veracity of all my outlandish claims.

"Alright," I said. "For me, it's not just about the food. It's about the thrill of the chase. Of finding a diamond in the culinary rough. A place that looks like it should've collapsed under its own weight a decade ago, but still pumps out delicious food by the basketful."

"And why is that important to you?"

I glanced at Shay. She peered back at me without an ounce of jest or malice in her eyes. She really wanted to know.

"I don't know," I said. "I guess it makes me feel...special. Like I know something others don't. Something I can share with them and then we can all enjoy."

Shay nodded. "I completely understand. I feel the exact same way about the places I share with you and Cairny and the guys."

"Yeah, but *my* places are dirt cheap," I said.

My partner smiled and rolled her eyes. "Fair enough."

We stepped back out onto the main thoroughfare and into the throng of beat cops and onlookers. The crowd had thinned—the appeal of a mud-caked dead hobo wears off quickly—but other than that, everything was as we'd left it. Except for the fact that the buildings at the alley's sides seemed lonelier than I remembered...

I ground my teeth and called for Phillips.

The young man came running. "Yes, sir, Detective Daggers, sir. At your service."

"Phillips," I said. "What the hell, man? Where are the suspects?"

"Suspects, sir?" he said.

"Don't play dumb," I said. "The witnesses! Our trio of servicemen and women."

Phillips fidgeted with his hands and refused to meet my eyes. "Um...yes. Well, about that. There was this, uh, army officer. A high ranking guy. A sergeant major, I think. He demanded we release the witnesses—err, I mean, suspects—to his custody, and—"

"Phillips! *Really?*"

Shay put a hand on my arm. "Calm down, Daggers. Phillips, please. Go ahead."

"Look, I'm sorry," said Phillips. "But I didn't know the proper protocol. The two of you were gone, as was Detective Quinto. I had nobody to go to for guidance. And the sergeant major—I forget his name—he said because of enlistees Holmes, Chavez, and Delvedeep's military status, the investigation into the victim's death was as much a military matter as a civilian one. He was very insistent."

"But you gave our only leads away," I said. "What if this major was an impostor? Did you think about that?"

"Daggers...really?" said Shay.

I recalled our last case. "Stranger things have happened."

"If he was an impostor," said Phillips, "then he was a really sharply-uniformed and well-armed impostor. And he had an entire troop, or brigade, or whatever of guys with him. A couple of them had swords. Honestly, there was nothing I could do."

I adopted my best disapproving father face—something I'd been working on as my tike grew older—and sicced it on Phillips. "I'm disappointed in you."

Phillips inspected his shoes. "Sorry, sir. But the sergeant major did say to tell you he was returning the recruits to the New Welwic Main base, and that if you had any further questions for them, you could inquire

about securing a meeting with them at the military police offices."

"Oh, I'll inquire," I said. "You can bet I'll inquire."

I meant it to sound tough, but 'inquire' was a difficult verb to put any gusto into.

Phillips slunk off, and Steele cast me a disapproving
glance.

"You didn't have to be so harsh with him," she said.

"Didn't I?" I said. "The kid needs to learn. You have
to watch suspects with hawk eyes. It's all too easy for
people to disappear in this city."

"Daggers, be real. I'm sure the major was who he
said he was, and besides, our suspects clearly aren't
flight risks. If they were, they would've fled before the
first bluecoats arrived. The fact that they stayed speaks
volumes."

"Yes," I replied. "It means they think their story is
solid enough to hold under scrutiny. And I know we'll
be able to find them at the base. But Phillips needs to
be held to a higher standard. It's a matter of principle."

Steele frowned and shook her head as Quinto returned.

"Everything all right?" he rumbled.

"Peachy," I said.

He blinked as he looked over my shoulder. "Hey,
what happened to the—"

"Don't ask," I said. "Learn anything useful?"

"Well, yes and no," he said. "I talked to a number of
patrons who were here early this morning, as well as a
couple of bar owners and waitresses who were nearby
at the time. They all told me basically the same story.
They heard screaming and yelling, including some dis-

tinct, high-pitched shrieking. Like serious, 'I'm flipping out' sorts of shrieks. But no one actually saw anything until after the fact. At that point, they describe seeing the three army folks here at the mouth of the alley, and the dead guy right where he is now. One waitress confirmed she saw Sergeant Holmes check the guy for a pulse, and another person said all three of them looked flustered. Other than that..." Quinto shrugged.

I rubbed my chin, which fought back against my hand with its untamed, day-old bristles. "So by your eyewitness accounts, the dead guy was right here in the street when people first saw him?"

Quinto nodded.

"And nobody saw Tim or Drake carrying him here?"

"Nope," said Quinto.

I grunted.

"What's on your mind?" asked Steele.

"Well, it's strange, isn't it?" I said. "If we're right about our theory, and our dead guy here—who really needs a nickname, by the way. I'm thinking Lanky—if he did assault Kelly in the alley, wouldn't the fight have taken place in the alley, too? So why would Tim and Drake drag him here after the fact? Where everyone could see him? Why not leave him in the alley?"

"Because they needed the evidence to support their story, probably," said Quinto.

"Well, sure. Right," I said. "But why not leave him in the alley and come up with a different story? A more believable and less convoluted one?"

"Maybe Drake and Tim didn't move the body," said Steele. "Maybe the fight naturally carried into the street. Or maybe the victim—"

"Lanky," I said.

Steele sighed. "Right. Lanky. Maybe Lanky tried to run away when he realized he wasn't going to win the fight. And that's when Tim or Drake ran him down and delivered the killing blow."

I snorted. "Could be."

My partner raised an eyebrow. "You don't sound convinced."

"I'm never convinced," I said. "Not until I have a preponderance of evidence to support my conclusions. It's one of the reasons I'm so good at my job."

"Don't be modest," said Quinto. "Tell us how you really feel."

I took one last look around the crime scene. "Quinto, you think you can help Phillips clean this mess up? Get the body back to Cairny and whatnot? I think it would be best if the kid gets a break from me for the time being."

Steele gave an approving nod, one I'm not entirely sure I was supposed to have noticed.

"Not a problem," said the big guy. "What are you two going to tackle next?"

"Oh, now the real fun begins," I said. "We get to unravel the tangled web of bureaucracy that holds together the armed forces. Should make a bout with the Captain feel like a walk in the park."

9

Shay and I headed west, in the direction of the army base. The churches and bars of the Delta district faded from view, replaced with row upon row of four- and five-story cookie cutter brownstones. Those in turn soon gave way to larger municipal buildings, many of them faced with banded columns and excessive amounts of polished granite. Down a cross-street, I even caught a glimpse of the famed Rucker Park, the city's one and only attempt at convincing the populace that a cluster of a half-dozen trees growing out of a sidewalk did not, in fact, constitute a forest. From there, it wasn't more than a few blocks to the edge of the New Welwic Main base.

The camp sprawled across a good dozen square blocks of prime city real estate, easily demarcated by the seemingly endless olive green fence that ran around its perimeter. I trailed my hand across the paint-slicked fence boards as we walked, my mind drifting to my little brother Jack.

I hadn't seen him in well over two years, and much to my chagrin, I couldn't with any degree of confidence say that I knew where in the world he was. I assumed he still drew breath, otherwise the army would've notified me via a sterile letter delivered with a stoic salute.

I suppose I couldn't blame him for his lack of written correspondence. We never enjoyed the sort of camaraderie that came naturally to most brothers, but who did Jack blame for that? Not our old man, of course, despite the fact that he never put forth the *slightest* modicum of effort after our mother died. *He* never noticed if Jack neglected to show up at school for a day, or even a whole week. *He* never chastised him for staying out too late, or beat him until he cried when he found an ounce of crank in his drawers. The old man was too far gone in his bottle, too lost in the possibilities of what could've been, to spare even an ounce of attention Jack's way. And so the responsibility fell onto me.

And how did Jack repay the old man's neglect, when he finally came of age? In the only way a boy ignored by his father could. By following in his steps and joining the army, same as my father had long before I'd been born—and, of course, by continuing to place the burden of his festering anger, resentment, and lack of self-worth onto my shoulders, rather than on my father's where it belonged.

Steele's voice reached through the cloud of my mind and brought me back to reality. "Daggers?"

I blinked. "Hmm?"

She nodded. In front of us stood the gate to the army base, guarded by a pair of burly young men holding halberds and wearing tan fatigues under similarly colored coats. I approached the pair and flashed my badge.

"Morning, soldiers," I said. "You mind pointing me in the direction of the MP offices?"

The pair glanced at each other, and the one on the right responded. "Um...what's this about, officer?"

"Detective," I corrected. "We're investigating a potential homicide that occurred this morning over in the Delta district. Involved a trio of your own. Who I now need to speak to."

The soldier I was talking to glanced at the other. "You familiar with the protocol on this?"

The second GI chewed his lip.

"Look you two," I said. "I'm fully aware the rules change when I cross the invisible line at our feet. I just need to talk to the suspects—who, I might add, were forcibly removed from my jurisdiction to your own. Now come on. Don't make me get somebody out here to rake you over the coals for refusing to let us in."

The soldiers shared another look before the one who'd found his voice responded. "Alright. Go straight and hook right at the parade grounds. Building A two-thirty."

I nodded and walked on through, Shay at my heels. We worked our way up the main thoroughfare, past a pair of grounds filled with squads of soldiers training in hand to hand combat. Beyond them, other groups worked on their marksmanship, taking turns firing crossbow bolts into life-sized, straw-filled targets. Their movements were exact, well-rehearsed, and methodical. The very definition of military precision—which I'd always found to be a baffling concept. How could the armed forces be so organized when the body that funded and dictated their actions, the government, was the exact opposite?

At the side of the marksmen, a team of army engineers wielding hammers and wrenches swarmed over one of those new-fangled Bock Industries reciprocating engines, although how they'd gotten their hands on one given the turmoil at Bock Industries, I couldn't be sure. The engineers lifted and banged and cranked as they attached the engine's drive shaft to what looked to my eyes like a ballista, except the implement of death in question had a large wooden drum sticking out of its backside.

I nudged Steele. "What do you suppose that is?"

My partner glanced at the contraption sadly. "I think that's what the military would call 'progress.' Let's hope we don't see too much of it too fast."

I blinked, but I think I got the gist of what she meant. And for my brother's sake, I hoped she was right.

We turned at the parade grounds, which looked as if they'd been trimmed by the army barbers, and walked until we found ourselves at the MP offices—a squat, boxy building slathered with several coats of the ubiquitous olive green army paint.

I pushed open the front doors and stepped inside. Corridors stretched out in three directions, but a low desk before me blocked my path. Behind it sat a pair of GIs, one male and one female. Both wore the same tan fatigues as the regular foot soldiers, but each had a white armband around their left arm, and on their right, an insignia patch with a prominently displayed pair of scales. It reminded me of my own badge, but instead of a soaring eagle holding the scales, a pair of swords crossed over them.

The woman looked up from her desk. "May I...help you?"

"I hope so," I said. "I'm Detective Daggers, and this is my partner, Detective Steele. NWPD. We're here to retrieve the suspects you stole from us."

The woman sat up and clasped her hands. "Excuse me?"

"Daggers..." said Steele, in that 'let me take it from here' tone of voice of hers.

I ignored her and kept going. I had a plan. "Three of them. Sergeant Tim Holmes. PFC Kelly Chavez. Private Drake Delvesdeep. Heavy drinkers. Look like they hit a rough patch this morning. Surely you saw them come through here. They'd be hard to miss."

"I'm sorry, detective," said the woman, "but I'm not familiar with any of those three individuals, and even if I were, I'm not at liberty to discuss such matters without prior authorization."

"Right, right," I said. "Nobody keeps you abreast of anything. I get it. Your job is to sit here and make life miserable for people who walk in the door." I leaned to my side to get a better look down the corridor behind the pair of desk jockeys. "Is that the sergeant major's office back there?"

The man stood. "Sir, I'm going to have to ask you to take a seat while we—"

"It is, isn't it?" I said. "Really, there's no need for you to get up. I can show myself in."

I took a step to the side, and the young man moved to block my way.

"I wouldn't do that if I were you, sir."

"And why not?" I asked. "What have you got back there? My suspects? Illicit hooch? Racy pinup mags?"

The scowl he wore on his face said he didn't care for my antics. Nor did he care who I was or what I thought I had the right to know. It did, however, tell me he'd be *happy* to put me down with excessive force should I be dumb enough to lay hands on him.

I gulped. My strategy of being an asshole to force someone to come deal with me wasn't going as planned. Or so I thought...

A strong, smooth voice made me turn. "I'll take it from here, Jenkins."

10

A pure blood elf, roughly my height, stood at the mouth of one of the corridors to my side. A crisp, clean uniform fit snugly over his lean, muscular frame. His pointed ears stood out sharply over the ultra-short stubble at the sides of his head, but the hair at his crown had been given a little more leeway. Dark brown and swept to the side with a touch of mousse, it lent his face a playful flair that contrasted with his straight nose and strong, smooth jaw. He peered at me judiciously with pale green eyes.

"And who are you?" I asked.

"Agent Elmorodil Blue," he said. "ACIC."

"Bless you," I said.

Blue gave me a perfunctory smile. "It stands for Army Criminal Investigative Command. It's essentially the army equivalent of your own civilian investigative unit."

Steele stepped forth and offered her hand. "Good to meet you, Agent Blue. I'm Detective Steele. Hopefully, you'll forgive my partner Daggers for his occasional failed attempts at wit."

Blue took her hand, and his smile transformed from a polite one to a genuine one. "Forgive *you*? I don't think that'll be a terribly difficult challenge."

My cheeks warmed as something bubbled up from the pit of my belly, something hollow and biting and angry all at the same time. Something that made my jaw and heart clench simultaneously. *Forgiving Steele wouldn't be terribly difficult*? What the heck did he mean by that?

"Please, Detectives," said the good-looking elf. "Accompany me to my office. We have things to discuss."

Without affording me the opportunity to come up with a clever response, Agent Blue turned and headed down the corridor, forcing me to follow. He led us past a cluster of cubicles before stopping at a door to a brightly lit corner office. He held his hand out in the direction of a couple of plain, solidly built chairs in front of his desk.

Shay took one of the proffered seats, but I elected to remain on my toes, circling the room as I analyzed its contents. A three-tiered letter tray graced one corner of the elf's desk, and an inclined wire file packed with manila envelopes perched on the other. Shiny, recently-waxed cherry wood dominated the chasm in-between.

A pair of bookshelves sparsely populated with reference texts leaned against the left-hand wall, while framed commendations and awards stretched in a neat line, at face level, along the right. I stopped in front of a diploma declaring one Elmorodil Blue a graduate of the criminal justice program from Rutherford University. A shiny, embossed gold seal caught my eye, as did the words 'With High Honors.'

Agent Blue followed Steele and sank into the chair behind his desk. "First of all, detectives, let me apologize for how the situation unfolded this morning. I myself didn't hear of the *incident*, should we say, until about an hour ago. At that point, Sergeant Major Keele had already made an executive decision to extract our soldiers from the scene."

"Wait," I said, glancing back. "You're not the sergeant major?"

Blue shook his head. "I don't rank quite that high—thankfully. I'm not sure I'd enjoy the responsibilities that go along with such a position. And for any other instance of misbehavior by enlisted personnel, I doubt Sergeant Major Keele would've made the trip himself. But when the events of the case suggest a possible homicide, our reaction must henceforth be different."

I moved to another wall-hung frame, this one containing a signed letter from a brigadier general thanking Agent Blue for his devotion and service. I frowned.

"So, Agent Blue," said Steele. "As you can probably imagine, Detective Daggers and I are feeling a bit out of our element following your intervention. How is this going to work, given we each have a legitimate juridical claim?"

"Well," said Blue, "if the evidence does point to a homicide, then we'll be dealing with a felony crime committed on civilian soil, which would make this primarily a New Welwic police investigation. We'll do our best not to interfere, but given the current three persons of interest—"

"Suspects," I said.

Blue glanced at me. *"Persons of interest.* Given all three are army enlistees, ACIC will conduct its own parallel investigation. Again, should the evidence point to a homicide, we'll let your jurisdiction take precedence, and beyond that, we'll happily share evidence we've gathered to support the case, as I'd hope you'd be willing to do the same for us. But if the facts point to something else, we still need to make sure the three servicemen and women in question maintained themselves in a fashion befitting of the army's code of conduct."

I glanced further down the wall at the rest of the plaques and awards. They made me want to puke.

"So, Elmo," I said. "Can I call you Elmo?"

"I'd prefer Elmorodil," he said. "Or Agent Blue."

I returned to Shay's side and took the remaining seat. "Alright. Sure. Let's talk about my suspects."

"Persons...of interest," corrected Agent Blue.

"It doesn't matter what we call them," I said. "I want them back."

"Do you, now?" he said.

"I do."

Elmorodil's chair squeaked as he straightened, and I heard a slight puff of air escape his nostrils. "I'm afraid I can't allow that, Detective."

"Why not?" I asked.

"Because privates Chavez and Delvesdeep and Sergeant Holmes are army enlistees," he said. "All three signed contracts committing them to service in defense of the country. Part of that commitment demands they adhere to the code of conduct to which I already referred, but more importantly, that contract stipulates they must follow our rules, regulations, and commands. Because they're army, they should be here, under our supervision, and in our care. Unless, of course, you have evidence with which to charge them for a crime." The man lifted an eyebrow. "Do you?"

"I can hold them in custody for twenty-four hours," I said. "Breathe on them a little. See what slips."

"That's unethical," said Blue. "And to be quite honest, I highly doubt it would get you anywhere. These aren't frightened street urchins or doped-up junkies, Detective. These are soldiers. Trained to stay calm under pressure."

I ground my teeth. Agent Blue knew too much for his own good—or at least for mine. He wasn't about to bend under the weight of my abrasive personality or official sounding demands. He wouldn't turn over the three GIs without some serious writs and warrants on my part, and even then he might fight it.

"What if they escape?" I asked.

"Daggers, this is a military base," said Steele.

Blue extended a couple fingers in Shay's direction, as if to say she'd made his case for him.

I sighed. "At least let us speak to them."

"What questions do you wish to ask?" asked Blue.

"I don't know," I said. "I tend to work off the cuff in that regard. Let my brain determine what's pertinent as the situation unfolds."

Agent Blue clasped his hands together. "As I said, I'll be happy to accommodate requests of that nature...assuming you can provide more concrete reasons for said requests."

I grunted, hoping the steam boiling inside me hadn't yet started to pour from my ears.

Shay cast a downturned lip and glance my way. "Let me again apologize for my partner, Agent Blue. He gets this way when he's hungry. Thanks for taking the time to talk to us, and we'll be sure to keep the communication routes open between us. Hopefully we'll be able to piece this thing together in short order."

"Wait." I waggled a pinky finger in my ear. "Did I hear that right? We're collaborating?"

"Yes," said Steele as she stood. "We are."

Her tone brooked no rebuke.

"Glad to hear it," said Agent Blue, standing in response. "I look forward to working with you, Detective Steele."

The army investigator smiled, and I swear I caught a hint of the same from Shay. I did my best not to growl.

11

We left the army base and headed back toward the precinct, though we took the scenic route by sweeping through Rucker Park on the way there. Many of the trees had already lost their leaves, so the walk wasn't quite as striking as it might've been a couple weeks prior with the park's canopy ablaze in reds, oranges, and yellows. Not that I cared. In the aftermath of my introduction to Agent Sweetcheeks, my mind had retreated into the dark hole it considered its safe place, taking with it the majority of my faculties.

Shay tried to engage me in conversation as we walked. I think I managed to respond to a grand total of thirteen inquiries with some form of a grunt, frown, or 'Mmm-hmm' before she noticed.

"In addition to her robe, did you accidentally slip on a pair of your wife's underwear this morning, too?" she asked.

I'd been dragging my eyes along the park's cobblestone path as we walked. I blinked and lifted them to meet Shay's gaze. "Say what?"

"I'm saying you're acting like your panties are in a bunch."

"Hardy-har har," I said.

We stood at the edge of an algae and lily pad-ridden pond, one surrounded by thick clusters of reeds and cattails. A lazy dragonfly alighted on the water's surface, only to get summarily introduced to a goldfish's gullet. Before me, the park's vegetation abruptly stopped as it met the packed earth of a main thoroughfare. Had we already traversed the entire thing?

"Seriously," said Steele. "What's up?"

"Nothing," I said.

Steele tilted her head and gave me a skeptical double eyebrow raise.

I grunted. Shay was almost as bad as my ex-wife Nicole in her ability to sniff out my bunkum and lies—and far more persistent in her search of a response. So I replied in the only way I knew how—by telling her the truth, but only a portion of it.

"It's that self-professed Agent Blue," I said. "I don't like him one bit."

"*Self-professed?*" said Steele.

"Yes," I said. "Detective, sure. Investigator. Why not? Officer. Well, given his military rank, probably. But *agent?* It's not like he's out there protecting generals and elected officials from assassination attempts."

"It's a perfectly suitable word," said Steele. "And I don't know what your issues with him are. He seemed eminently professional."

I tried not to snort. *Right. The manner in which he took your hand as he introduced himself was nothing if not professional.*

"He's going to be a pain in our backsides," I said. "Mark my words. Lanky hadn't even cooled to an acceptable temperature before he stuck his meddling fingers in our investigation."

"It sounded like he had nothing to do with that," said Steele. "The sergeant major acted on his own."

"And you believed him?" I shook my head.

Shay rolled her eyes. "You know, I was mostly joking about you being cranky because of hunger pangs, but your attitude is convincing me otherwise." She pointed across the street. "Want to try that place for lunch? I've heard good things. Inexpensive, high quality ingredients, and fast."

I followed her finger to a sign that had an enormous steel frying pan attached to it, and to the right, the words 'Speed Wok.'

"Stir fry?" I asked. "Really?"

"Why not?" said Steele. "And it's not like you have any say in the matter. It's my turn to choose."

We crossed the road and stepped into the eatery, which had a different layout than any I'd seen before. The establishment contained no walls or partitions. It was just one big room filled with neatly arranged tables, and in the back, the kitchen, its hustle and bustle and noise and heat open for all to see and experience—not a bad idea in the cool winter months, but a questionable strategy come June.

Before us, a short line stretched to a counter manned by a gnome—of *course* it was a gnome—taking orders which he scribbled onto a notepad. As he finished each order, he yelled it to the kitchen staff, who repeated it three times in what I assumed was a ritual to help keep them from forgetting it. At the gnome's side, a blackboard listed the menu in variegated colors of chalk.

I refused to let the restaurant's flashy, new design deviate my stream of thought. "You see, the problem with stir fry is the name is so deceptive. I mean, it *sounds* great. The word 'fry' is right there in the title. But when you sit down to eat it, it's just a bunch of noodles and vegetables and sauce."

Shay narrowed her eyes as she peered at the chalkboard. "You're confusing frying and deep-frying."

"Well maybe next time we should try a deep stir fry joint," I said. "Or would it be stir deep fry? Neither one sounds quite right..." I twisted my face in thought.

"Just get the tempura bowl..." said Steele.

I detected a hint of annoyance in her voice, so I closed my yapper and did as she suggested. After ordering, we shuffled along in the line toward the end of the kitchen, where after no more than a minute and a half, one of the apron-clad cooks set a couple bowls on the counter, rang a bell, and shouted out our order.

I gaped as I picked up my meal. Other than the noodles forming the entrée's bed, everything in the tasteful blue and while filigreed bowl was coated in a crispy layer of fried batter.

"You're welcome," said Steele.

We found a table and shoveled food in our mouths, and as the fried meats and crunchy vegetables sent energy flowing through my stomach and into my extremities, I felt my mood improve. Perhaps Shay had been right and all I needed was a bite to eat. And perhaps I'd overreacted with regards to Elmo Blue. Not in the sense that he wouldn't be a thorn in our sides—I was sure he'd be—but in the hidden meanings I'd uncovered in his behavior toward Shay. Perhaps he *was* simply being nice, and he hadn't afforded me the same courtesy because I was an abrasive A-hole.

Steele made it clear through her devoted chewing efforts that she'd expended enough energy trying to engage me in discussion during our park foray, leaving the burden of conversation up to me. Hence, we ate in silence. After all, my mood hadn't improved *that* much.

After lunch, we returned to the station. Clouds momentarily hid the sun, casting a shadow across the huge seal of justice that hung over the precinct's iron-banded front double doors. I gazed at the soaring eagle holding a pair of scales in its claws and snorted.

Swords. Bah. Even without the sun's bright rays sparkling its edges, the seal put Agent Blue's pale imitation to shame.

I held the door open for Shay and plowed my way into the cluster of beat-to-hell desks, stale coffee smell, and gloom we detectives lovingly referred to as 'the pit.' I passed Rodgers and Quinto's desks—both empty—as I waltzed to my own, situated across from Shay's. Mine, of course, was the better of the pair, not only because it sat in a thin sliver of light that weaseled its way from outside, though the windows in the Captain's office, and over to my patch of real estate, but also because it held my trusty chair. Over years of toil and sloth, I'd worn a perfectly-shaped Jake Daggers butt groove into the seat, which was no small feat given the thing's oaken construction.

Barely had I swung my body about and positioned it above the groove before I heard the Captain's harsh voice.

"Daggers. Steele. There you are!"

I straightened as the old bulldog approached. The years had softened some of his muscle into flab, but not much, and they hadn't quenched the heat of his bark in the least. The old guy had honed his vocal abilities during his stint in the marines, and as far as I was aware, the only opponent that had ever silenced him was laryngitis. What remained of his hair had recently been buzzed, and his jowls—the only part of his face that *didn't* look as if it was carved from granite—pulled as he frowned.

"I think this a new record, even for you, Daggers," he said. "What is it? After noon?"

"Don't give me that," I said. "I've been on the job since I woke up. And no, before you ask, that was not fifteen minutes ago. It was early this morning, when Quinto and Steele brought the joys of this profession straight to my door."

"I know," said the Captain. "That was a joke."

Really? The Captain's lips didn't show even the slightest hint of an upward curl. He could've fooled me—but maybe therein lay the joke.

"Do you have an update for us, sir?" asked Steele.

"Actually, I was hoping you'd have one for me," he said. "Detective Quinto came back about half an hour ago and said you encountered some unexpected *resistance* in the form of one of our government's other law enforcement agencies."

I snorted. "You could say that."

The Captain lifted an eyebrow in my direction. Apparently he'd finally learned that trick from either Steele or me, though it lessened his face's illusion of immobility.

"The suspects in the case—or persons of interest, rather," said Steele, "are all army servicemen and women. A team came and returned them to the New Welwic Main base. Now they're in the care of the military police and under investigation by an Agent Elmorodil Blue, a member of the Army Criminal Investigative Command."

While Steele explained the situation to the Captain, I dug my thermos—now empty—out of my pocket and placed it on my desk. The pocket flopped open, like the mouth of a dead fish. Hopefully I hadn't stretched it beyond the limits of elasticity. I still planned on getting another twenty good years out of my jacket.

"Yeah," I said, still eyeing the deformation in my coat. "And this Agent Blue is a real piece of work. It's going to be a *blast* prying information out of him."

Steele blinked and gave me a dissenting glance.

The Captain noticed. "Has he been like this all day?"

"How did you guess?" said Steele.

The bulldog groaned and rolled his eyes in the surliest way possible. "Listen up, Daggers, as I'm only going to say this once. I've no doubt you harbor a high level of distaste for this Blue individual, because you don't like much of anyone. Guess what? I don't care. Your job is to follow the rules, work with other government agencies where necessary, and to solve the crimes that are thrust in front of your crooked nose."

"*Crooked?*"

"Shut up," he said. "I'm not done. The point is, I expect you to get to the bottom of this, despite whatever hurdles are in your way, and I expect you to do it with a smile on your face. Detective Steele? Inform me if he becomes a problem—by which I mean a greater one than he normally is. Understood?"

The Captain waggled his finger between the two of us. Steele nodded. I grudgingly did the same.

"Good. Now, seeing as you've already eaten—" The bulldog indicated a spot of sauce on my jacket that had somehow eluded my attention. "—I'd suggest you get to work. From everything Quinto told me, this shouldn't be that hard of a case to unravel."

The Captain turned and headed back toward his office, but he paused halfway there. "Oh, and one more thing. I was informed late last night that Detective Rodgers suffered a death in his family."

"*What?*" said Steele. "Who?"

"Not his wife or kids," said the Captain. "Extended family. He'll be out of town for a few days as he deals with the aftermath. But it means the two of you and Quinto will have to shoulder the load until he returns. I figured you should know. If nothing else, perhaps that knowledge will *encourage* you to strive for increased efficiency."

Based on the bulldog's smirk, I knew he directed that last bit toward me, but it was an unneeded jab. I was a master of efficiency—mostly because I delegated as much of the grunt work to others as I could. But I don't think that's what he meant...

12

Shay and I headed downstairs to the dungeon, which, despite persistent rumors to the contrary, wasn't a *real* dungeon, populated with the emaciated remains of poor saps who'd never made bail and the Captain's own staunchest adversaries. Not that I'd explored the underground portions of the precinct to their fullest, mind you, but if the rumors held even a shred of truth, surely I would've been one of the first to be shackled and imprisoned for my gross insubordination.

Rather, 'the dungeon' encompassed the precinct's morgue, so named for its complete lack of natural light, musty smell, and overall cheery atmosphere. Oh, and the dead people. There were lots of dead people.

I shivered as we reached the bottom of the steps and gave my head a shake. "I don't know how Cairny manages. Especially in the winter."

"Well," said Steele, "there are these things called sweaters..."

"Oh, come off it," I said. "If it were you down here, you could throw on a half-dozen layers, and you'd still turn into a half-elf popsicle. Chances are they'd send me down with an ice pick to free you from the frost."

We stepped into the morgue proper, a cavernous room sparsely filled with examination tables, surgical instruments, and coat racks pre-supplied with long, white coats. Cadaver vaults with shiny steel handles, stacked three high, lined the far wall—dozens of temporary homes for the recently living. The room smelled of lemon and industrial solvents, and the floors seemed shinier than I remembered. Either the janitor had just completed his bi-monthly visit, or Cairny had gotten bored and stooped to tasks far beneath her pay grade. Well...not *that* far. None of us public servants earned much.

Only one of the exam tables was currently in use, its occupant's form shrouded by a pristine white sheet. I guessed it had to be Lanky, based on the size of the body. Of Cairny, however, I saw neither hide nor hair. I'd hoped to inquire if she'd had time to examine the corpse yet. Our leads were limited, but a confirmation of blunt force trauma as the method by which Lanky had been slain would go a long way toward confirming our theory involving Private Delvesdeep and Sergeant Timmy.

I glanced at Shay. "So...where's Cairny, I wonder?"

"Why do you assume I know?" she said. "I came down with you, remember?"

"Well, you're friends and all," I offered. "Plus there's that prescient insight of yours."

"That'll never get old, will it?"

I shook my head.

"Maybe she's warming her hands by a roaring fire?" said Steele.

I grunted, doubtful. The Captain would never spring for firewood.

After a lengthy circuit of the precinct that had us visit the lonelier portions of the dungeon and the holding cells, not to mention the building's second and third floors, Shay and I eventually returned to the pit, whereupon we spotted Cairny lounging on a couch in the break room, Quinto's wide frame and smiling, brick-toothed mug at her side.

"There you are," I said as I walked through the doorway.

"Hey Daggers," she said, and then as she eyed Steele, "Looking good, bestie. I like the jacket."

"Thanks," said Shay. "The color's kind of fun, isn't it?"

Cairny nodded, which I found amusing given her own closet probably resembled a mortician's. She rarely wore anything other than black, likely because the color paired so well with her long, jet-black hair and ivory skin, but today she'd decided to get *crazy* and wear a grey cowl neck sweater—points to Shay for calling that—which she'd matched with a pair of voluminous charcoal-colored pants that helped disguise her gangly legs. In the delicate fingers of her right hand she held a few thin cuts of deli meat sandwiched between slices of bread that appeared to have been trampled by a herd of large ruminating mammals.

"What in the world are you eating?" I asked.

Cairny stared at me with those large, vacant eyes of hers. "Roast beef. On white."

"Yes, I can see that," I said. "But what in the world happened to it? It looks so...sad."

Shay pressed a hand against my arm and pointed at Cairny and Quinto. "Hold on. You guys heard that, right?"

"Heard what?" I asked.

"You," she said, a look of triumph on her face. "You condemned a sandwich...*for its simplicity.*"

I felt the heat rise in my face. "No, no, no. That's not—"

"It's true," said Quinto. "I heard it. Straight from the horse's mouth."

Was the big guy calling me horse-faced? "That's not what I meant. I—"

"Oh, admit it," said Shay with a smile. "Try as you might to fight it, your culinary tastes are changing. Soon enough you won't even look twice at a sandwich unless it's topped with melted cheese, crisp lettuce, and a housemade aioli."

I wasn't even sure what that last word meant, but I was too flustered to argue. Was Shay right? Were my tastes actually changing? And by *her* influence? By the gods, we weren't even officially dating. What sorts of transformations could I expect if our relationship progressed to a more serious level?

I changed the subject. "Never you mind about that. The important question is, where have the two of you been?" I gestured at Cairny and Quinto and raised an inquisitive eyebrow, trying to make the action look risqué. "We looked all over for you."

Cairny blinked. "And? You found us."

I sighed and wiped a hand across my face. The subtleties of speech—and, in fact, regular humanoid interaction—were often lost on her. "Never mind. Have you had a chance to look at the body yet?"

"What body?" she asked.

I glanced at Quinto. "Didn't you fill her in?"

The big guy nodded. "Yeah. It's this case I was telling you about, Cairny. You remember, right? The one in the Delta district, with the dead hobo?"

"Oh. Right." Cairny blinked. "Yes, well, I haven't been around the crypt much today."

"Too cold?" Shay gave me a sideways glance as she asked that.

Cairny shook her head. "I've simply had other things to attend to."

"I'm sure you did." I eyed Quinto and tried my eyebrow trick again, leaning in so that Cairny would be sure to notice.

She blinked and squinted at me, head slightly tilted to the side. "Pardon?"

I rolled my eyes. "I don't know why I try. Look, do you mind accompanying us to the morgue to take a look at Lanky? We're not exactly overflowing with leads, and your expertise could help clear up who committed the murder."

Cairny glanced at Steele. "Lanky?"

"You know Daggers' proclivity for witty nicknames," she said. "Admittedly, this one's not as inspired as most, but I'm sure you can figure it out."

Cairny gave Quinto a pat on the shoulder. "Well...duty calls."

"Oh, I'll come," said Quinto. "Not like I have any-thing else to do. But don't tell the Captain that."

The awkward pair stood, Cairny with sandwich still in hand.

"Wait," I said. "You're bringing that?"

"Why not?" The pale-skinned, fae-blooded coroner waved the layers of meat and bread in my face before taking a bite. "Does it bother you that I'd eat while in-specting cadavers?"

"Me?" I said. "I was thinking more him."

I gestured at Quinto. He peered back at me quizzi-cally.

"You know, because she might get cadaver breath," I said.

More quizzical looks, from all present.

"Like, it might waft off the corpse. Or the smell of the room maybe. Get caught in the bread..."

Steele crossed her arms. "You're really off today. Is there something going on I should know about?"

Apparently my encounter with Blue had rattled me more than I'd realized. Even my quips were falling flat. One more reason to dislike the guy.

"Come on," I said. "Let's get to the exam room before I make an even bigger fool of myself."

Nobody argued, and we headed down the stairs into the dungeon. As we reached Cairny's workspace, I led the congregation toward the body.

"So, Cairny," I said. "What we're trying to confirm is whether our dead guy, Lanky, died of blunt force trauma or not. It seems pretty obvious he did, but that's why we've got you around. Now, beyond that, the real question is, was there a murder weapon?"

Cairny stuck out the index finger of her sandwich-free hand. "Um, Daggers..."

"Now, now," I said as I reached the side of the white sheet-draped body. "I know what you're going to say. You need time to perform your investigation. I get it. But we don't need a full report. If you could just tell us whether the guy was beaten to death by hand or with a murder weapon, that'll do. If the latter, then better if you can give us some idea of the weapon, but you know." I shrugged.

"No, Daggers," said Cairny. "That wasn't what I was going to say. It's that—"

I ignored our coroner's protests and flipped up the sheet. Then I blinked a few times.

13

A guy with a bloated, black and blue face, long sandy blond hair, and a thin moustache stared at the ceiling with dead eyes.

"Who the hell is this?" I asked.

Cairny joined me at my side. "A narc. A good one, by all accounts. Morales found him in his apartment yesterday afternoon, along with quite a bit of drug paraphernalia. Looks like he relapsed without anyone knowing. The evidence in his place was pretty damning, but Morales asked me to take a look at him. Make sure his death was an overdose and not something more nefarious disguised to look as such."

"Ok..." I said slowly. "That's a nice story. But what I meant was, where the hell is our stiff? Where's Lanky?"

I glanced around the examination room, which stubbornly remained as empty as when I'd first entered it thirty minutes ago.

Cairny shrugged. "Beats me. As I said, I've been out most of the day."

I glanced at Quinto, who stood next to Shay with his hands in his pockets and a puzzled expression on his face.

"Well?" I asked.

The big guy met my eyes. "You talking to me?"

"No, I'm talking to the enormous lug behind you who's also wearing an oversized purple duster," I said. "Didn't you help Phillips bring Lanky back to the precinct?"

"Well, yes and no," he said.

I rolled my fingers in the air. "The no part being?"

"I accompanied Phillips and the stiff back to the station," said Quinto, "but I didn't help bring the body to the morgue. I let Phillips and those other beat cops take care of it. I figured they would." He scratched his head.

"Really?" I said. "You're the size of a small barge, and you made other people do the heavy lifting?"

"Just because I *can* do something doesn't mean I relish it," he said. "Honestly, do you have any idea how often people ask me to help them move?"

I planted my hands on my hips and shook my head. "I can't believe that Phillips character..."

Steele pointed a stern finger in my direction. "You be nice to him, now."

"What?" I said. "What did I do?"

"You were unnecessarily mean to him back at the crime scene," said Shay. "You know as well as I do there was nothing he could've done to prevent that sergeant major from taking charge of the army enlistees. I'm sure whatever happened here, he's not to blame."

I grunted. Steele was far more trusting than I. "Fine. Whatever. I'll do my best to be nice." Which was a clever way of hedging my bets in case the eager beaver had done something *really* stupid. "Now why don't we find Phillips to see what exactly *did* happen."

Cairny stayed behind, citing the need to get back to work on the ragged narc, but Quinto joined us as we embarked on our second straight tour of the precinct grounds. After not finding Phillips anywhere, I stopped by the Captain's office and asked the bulldog for his beat. With the information in hand, I grudgingly stepped back outside, mentally preparing my feet for the long journey that was sure to follow. Before I'd even taken three steps up 5th Street, however, I heard a few chuckles and guffaws, as well as a voice: Phillips', coming from nearby.

We found our prey in the alley adjacent to the station, chatting with a pair of other bluecoats, one of whom took a long draught from a briar pipe and puffed the smoke out of the corner of his lips.

"Phillips!" I said. "Where the hell have you been!"

Thankfully for Phillips, he wasn't the one sucking on the pipe, otherwise the thing might've gone flying.

"Daggers! Sir," he said as he came to attention. "What can I do for you?"

Steele dug her fingers into my side and whispered in my ear. "Remember. Be nice."

I forced myself to take a deep breath before continuing. "The body, Phillips. What happened to it?"

"The body, sir?"

"Yes," I said. "Lanky. The corpse from the crime scene this morning. With the hair and the beard and the noticeable funk. I understand you brought it back to the precinct alongside Detective Quinto." I jerked my thumb in the big guy's direction, who did his best to block out the sun at the alley's mouth. "Where is it?"

"I...delivered it," said Phillips.

"Where?" I asked.

"To the morgue."

"*Our* morgue?"

"Of course."

I lifted an eyebrow. "Are you *sure* about that?"

I flinched as Steele's claws dug into my ribcage.

Phillips' lips flattened as he pushed them together, but other than that he did a good job of hiding his displeasure. "Absolutely. Ask Poundstone, or the other beat cop who helped us out. Whatever his name is. Ferguson, I think."

I frowned, but I also kept my composure—thanks in large part to Shay and her needlelike fingers. "Perhaps you could show us exactly where you left it?"

Phillips nodded and pushed his way past me and the living wall of muscle that constituted Quinto. We followed him back inside the precinct, down the stairs, and into the morgue, where we found Cairny slicing into the narc's throat with a wicked-looking scalpel.

"You're back!" Cairny smiled and waved with the scalpel in hand.

I averted my eyes from the cadaver's skin flaps by resting them on Phillips. His jaw fell, and I saw his tongue twist as he raked it across his teeth. His eyes darted back and forth across the room, and he blinked.

"I...don't understand," he said. "The body's gone."

I thought of a vulgar response, but pared it down for Shay's benefit. "No kidding."

I leveled a cool glance at Phillips, but I needn't have. As the gravity of the charge settled in, the poor kid's attitude spontaneously melted from a frosty frustration to a blubbering puddle of ass-covering.

"Sir, you've got to believe me. We left the body right there, on that table." Phillips pointed it out. "Pound-stone and Ferguson will back me up, I swear. We even filled out and stamped the clipboard at the door!"

Quinto walked over and glanced at the clipboard in question. He nodded. "They did. Ink's still fresh."

"Did anyone sign the body out?" I asked.

If family members came to collect the body for burial or cremation, they'd need proper authorization, and the event would be recorded on the clipboard, among other places. Not that anyone could sign off on the collection of a murder victim before Cairny conducted her investigation, or that any family members would be around to collect Lanky at all. We didn't even know his real name yet, much less had we contacted his next of kin.

Quinto looked again. "Nope."

Steele pressed her lips together and wet them with her tongue. "So...what? Are we to assume someone broke in here and stole the body? Who would do such a thing?"

I ground my teeth together and growled under my breath. "I think I have a pretty good idea."

14

I burst into the military police offices at the New Welwic Main army base like a tornado of piss and vinegar, spraying everything and everyone in my way with the unsavory cocktail.

"Where's Agent Blue?" I demanded. "Where is that sneak thief? In his office?"

The same man and woman as before guarded the castle gates, but this time, both of them stood in response to my appearance. The woman, sensing the potential ramifications of my violent outburst, sped off down the hallway in the direction of Blue's office, while the young man moved to intercept me. A mask of impassiveness covered his face, but he hunched slightly as he approached me, his arms held at his sides, ready for action.

"Sir," he said. "You need to calm down."

"Calm down?" I said. "*Calm down?* What I need are answers. Explanations. And an apology. Quite frankly, this is absurd! In all my years on the force, I've never had to deal with such blatant disrespect for established police etiquette."

"Sir," said the young man, approaching me as if I were a wild animal that might bolt as easily as strike, "I don't know what you're talking about. But I'm sure if we calm down we'll—"

The front door creaked behind me. I spared a glance its way and spotted Shay entering the building, looking even more mortified than she'd been for the last fifteen minutes of our walk. She didn't even meet my eyes.

The look of despondency almost made me reconsider my strategy, but gosh darn it, if I didn't create a scene, then who would? Shay wasn't anywhere near as confrontational as I was, and given Quinto had elected to stay at the precinct—ostensibly to catch up on paperwork, but probably to spend more time around his fair-skinned, death-obsessed belle—then by default, the task fell upon my shoulders. And I didn't for a minute think a goody two shoes, 'please and thank you, ma'am' approach would get us anywhere with Agent Blue and his well-dressed army of bootlickers. They needed to know Shay and I and the rest of the police department meant business, and that we wouldn't stand for surreptitious body-snatching shenanigans and insincere tidings of camaraderie and goodwill delivered with a white-toothed smile.

I ranted and raved a bit more, trying to retain the heat in my blood until Agent Blue showed up, but I found I didn't have to try hard. I'd worked myself into a frenzy, and to be fair, it wasn't all an act. I *was* angry.

I also didn't have to wait long. Agent Blue sprinted up the hall, with the female soldier hot on his heels. His lips pressed tightly against one another, and his clenched jaw hardened his face.

"What in the world is going on here?" he asked.

"You tell me," I said. "When last we parted ways, you made a grand show of how you wanted to pool our resources and work together. How if you were in our shoes, you'd be the grand poobah of cooperation. So what exactly happened to that? Change your mind? Or was it a disingenuous platitude all along?"

Blue nodded at the female soldier in a 'Scram, I've got this' sort of way. She retreated to her desk, and the ACIC officer held his hand out down the hallway. "I'll be happy to discuss whatever problem has arisen, Detective Daggers, as long as you can rein in your anger and discuss this in a fashion fit for adults. Now...my office, if you please?"

I grunted and stomped off in the indicated direction. Behind me, I heard the soft patter of Shay's feet as she followed, and picked up on a quiet, "I'm sorry." I couldn't see the shake of her head that surely accompanied the apology, but her efforts to undermine me in front of Agent Blue did nothing to help my mood.

I settled myself in one of the investigator's chairs. Shay followed suit, as did Blue behind his desk.

"Now," said Blue. "Perhaps you could explain to me what this is all about?"

"Don't play dumb, Blue," I said. "The body. Where is it?"

"Excuse me?"

"You said you wanted to work together," I said. "But now you go and steal the body from us? And right out from under our own noses, without alerting anyone or filing any paperwork. It would be one thing to have done so when you took back your recruits, but to wait until we'd already returned the body to our own morgue? That's a *really* low blow. Like right in the gonads."

Blue glanced at Steele with narrowed eyes.

"The slain transient's body was delivered to our precinct earlier today," explained Steele. "It's since gone missing."

Blue shifted his eyes back to me. "And you think I had *my* men take it?"

I gave the elf a fake, toothless smile and flicked my hands in the air.

"But why would we want the cadaver?" asked Agent Blue.

"That's what I argued," said Steele.

I shook my head. Apparently Agent Blue, like my partner, lacked the sort of overactive imagination that came from reading large amounts of speculative fiction. "I can think of several reasons. But, to give you the condensed version, I think there's some clue about the manner of the man's death you—or the army as a whole—doesn't want leaking out."

Agent Blue snorted. "Detective Daggers, I assure you I didn't instruct any of my men to take the victim from your morgue. And I can also assure you none of my men acted in such a capacity without my knowledge. That's simply not how things are done in the army. And beyond that, I was fully honest in my stated desire to work together. You seem to think otherwise, but we're allies in this investigation, and I'm fully capable of admitting your forensics team is probably better versed than mine. Frankly, I'd *prefer* your team examine the body."

"You see, Daggers?" said Steele. "This is exactly what I told him on our way here, Agent Blue."

"And I thank you for the vote of confidence, Detective Steele." Elmorodil smiled, and his eyes twinkled.

One of the demons inside me reared its ugly head again. I tried to slap it down, but it growled and threatened to bite me. "So... Let's assume you're telling the truth. If you didn't take the body, then who did? And why?"

The ACIC agent leaned back in his chair and stroked his smooth jaw. "Well, that's an interesting question, isn't it? As you said, it would have to be a party that didn't want some piece of evidence to be uncovered. But who? Even though they're persons of interest, Sergeant Holmes and Privates Chavez and Delvesdeep have been on base since the incident this morning."

I drummed my fingers on my chair's armrest. "Perhaps *this* is a question we could pose to that trio directly."

Blue snorted, but his face softened. "I did say I'd be willing to let you talk to my men and women assuming you had valid reasons. Well, I admit this qualifies. And you have my attention as well. I'm assuming you're both currently available?"

Steele and I nodded.

"Good," said Blue. "We can start with Sergeant Holmes. To the best of my knowledge, he's in the infirmary having his wounds attended to. Follow me."

15

We dogged Blue's footsteps as he stepped outside, skirted the perimeter of the perfectly manicured lawn, and headed north at a cross street. Though part of me wanted to badger the ACIC agent into releasing more useful tidbits of information regarding our case, that desire was tempered by the fact that I'd have to talk to the smug-faced elf to do so. Luckily, my years in the force prior to Steele's arrival—years spent alongside my stone-faced fossil of an ex-partner, Griggs—had helped me develop my non-verbal communication skills. I stuffed my hands in my pockets and glared at the back of Blue's skull in what I imagined to be an intimidating and disapproving manner.

We soon arrived at a three-story rectangular box that displayed all the best architectural design elements of military construction—namely four walls and a roof—but despite its uninspired construction, the thing stuck out among its counterparts like a sore thumb. The structure blazed a brilliant white, like a daisy in a field of grass, albeit grass with a decidedly unhealthy olive hue. I rubbed my thumb against the side of the building as we approached, and it came away clean as it would from paint, not whitewash—which didn't surprise me, given the military budget.

It seemed grossly unfair that between our two ostensible peace-keeping organizations, the police department got such a short end of the cash stick. Then again, the chance of dying in the line of police duty was markedly lower than in the army, and while the GIs had no shortage of coin to buy fancy equipment and to hire fire- and lightning-wielding magical bigwigs, the guys doing the majority of the dying out on the front lines tended to be paid even worse than I was. I told myself to keep that in mind the next time we ran out of coffee or the Captain decided to treat me as his own personal side of beef jerky.

Blue pushed on into the hospital, and Shay and I followed. More white covered the walls, and ceramic tiles sparkled underfoot, freshly mopped with a cleaner that had left behind a faint smell of orange peels and ammonia. Metal-framed cots lined the walls, each with a partition between them—a steel bar fitted with metal rings and a curtain, much like one might find around a shower. All the curtains had been pushed back, revealing the beds as empty.

In response to the front door's creak, a nurse approached us from the far side. I glanced at her, blinked, and tried not to look disappointed. Rather than the tight white miniskirt and matching red-trimmed corset I'd come to expect from the history course I'd taken at the local gentleman's club, the nurse wore a long-sleeved checkered dress shirt, over which lay a white apron and skirt combo that came to her mid shin. In addition, the nurse underneath the outfit wasn't much to look at. Between her motley collection of chocolate-brown skin, pale hair, mismatched eyes, and ears that looked like they might help her take flight at any moment, I wasn't even sure if she was human.

She saluted as she stopped in front of Agent Blue. "Nurse Billings, at your service sir."

Blue responded in kind. "We're looking for Sergeant Timothy Holmes. Know where we can find him?"

"Yes, sir," she said. "Second floor. Far side of the building. Should be easy to find, sir. Only occupied bed on that side at the moment."

Blue nodded and headed toward the nearest stairwell. I mounted the steps behind him.

We found Timmy propped up on a stack of pillows. His tan fatigue-clad legs stretched out before him on the bed, but he'd shrugged out of his official-looking top and into a white undershirt that showed off his muscular arms. As I'd predicted, the bruise underneath his eye had spread, coloring his skin with a brilliant shade of violet that would've looked far more appealing in the setting sky than it did on his face. Black stitches peeked through his bushy eyebrow, and given his reduction in clothing, I was able to make out a number of other bruises blotching his chest and arms.

To Timmy's right, a young bruiser wearing full fatigues and the now familiar white MP armband stood at attention. He eyed us and saluted as Blue approached, but otherwise he didn't move. Sergeant Holmes saluted Agent Blue as well, making me wonder what the elf detective's rank was.

"At ease, Sergeant," said Blue. "How are you feeling?"

"Better," he said. "A little sore, but far from the worst I've been through. The orderly said I'll be released this afternoon."

Blue gave the MP bruiser a nod, which I gathered was his way of making sure the guy stuck to Holmes like glue.

"Excellent." Blue tilted his head toward me and Steele. "I'm assuming you remember detectives Steele and Daggers?"

I took note of the order in which he named us.

"Yeah. Sure," said Holmes.

"Good," said Blue. "They've had a...*development* in their case, and they'd like to ask you a few more questions. I assured them you'd be amenable to that."

Timmy showcased his need for a thesaurus in his response. "Yeah. Sure. What do you need?"

"Where's the body, Timmy?" I asked.

"Huh?" said the Sergeant.

Blue snorted, almost imperceptibly. "Straight and to the point, I see." Which he appended with a muttered, "Not that I expected anything else..."

"Excuse me?" I said.

I'm not sure if curiosity or a desire to keep the peace motivated Shay, but she filled the auditory void before either of us could say anything else. "Sergeant Holmes, do you have any idea as to the identity of the man who died following his encounter with you earlier today?"

The muscular guy shook his head. "No. I told you this morning. I'd never seen that guy before in my life."

"Are you sure the man was alone when he approached you?" asked Shay. "Did he have any friends nearby? Or anyone following him?"

"What?" said Tim. "No. Why would he?"

Shay clasped her hands. "Someone attacked him. If he approached you in the alley already wounded, there's a good chance his attacker was nearby."

I forced my glaring eyes from Agent Blue to Timmy. He blinked and gave us a shifty-eyed sort of look. I don't think he thought through his response.

"The body, Timmy," I repeated. "It was delivered to our morgue and now it's gone. So where is it?"

I didn't think he'd know, just as I was sure Steele didn't believe Lanky stumbled into Timmy in the alley as he'd claimed, but like my partner I asked anyway, partly because I had to and partly because it might grease Tim's lips into letting something slip—or force the elf at my side to say something that might reveal more of what *he* knew and refused to share.

"The *name's* Tim," growled the sergeant. "And I didn't steal a body from your morgue, if that's what you're insinuating."

"It wasn't," I said.

Tim looked at me cross-wise. A voice from the stairwell diverted our attention.

"Agent Blue?" The nurse from downstairs poked her head through the door. "A message for you, sir."

Elmorodil glanced at Shay and me, his brow furrowed. "I'll be right back. Please refrain from any questions until I return."

He slipped off and disappeared down the stairs. I gave Shay a look. She shrugged in response. I couldn't

tell what she meant by that. Was it a shrug of resigna-
tion, or a complicit one, agreeing that we should ignore
the guy?

I took another look at Timmy and his impressive collection of bruises. The MP guard peered at me impas-
sively. He didn't seem to have any skin in the game.

I figured a question or two unrelated to Lanky's disappearance couldn't hurt. "You suffer from vertigo,
Tim?"

"What?"

"Vertigo," I said. "A dizzying sensation, as if your
surroundings are tilting or spinning."

"I know what it is," he said.

I lifted an eyebrow. "Well then?"

"No."

"You drink often?" I asked.

"Sometimes," he said. "When I'm off duty. Why?"

I shrugged. "Big guy like you? Regular at the bars?
You must be able to hold your liquor pretty well. And if
your sense of balance is fine..."

"I told you, I was drunk," said Tim. "I fell down."

"I can't imagine that happens a lot," I said. "Or, you
know...ever. Funny it should happen the same night a
guy shows up dead."

I felt Shay's light touch on my elbow. "Daggers..."

The sergeant's eyes narrowed, and I could hear his
teeth squeak as they ground together. He sat up. "If
you've got something to say, then say it, asshole."

Between the loss of our cadaver, the black cloud
hanging over me today, and the whole Sweetcheeks
Blue situation, I was already emotionally balanced on a

razor's edge. The punk-ass twenty-something's mouth just happened to push me over.

"*Fine*," I said, slamming my hand into his bed frame. "I'll say it. I think you're a damned liar who beat a hobo to death, and regardless of whether or not that bastard deserved it, you can bet your sweet ass I'm going to come after you for it. Because if there's anything I like less than murderers, it's cocky SOBs who think they can get away with it!"

The sergeant cocked his arm and leaned forward. The MP darted forward and pushed me back as he yanked on Tim from behind. At the same time, Steele grabbed my coat.

"Daggers, what the hell do you think you're doing?" she hissed. "This isn't the precinct! You can't do that!"

"WHAT is going on here?" Agent Blue stormed back with perfect timing, the air around him crackling with ill-restrained fury.

Sergeant Timmy pointed a finger at me. "This asshole tried to—"

Blue silenced him with a glare. "I expect you to conduct yourself in a manner befitting your uniform, *soldier*, even if you might not be wearing it at this moment. That includes your speech as well as your actions."

I dusted my jacket, feeling pleased.

"And as for you—" Blue turned to me. "You need to leave."

"Fine by me," I said. "Sergeant Tim and I aren't exactly on the best of terms. Let's go see if Kelly and Drake have anything useful to say."

"You misunderstand me," said the army investigator in a slow voice. "You need to get off this base. *Now*. Go home and cool off. Or go to your station. I don't really care. But I won't have you here, insulting my men and picking fights with my charges."

He turned to Shay. "Detective Steele, I'm sorry it has to be this way. I'd still like to work together on this investigation, but if your partner can't control himself, then I'm afraid that won't be possible. At least not in face to face meetings, not with him present. Now, unless there's some urgent matter to attend to before you leave...?"

Shay shot me a chilling glance. "I understand, Agent Blue. I'll have a word with Detective Daggers. Several, actually. All I ask is that you update us if you get any further information from privates Chavez and Delvesdeep. And, if it wouldn't be too much trouble, could we have a copy of theirs, as well as Sergeant Holmes', personnel files?"

"Absolutely," said Blue with thin smile and a nod. "We'll stop at Admissions and Records as I escort you out."

The agent held his arm in the direction of the stairs. Under normal circumstances, I might've fought back against his commands, but for the time being, I was too preoccupied with Steele's fierce scowl to care.

16

The shops and eateries that lined Ley Street stretched out before me, surrounded by clusters of humans and half-breeds chatting and smoking cigarillos and warily eyeing the clouds above for traces of rain.

I barely saw them. A smug face with close-cropped dark hair and a jaw that looked as if it had been modeled out of clay filled my field of vision. The face sneered at me and lifted an eyebrow, taunting me with its elven perfection.

I blinked, trying to banish the apparition, but my own insecurities decided I hadn't suffered enough. Agent Blue's full form materialized, and the Captain appeared behind him. The bulldog clapped the elf on the shoulder, and I heard his gruff voice in my mind.

Daggers. I assume you've heard the news, he said. *Due to his exemplary performance on your most recent case, we've decided to bring Agent Blue on board. Of course, given his track record and education, I'm promoting him to a senior de-*

tective position, effective immediately. And he'll need a partner. Someone worthy of his skill...

I sucked air in through my teeth as Steele coalesced into form beside the pair. Blue smiled and put an arm around her shoulders.

"Daggers!"

I felt my arm yanked to the side, and a rush of air flapped the hem of my coat. A rickshaw careened past, evoking a chain reaction of yells that started from the driver and spilled to the loiterers at my side before bouncing back to the patron in the back seat.

Steele clutched my arm in a vice grip. Her eyes radiated concern. "Are you even paying attention?"

"Huh?" I said.

"That answers that." She let go of my elbow and shook her head. "Look, I know you're the dark and brooding sort, but try not to get yourself killed, ok?"

"Um...right." I flattened my coat back into place.

Steele's boots crunched on the gravel underfoot as she started to walk again, and she shifted the manila folder with the files we'd received from the Admissions and Records office higher under her arm. "What in the world is going on with you today, anyway?"

Where should I start? I wasn't sure if I could successfully lie to Steele about such a matter, but I could at least obfuscate my root issues with partial truths. "It's that Agent Blue. He's in on it. And I don't even know what *it* is yet, but he's involved."

Steele rolled her eyes. "Not this again."

"Yes, *this* again," I said. "Think about it. Why else wouldn't he allow us to speak with Privates Chavez and Delvesdeep? Unless, of course, *he* knows *they* know something he doesn't want *us* knowing. Like, say, regarding the disappearance of Lanky's corpse."

"Right," said Steele. "Like how maybe Lanky was really an army special forces ranger who died after being injected with lab-grown mutagens that were *supposed* to transform him into a super soldier but instead killed him and now the whole army wants to cover it up."

I snapped my fingers. "Exactly. I mean...*what?*"

"Oh, that's not plausible to you?" asked Steele.

"You're making fun of me, aren't you?"

"You think?"

"Ok," I said. "Why don't you suggest a more rational theory?"

"Ok. Here's one," said Steele. "Maybe—and I know this is a stretch—Agent Blue is actually telling the truth. Maybe he doesn't like the fact that you're throwing your weight around with the same enthusiasm as the insults you're slinging, and that he can't trust you not to instigate the army's next major armed conflict. Oh, and that he just plain doesn't like you because you've been an irritable ass around him."

I gaped at my partner. She didn't believe all that, did she? Not the first parts. I'd intentionally acted like a force of nature in the Agent's presence, for precisely the reasons I'd told Shay. I'd hoped to knock some truth off the walls by the gravity of my presence. No, I meant the last part. Was she really taking the pretty elf dude's side? And more importantly...*why?*

Steele took one look at my face and reacted accordingly. "Look, why don't we talk about something else?"

I nodded dumbly, unsure if I'd managed to ratchet my jaw up to its regular position.

Steele stuck her hands in her blazer pockets—a move that seemed silly given the length of her coat sleeves—and glanced at me furtively. "So, anyway, I wanted to ask you something. Have you ever been to the Dogfish Club?"

I wracked my brain. "Is that the place over on Wadsworth and 7th?"

Steele nodded.

I shook my head. "Not unless you count a stakeout I once had across the street from there. What about it?"

"I've heard Marko Prizek is going to be there next week. Three nights only. Tuesday through Thursday."

"Am I supposed to know who that is?"

"He's a famous pianist," said Shay. "Performs ragtime, mostly, though he's been known to dabble in jazz every now and then."

I blinked.

Shay's brow furrowed. "What are you confused about? Ragtime? It's a musical genre featuring a syncopated, ragged rhythm. Typically it—"

I held up a hand. "I know what it is. I'm just blown away anybody still listens to that crap. I thought it went out of style a century ago."

Shay glanced at me, a slight crease in her forehead. She opened her mouth and took a breath, then closed it as she exhaled. "I... I mean, some people still like it."

"They must," I said, "otherwise the Dogfish Club isn't going to be in business much longer. So what did you want to tell me about this Marko guy?"

Steele sighed and turned her attention to the gravel at her feet. "Nothing. Heard he was going to be around, is all."

I chuckled as a stray thought crossed my mind. "Hey, speaking of pianists—"

"Stop it, Daggers," said Steele, without looking my way. "I don't want to hear any of your stupid jokes right now."

"Hey now, that's not fair. I wasn't going to make a dumb joke. I was going to share some choice tidbits about the origin of the piano which I thought you'd be interested in." Which was a total fabrication. I did have a crude joke on my mind, one involving a genie and a miniature version of the aforementioned piano player. The joke absolutely *killed* the first time I told it to Quinto.

Steele didn't even glance at me.

Following her lead, I stuffed my hands in my pockets and snorted. "And to think you've been bugging me about *my* attitude. What's *your* problem all of a sudden?"

"Nothing," she snapped. "Let's get back to the precinct, ok?"

Steele surged forward, her legs carrying her at twice their usual rate, leaving me in the dust and wondering what exactly I'd done to piss her off.

17

Steele and I walked into the precinct, both of us still refusing to brush the encroaching winter chill from our shoulders. We sauntered past Rodgers' and Quinto's empty desks on our way to our own. When we arrived, Steele slumped into her chair and immediately flipped open the manila folder, glancing at the contents within.

I collapsed in my throne and leaned back, glancing across the conjoined pair of desks at my partner. The folder obscured her face, though the voluminous hair treatment she'd undergone at least made it so I could see a wave of chocolate brown around the edges of the thick manila paper stock.

Clever me, I gathered the placement of the folder wasn't an accident. I rubbed my thumb against my index finger as I considered how to proceed.

I went with the straightforward route. "So, what do you think we should do now?"

"Isn't determining that more your area of expertise?" The creased manila portfolio didn't move. "My job is to make keen observations and look pretty."

I continued to rub my fingers together. With any luck, I'd start a fire, immolate myself, and never again have to try and understand the inner workings of the female mind. What did she mean by that last statement, anyway? Was she throwing something back in my face? I didn't recall ever saying anything of the sort to her, or to someone else while in her presence. And wasn't *I* the one whose day was turning out less than stellar? What did she have to be upset about, other than being subjected to the constant demands of my own waffling misery?

I cached that last thought. It hit too close to home. "I...don't recall anyone around here ever expressing that thought. Besides, I'm being serious. Do you have any ideas about where to point the investigation next, because I'm running low on ingenuity at the moment."

The manila folder remained immobile, but the voice that drifted over to my ears was decidedly less hostile than before. "I don't know, Daggers."

Shay closed the folder and set it on the corner of her desk. She stood, neglecting to make eye contact with me. "I've got paperwork I need to catch up on. I'll be back."

She strode off in the direction of the form office, leaving me to wonder what form, exactly, she intended to file. A 1053B? Not until we'd officially charged someone with the murder. Maybe a 799, but that could wait until the morning. I drummed my fingers on my desk, and after a minute or two of waiting, the truth dawned on me.

She wasn't coming back. Not any time soon.

I felt a churning in my well of emotions, analogous to alcohol-induced stomach queasiness but not as frightening for nearby parties.

I took a deep breath and quashed it as best I could. No worries. I'd survived life on the force alone before. Admittedly, my most recent stint between partners had left me a gibbering mess, but most of that had to do with the sheer amount of paperwork inflicted upon me by the Captain.

I stood and stretched, glancing in the direction of Quinto's desk. Unfortunately, the big guy remained invisible. I would've gladly bounced ideas off him—he, unlike my current partner, was almost always amenable to conversation—but as I stood there looking in his workspace's direction, my thoughts drifted to Rodgers. Hopefully the cheery guy's spirits wouldn't be too negatively affected by the death of his relative, whoever it happened to be. Of course, he probably wasn't the one who needed my thoughts the most. Poor Allison. I could envision her now, struggling to wrangle their two sprightly little ones without any help from Rodgers. I made a mental note to stop by her place later with some food—preferably something without any sugar in it.

Determined to make myself useful—and keep any encroaching dark thoughts at bay—I headed back down to the morgue, where I found Cairny still poking at the corpse of the deceased drug addict. She'd peeled several more layers of flesh off the guy in search of who knows what, but for some reason the sliced up cadaver didn't bother me as it had earlier in the morning.

Cairny glanced at me as I entered her sphere of interaction. "Daggers. You came back."

"I always do," I said. "I've been told I'm like a lost dog in that respect."

"You look way too well fed for that analogy to work."

I lifted a brow. "Are you saying I'm fat? I'll have you know I've lost a good ten or fifteen pounds since the summer."

Cairny kept her eyes trained on the corpse. "What do you want, Daggers?"

"Have you seen Quinto?"

"Not recently. Anything else?"

"I don't suppose the body we misplaced magically reappeared?"

Cairny set her big moon eyes on me, a viscera-encrusted scalpel in hand. "I take it your return trip to see the army investigator didn't go so well?"

I snorted. "That's putting it mildly."

"Interesting." She blinked and dove back into her autopsy.

"I don't suppose you have any additional insights you've gathered since our last conversation?" I asked.

"Actually, I do." Cairny pushed her scalpel into the dead guy's chest cavity, using it as a pointer. "See here? I found some waxy accumulations in this man's ventricles, which indicates—"

"Cairny, I meant about Lanky. *My* dead guy."

The dark-haired coroner tilted her head. "Oh. No. Sorry."

"Ok. Thanks anyway. Stay frosty, Cairny."

Based on the look she gave me, I don't think she got my particular bit of morgue humor. Then again, the looks Cairny gave everyone were usually off.

I excused myself and spent the next hour combing the precinct for anyone and everyone who might've spent time in and around the morgue during the period after which Phillips delivered Lanky to our subterranean storage facility. I talked to beat cops and runners, street urchins and detectives. I even found the janitor I'd suspected of having cleaned the morgue, but he didn't have anything useful to tell me other than to grumble about the continued deterioration in quality of his detergent brands. While several people remembered Phillips' delivery earlier this morning, nobody could recall any group of people carrying a body *out* of the morgue.

The more I investigated, the less I found, and I became more and more certain something nefarious had taken place with Lanky's body. After all, corpses didn't plum disappear by themselves, and as much as I disliked the guy, I had to admit Agent Blue *probably* didn't take back the body—which meant my simple case of hobo beating gone sour had morphed into something far more complicated. But as compelling as the questions of *how* the body had been removed and *who* did it were, the most head-scratching part of it all was *why* anyone had bothered to take it.

I pictured Lanky in my mind's eye, specifically the wound he'd suffered on the back of his head. First appearances indicated the man had been beaten to death. If so, perhaps whatever weapon had delivered the killing blow was so distinctive we'd be able to identify it right off.

I supposed that might be possible, but it would suggest we'd come so close to our killer already that we'd spooked him or her into an otherwise insane course of action—to break into a police station and steal a dead body. And try as I might to think of any organization capable of pulling off such a feat, I couldn't come up with anyone that fit the bill other than the army. But our three hungover GIs couldn't have done it themselves, not in their state, and not while in custody—if we believed Agent Blue. But even if I was right and Lanky's disappearance was a convoluted government plot, why steal him? What was Agent Blue, or the Sergeant Major above him, trying to hide?

As I filled my brain to near bursting with conspiracy theories, my paranoia got the best of me. I headed to the precinct's second floor and searched out our sketch artist Boatreng, a short, bald-headed man whose artistic needs went sorely unmet by the police department's demands. I found him at his desk, shading the left side of a drawing on his pad, something depicting a dark alley and a man in black under a night sky. At least, that's what it looked like to me. It wasn't particularly detailed yet. And many of shapes seemed somehow *off*.

"Nice piece," I said as I walked up.

Boatreng eyed me dubiously. He and I weren't exactly on the best of terms, but we'd made quite a bit of headway since Shay's arrival. We could go for whole stretches of conversation now without anyone frowning or snarling.

"You like expressionism?" he asked.

I shrugged. "Beats me. I couldn't even define it if you asked me to. But that drawing of yours looks cool. Gives me a grizzled, dark sort of feeling."

Boatreng smiled. "Well, that's expressionism for you."

"You mind doing a sketch for me?" I asked.

He nodded. "Point me in the direction of the witness."

"You're looking at him."

Boatreng lifted an eyebrow. "You witnessed a murder?"

"Not exactly," I said. "But our victim has, um...gone missing. And I'd like to get a reference of the guy while he's still fresh in my mind. Two, actually. I'll need you to draw me a spare."

Boatreng snorted. "Not a problem. Have a seat."

The sketch artist flipped to a new page in his pad, and I sat. After three-quarters of an hour of questioning and drawing, I walked away with two nearly identical renditions of Lanky's face exactly as I remembered it, complete with his mud-caked beard and altercation-induced scrapes. I took the drawings back with me downstairs to the pit, eager to share them and my newly forged theories with my partner.

That's when I recalled the state of our relationship. I took a deep breath and steeled myself for the inevitable, but apparently fate had other plans for me.

18

I returned to my desk, drawings in hand, but rather than being faced with my partner's thin lips, cool azure eyes, and cheeks made rosy by pent frustration, I found myself staring at her empty chair and the manila folder from the army base, which appeared untouched from when she'd left it. I glanced in the direction of the form office before remembering she'd probably never gone there in the first place.

A slurp and a hearty clearing of a throat brought my attention across the pit to Quinto's backside. I walked over to find the big guy seated at his desk, surrounded by administrative documents and with a steaming mug of dark liquid at his elbow. An earthy smell worked its way into my nose alongside a hint of something spicy—perhaps anise. Either Quinto had developed a taste for licorice, or he'd found a new favorite variety of tea.

"Holy cow," I said as I approached. "You weren't kidding about the paperwork earlier."

Quinto gave me a resigned glance. "You of all people should know how the Captain operates. Your partner goes missing, and all of a sudden, the skies part and ten years worth of back-catalogued crap falls on your head. All of which, incredibly, needed to get done yesterday."

I shook my head. "You'd think if anyone would be exempt from that treatment, it would be you. I mean, honestly, what's the worst that could happen to you if you went out alone? You took on a seven foot tall werewolf and barely came away with a scratch."

"That scratch required stitches," said Quinto as he ran his hand across the forearm in question, "but I don't think the Captain's policy has anything to do with physical danger. I think he's more concerned with what goes on up here when we're alone." He tapped the side of his head.

I snorted. I didn't think Quinto had anything to fear from what lingered in *his* mind. Me, on the other hand...

"Speaking of which," I said. "Have you seen Steele recently?"

"Yeah. About twenty minutes ago. I think she left."

"Really?" I glanced at the windows on the far side of the Captain's office. The day's light was fading, but with winter approaching, that didn't necessarily mean it was time to cut and run. Besides, Steele never left work before I did, not with her can-do attitude and my aversion to putting in more than six hours a day unless I absolutely had to.

Quinto slurped his tea, bringing my attention back to reality. "Everything...ok between you two?"

I blinked. "Huh? Yeah, yeah. Sure."

I introduced my hands to my coat pockets, and Quinto took another sip of tea, possibly as a way to give his own enormous mitts something to do.

"So," he said, eventually breaking the silence. "How's the case going?"

I grunted.

"That bad, huh?"

I nodded. "I haven't made any progress at all with the three army enlistees. And Lanky's disappearance is driving me up the walls—mostly because it puts me at square one regarding his identity and the manner of his death."

"Have you considered it might've been a clerical error?" asked Quinto. "His disappearance, I mean."

"C'mon, big guy. You think he got transferred to a different morgue without *anyone* here knowing? *Really?*"

"It's possible," said Quinto. "Have you talked to the Captain about it?"

"Not yet," I said. "I'm afraid of how he'll take it. You know he's a stickler for security. Or, alternatively, he'll think I'm nuts and that there's a perfectly rational explanation for everything."

Quinto rolled his eyes in a way that made me think he also believed the latter. "Well, don't worry about it, Daggers. We'll sort through it in the morning, I'm sure."

"*We?*" I asked.

Quinto shrugged. "What? I'm optimistic about how quickly I can get through this paperwork. Captain'll let me come with you guys if I do."

I nodded and returned to my desk, secretly thinking the only way Quinto would reach his goal was if his desk spontaneously combusted. After seating myself in my chair, I tried to engage my mental faculties in more harebrained theorizing, but I couldn't focus. My thoughts kept drifting to Shay.

Why had she left so early? Had I crossed a line, and if so, which one? Professional, or personal? Yes, I knew I'd acted like a jerk throughout parts of the day, but wasn't that one of my charming, affable qualities? One of the things that made me irresistible?

I glanced at her empty desk, and my eyes fell upon the manila folder. Feeling the need for a distraction, I reached over, grabbed it, and helped myself to the contents. First in line was Sergeant Timmy's file, four sheets held together by a paper clip, which appeared to be presented in the order of: personal information, a perfunctory psychiatric evaluation, citations of exceptional service, and indictments for the exact opposite.

I scanned the pages in order.

First page. Full name Timothy Robin Holmes. *Robin? Really? Had his parents secretly desired a girl?* Born in New Welwic. Raised on the southeastern side. Twenty-seven years old. No disclosed allergies or preexisting medical conditions. Fingerprints were attached.

Flip.

Second page. A fairly unspectacular psych eval, full of the sorts of things you'd expect from an army sergeant. Bull headed, liked to hit things and boss people around, but followed orders. Not much of an intellectual.

Flip.

Third page. One single commendation, for exceptional performance on an athletic challenge performed during basic training, something imaginatively called 'The Gauntlet.' Not a single mention of his performance as a sergeant, however. That was a little surprising.

Flip.

Fourth page. Jackpot. Four incidents and complaints. Two of them involved physical altercations with other recruits, once as a private and the other as a corporal. The other two incidents had occurred during Timmy's stint as a sergeant.

The first involved a case of neglect. Apparently someone in Tim's charge had overheated, collapsed, and nearly died during a training exercise. At the bottom of that summary was a stamp reading 'Closed, Nolle Prosse,' which meant the prosecutor in charge of the case had decided not to file charges. In all likelihood, no one could prove whether or not Sergeant Holmes had pushed the soldier to the brink of death or if the soldier had pushed himself there.

The last incident was recent, only three months old. A private Bernadette Chesterfield had filed a complaint against Timmy for 'promoting a hostile work environment' and 'using language unbefitting the workplace.' Another stamp had been affixed to the bottom of the synopsis, this one bearing the word 'Withdrawn' and a date two months past.

I made some mental notes before moving on to the remaining two files in the folder. If I hadn't been particularly impressed with the wealth of information available on Sergeant Holmes, then I was downright disappointed with the files on privates Chavez and Delvesdeep.

I supposed it was to be expected. Both were relatively new enlistees, having joined five months back, on the exact same date no less. Both also hailed from the same town, a flyspeck on the map a few days north of the city by boat. I assumed the two had known each other prior to enlisting.

While I didn't glean much about the pair from the army documentation, I did note the psych evals listed Chavez as 'argumentative' and Delvesdeep as 'aloof' and 'potentially uncooperative.' Which got me to thinking—who, exactly, did the army turn away? Of the three evaluations I'd read, not one had been filled with glitter and affixed with gold stars.

I replaced the pages in the manila folder and set the pile back in its rightful spot on Shay's desk. A long shadow stretched across the floor, and as I looked up, I spotted Quinto standing beside his chair, shrugging into his enormous purple duster that contained enough fabric to clothe an entire village in loincloths.

I hustled to catch up to him before he vanished. "Hey, big guy. Headed out?"

"Yup," he said. "Taking Cairny to a new restaurant a few blocks south of the station. A place called Flim-flame. Heard of it?"

I bit down on my tongue. I'd planned on asking Quinto if he wanted to join me at Jjade's, my watering hole of choice. "Um...no. Can't say I have."

"Well, I'll let you know how it is," he said. "If it's good, maybe we can all head there sometime. Though we should wait until Rodgers returns. You know how he gets about being left out."

I nodded. "Yeah."

Quinto gave me a nod. "Anyway. See you tomorrow."

"Right. You, too." I paired my farewell with a half-hearted wave.

Thumping footsteps dogged Quinto's departure, and I found myself standing in the pit, surrounded by polished wood and gleaming metal, chatting cops and coffee-fueled investigators and the Captain's lingering aura, but still feeling very much alone.

19

A chill morning fog hung to my shoulders and prickled the skin at the base of my neck as I marched
down Schumacher onto 5th. I grumbled under my
breath, but I didn't fight it—not only because doing so
would've marked me as loonier than a brace of ducks,
but also because the cold mist seemed like such a fitting
complement to my mood.

I pushed through the station's heavy double doors,
letting traces of fog sweep in behind me, and headed
toward my desk. Quinto's empty chair gave me a wink
and a smile as I passed, relishing in its temporary liberation from the big guy's weighty hindquarters.
Steele's chair couldn't give me the same salutation, but
then again, it probably liked the attention *it* got.

Shay sat, back to me, her still-curled chocolate
brown hair spilling over a maroon jacket, one that featured full length sleeves, a notched lapel, and a heavier
weave than yesterday's version. A cream-colored scarf
curled in a tight spiral in the spot where I'd last seen
the army admissions folder reside, and an umbrella

rested against the side of the desk, its oiled fabric dry
and its clasp still attached. Though the skies threatened,
so far all we'd gotten was fog.

Shay heard the thumping of my feet and turned to
face me. Her cheeks were smooth and the line made by
her mouth flat, but other than the cool air about her, I
didn't detect any hints of malice. I took that as a good
sign.

"You're in early." She glanced at my face and did a
double take. "You look terrible, by the way."

I frowned. "Thanks...?"

"Oh come on. You know what I mean. It's early—"
She glanced at the windows, where a stray ray of light
had burst through the low cloud cover. "—at least for
you—but it's not *that* early."

I settled into my seat. "I suffered through some ex-
tenuating circumstances."

Steele tilted her head and lifted a brow. "Of the pro-
jectile vomit variety?"

"*What?* No." I sniffed my coat. "Is that what I smell
like?"

Shay shook her head. "You're emitting your usual
aroma—"

I wondered what she meant by that comment.

"—but I assumed based on past events. Given your
appearance, I figured...Jjade's, heavy drinking, and the
inevitable conclusion of the first two."

"Well, I'm sorry to disappoint you, Miss Clairvoy-
ant," I said. "But you're batting one for three this morning."

"You tried a different bar?" said Shay. "How adven-
turous of you."

I snorted. "Your unshakable belief in my alcoholism is reassuring, but no. I went to Jjade's. I did not consume any potent potables. And I did not get sick afterwards."

Shay smiled an evil grin. "So you're telling me you look this bad because you *didn't* drink?"

"I look like this because of when I got up."

"Daggers, really. I know you're in your own league in that regard, but it's not *that* early."

"I've been up for over two hours," I said.

"*You have?*" Shay's eyes narrowed. "Why?"

"I picked up bagels, cream cheese, and coffee, not to mention some kolaches, and went over to Rodgers' place. Checked in with Allison—who's doing fine, by the way, thanks for asking—and had breakfast with her and the kids."

Shay blinked. "Really?"

"Yes, really," I said. "I've known Rodgers for almost a decade, and I've always been fond of Allison—in a purely platonic way, mind you. It's the least I could do to drop off food along with my condolences."

My partner's face softened, and she seemed to regard me in a new light—though it could've been the strengthening sun burning its way through the mist and into the pit.

"Well...that was very thoughtful of you, Daggers."

I nodded.

Shay played with the tassels on the end of her scarf. "Did you find out who died?"

"His father."

My partner took a sharp breath. "Oh, no. Poor Rodgers."

"Yeah," I said. "He suffered a stroke. Totally unexpected. Well...not totally. The guy was pretty old, apparently. Did you know Rodgers is the youngest of five?"

Shay shook her head.

"Yeah. Anyway, it sounds like Rodgers will be gone for at least a week. I hope he doesn't lose that trademark smile of his. Losing a parent...can be tough."

Steele seemed to have lost her taste for speech. She regarded me with soulful eyes and nodded.

"So where's Quinto?" I asked.

"In self-imposed solitary confinement," said Steele. "He's trying to churn through the Captain's paperwork in record time."

I snorted. Apparently the big guy didn't realize the key to survival wasn't to wade through the stacks of work but to simply weather the storm until it passed.

A flash of sunlight shimmering through fog caught my eye. A runner, no more than ten years old, pushed his way through the front doors and headed in the direction of the Captain's quarters. *Just what the doctor ordered...*

Shay noticed him about the time he reached the bulldog's office. "Oh, no. I could've gone without that this morning."

"You're preaching to the choir, sister," I said. "Why is it people always get forked in the kidneys at night?"

"That's a rhetorical question, I presume?" asked Steele.

"Mostly," I said. "But killers need sleep, too."

Within a minute, the Captain emerged from his office and motioned to the two of us. "Daggers? Steele? A minute."

The runner made himself scarce, and we joined the Captain, who leaned against his door frame. A grim frown stretched across his lips.

"Let me guess," I said. "Another murder?"

The bulldog didn't bother to rib me over my patent observation. "Possibly. The runner's description was unclear. I'll need the two of you to check into it."

"Where are we headed?" asked Steele.

"Back to the Delta district," said the Captain. "Outside, on a street corner, near Cross and Sweetgum."

I shot Steele a suspicious glance. "Wait...that's not far from where we found Lanky yesterday. A few blocks at most." The Delta district could get rough at night, but not *that* rough.

"Think I don't know that?" said the Captain. "Like I said, the details are confusing at the moment. But given yesterday's events, I want the two of you to investigate the matter. Speaking of which...any leads on yesterday's murder?"

"We're working on it, sir," said Steele.

The bulldog snorted, and his lip curled upward in an approximation of a smile. "What a wonderfully vague response."

"She learned from the best, Captain," I said with a grin.

"I can't tell if you're talking about yourself or me." The grizzled commander-in-chief nodded toward the door. "Now quit yapping and get moving. The murders won't solve themselves, detectives."

Shay stopped by her desk to grab her scarf. I watched her, transfixed, as she wrapped the napped wool around her slender neck, looping it once, then twice with a casual grace. There was a feminine, sensual element to the way she did it, the way she flicked her fingers and elongated her neck opposite the motion of her arms.

Shay glanced at me curiously as she settled the last end in place over her shoulder. "You...ready to go?"

Based on the look in her eyes, I knew yesterday's storm had passed. The question of how to prevent another squall from blowing in, however, still lingered.

I nodded. "Let's hoof it."

20

The sun burned off the last of the mist as we reached the outskirts of the Delta district, though it wasn't strong enough to displace the droplets of water clinging desperately to awnings or to banish the thin, glimmering sheen coating the exterior of residences both old and ostentatious enough to be built out of stone. Cats mewled from within alleys, their calls followed by the patter of small, clawed feet scrabbling for purchase on damp earth and fog-slicked cobblestones. As I skirted a rat that dove out of a back street in front of me, I couldn't help but reflect upon what the city's vermin infestation said about the homeless population: either felines and rodents reproduced faster than they could be skewered and eaten, or New Welwic's soup kitchens were flush with cash.

After fumbling about at the intersection the Captain had directed us to, Shay and I eventually found our crime scene hidden amongst a couple smaller cross streets nearby, sandwiched between an embroidery shop by the name of Needle in a Haystack and a shoe store that specialized in anything dull, brown, and ugly. Probably because of the location, gawkers were nonexistent. Besides me and Shay, I only spotted a couple of bluecoats, a young couple with bags under their eyes, and a rough around the edges stiff laying on his side in the dirt.

One of the two beat cops approached me, one of the guys who'd been at yesterday's scene but whose name I couldn't remember—if, indeed, I'd ever learned it. An ill-advised chinstrap beard grew from his face, and when he opened his mouth to speak, I found I couldn't take my eyes off his severe underbite.

"You're Detectives Daggers and Steele, right?" he asked.

I forced my gaze north of the mouth border with a practiced ease, born from years of tearing my eyes away from prominently displayed female knockers. "That's right. And you are...?"

"Officer Peabody." He jerked a thumb toward the other bluecoat. "That's Carter. You need a rundown?"

"That would be helpful," said Shay.

"Alright," he said. "Not much to tell, really. Gary and Norma, here—that's the couple, see—flagged me and Carter down 'bout an hour ago. Said they ran into this guy who wasn't doing so good. Collapsed and fell down right on the spot. So they brought us here and showed us who it was. And that's the guy. The one on the ground, there."

"Yes," I said. "We're crack detectives. We identified which of the five of you wasn't looking so hot right from the get-go."

Peabody eyed me with a furrowed brow and a jutting lower lip, which was impressive thanks to his underbite. Clearly, he didn't appreciate my humor. Where was Phillips when you needed him? That kid would laugh at anything I said or click his heels at a moment's notice. Maybe Shay had been right. I'd probably treated him unfairly.

"Anything else you can tell us?" asked Shay.

The guy shrugged, and I felt confident in my assessment that he probably wouldn't rise above his current station even if he stayed on the force another forty years.

"Thanks," said Shay before brushing him off and kneeling beside the body.

I joined her. "Spooky, isn't it?"

"What is?"

"The resemblance," I said.

The stiff was a dead ringer—no pun intended—for Lanky. Long hair, thick beard, wide frame, and big hands. He wore a tattered chestnut brown coat and matching, moth-eaten trousers. If anything, he was burlier than Lanky, which was a surprising quality for a transient—of which the new guy undoubtedly was. The clothes, beard, and hair gave it away. Unlike Lanky, however, he was in pretty rough shape. Lesions covered much of his face, and his skin had an unhealthy pallor to it—whether from disease or from some orc or ogre blood in his lineage, I couldn't tell. He also smelled. *Bad.*

"He does look a lot like yesterday's victim, doesn't he?" said Steele. "And the similarities between him and Lanky don't end at the superficial. Look at this."

She pointed at the vagrant's backside, and I leaned over so I could follow her finger. At the base of the man's skull was, for lack of a better word, a dent, caked with mud and dried blood and bits of hair and gristle. I held a couple fingers to the wound. Two wide, as with Lanky.

I took a deep breath and exhaled slowly as I rubbed my chin.

"What're you thinking?" asked Steele.

"I'm thinking this case just got a lot more complicated," I said. "Never mind Lanky's disappearance. We now have two murders with the same M.O., and I'm struggling to understand how our GI friends from yesterday fit into all this."

"Yeah," said Shay. "Me, too."

She reached out and rifled through his pockets. I fully expected her to come away empty handed, but upon checking his right coat pocket, Shay pulled out a shiny coin.

"Oh my gosh," I said. "Looks like Burly here was holding out on his hobo buddies. He's rich!"

"Not quite."

Steele handed me the coin, which upon further inspection turned out not to be legal tender, but rather a token. On its face, a geometrically-designed vortex swirled around a perfect circle. I flipped the token over. The back was blank.

"You ever seen anything like this?" I asked.

My partner shook her head as she completed her search. "Can't say I have. But any evidence is better than no evidence, right?"

I mumbled my agreement as I stood. "I suppose. Let's see what our concerned citizens can add to this mess."

I pocketed the coin and gave Shay a hand before turning to the witnesses, both of whom leaned against the side of the embroidery store. They held their arms folded across their chests as they talked in hushed voices.

"Gary and Norma?" I asked.

They nodded, and Gary responded. "That's right."

"I'm Detective Daggers, and this is Detective Steele," I said. "We understand you were the first ones to come across the body?"

Gary bobbed his head again as he pushed a mop of hair across his face and over to the side. A flashy suit jacket draped over his shoulders, partially concealing a shirt with far too many unbuttoned buttons. Based on his haircut and almost complete lack of chest hair, I placed him in his early twenties.

His date/girlfriend/courtesan Norma, on the other hand, probably hadn't even made it that far in life. She wore a diaphanous yellow dress under a heavy, knee-length overcoat, and her shoes were strictly of the flattering but impractical variety. Like the soldiers from twenty-four hours ago, both she and her boy toy reeked of alcohol.

"Yeah, yeah, man," said Gary. "We ran into the guy. I did, really. But he wasn't dead when we found him."

"Says you," said Norma. "That guy was dead as a doornail."

"If he was dead, then how did he bump into me?" he asked.

"He didn't," said Norma. "You ran into *him*. And if he wasn't dead already, then you killed him when you knocked him to the ground, you stupid gump."

Gary's eyes widened into saucers, and his hands turned into claws. "*Norma!* Shut up! You can't joke about that kind of thing. These are cops!"

"Whatever." The girl rolled her eyes.

Steele glanced at me with narrowed eyes before turning the suspicious peepers onto the young couple. "Why don't you two explain exactly what happened? Start at the beginning."

"Ok," said Gary. "So, Norma and I, we went out for drinks. Stopped at the Crown and Rose first, but that place was lame. So we cut out of there. Then we heard about a party over at the Flapping Gander. You know, that new jazz club? And man, it was hoppin'. The drinks were wicked strong, and the bartenders were pouring them as fast as the nozzles would let 'em. And the band? They had this crazy guy on the horn. Best trumpet player you ever heard, man. The music was flowing through me. I could feel it in my body, man. And—"

Shay jerked her thumb at Burly. "Why don't we skip to the part where this guy entered the picture?"

"Oh. Right, right," said Gary. "So anyway, Norma and I leave the club late. Real late. Like early morning late. And there's this fog everywhere. Thick as soup. Can't see a thing. So we start walking back to our place—"

Norma huffed. "Because *apparently* there aren't any rickshaw drivers around these parts at six or seven or whatever it was. Told you we should've gone to the Pearl instead."

"*What?*" said Gary. "You can't get jazz like that in the Pearl. With that kind of flow? That kind of soul? No way."

"Guys, focus," said Steele.

"Right," said Gary. "So we're walking along, looking for a rickshaw. But we can't find one because of the fog. Can't see anything 'cause of the fog. And then this guy comes out of nowhere. Barrels into me and almost knocks me over, and—"

Norma rolled her eyes again. "*Please...*"

"You remember things differently?" I asked.

The young lady—if, indeed, that word applied—flicked an idle hand. "Gary's embellishing everything. He was drunk as a skunk. Couldn't walk straight. Lost his balance and fell into the side of the building. 'Cept there was a guy standing there. That homeless man. Knocked him over."

"I didn't knock him over," said Gary. "The guy bounced off me."

"Alright," said Steele. "So what happened after he fell or was knocked over?"

"Well," said Gary. "I think I knocked the wind out of the guy, and—"

"Wait," I said. "I thought he bumped into you?"

"Yeah, yeah," said Gary. "Same difference. So he careens into me, losing his wind, and he grunts—"

"He did not grunt," said Norma.

Gary tossed his hands in the air. "Is anybody going to let me finish this story?"

Norma ignored her beau and eyed Steele and me. "He didn't grunt. Just fell over like a log. *Splat.*"

"He *grunted*," said Gary. "I heard him. Anyway, I bend over to help him. See if he's ok, right?"

"Really?" I eyed the kid's expensive jacket and considered how much money he must've blown on drinks through the course of the night. "*You* stopped to help a homeless guy?"

Gary tried his best to look offended. "Hey...what's that supposed to mean?"

"He didn't realize the guy was a hobo," said Norma. "Couldn't see in the fog."

Steele rolled her hand in the air. "Can we wrap this up? Preferably before lunch."

The tension in Gary's jaw was a clear sign of his annoyance, but I couldn't tell if it was due to our line of questioning or Norma's constant undermining of his story.

"Yeah," he said. "So I kneel down to help him. And that's when I notice this glimmer. On his head. Like blood. And I think, holy crap, somebody must've mugged this poor bastard. And at that point, I start to freak out. I'm not even sure if the guy's breathing any more. So Norma and I, we call out for help. Eventually find these two cops here and bring them back. But by that point the guy was dead."

I glanced at Norma to see if she felt the need to contradict any of that last part. She shrugged in acquiescence.

"I'm assuming neither of you know who this is?" said Steele, pointing at Burly.

"No idea," said Gary.

"Do you remember hearing any shouts or yells or screams before you stumbled across this man?" asked Steele.

Gary and Norma shook their heads.

"Did you see anyone suspicious either before or after the incident?" I asked. "Anyone carrying a weapon?"

Norma gave me a mocking glance. "How many times do we have to tell you it was foggy?"

"A simple *no* would suffice." I dug the coin out of my pocket and showed the young couple the face. "This ring any bells in either of your belfries?"

"Belfries?" said Gary.

"What is that thing?" asked Norma, squinting as she gazed upon it.

"I'm guessing that's another no," said Steele.

Norma stifled a yawn. "So...like, can we go now?"

I pocketed the coin and held up a finger. "Just a moment."

I pulled Steele back out of earshot. "So...what do you think?"

"About these two?" She glanced at Gary and Norma. "I don't think they could be any more clueless if they tried."

I nodded. "Yeah, I think they might be able to give Officer Peabody over there some competition for his title. So we're in agreement they're not involved in the murder?"

"Correct."

"What about their stories?" I said. "Who do you believe?"

"Both. Neither?" said Steele. "It's probably somewhere in the middle."

I grunted in agreement and pursed my lips.

"Detectives Daggers? Steele?"

I turned to find the runner who'd burst into the precinct this morning tugging at the hem of my jacket.

"That's us," I said. "What's new?"

"I'm relaying a message that arrived at the police station not long after you left," said the kid. "An Agent Blue at the New Welwic Main army base has requested a meeting with you. He said it's urgent."

I snorted. "I rather doubt that. I'm not allowed to play over at his house anymore."

The kid got the gist of my turn of phrase. "No. The other runner was very specific. He said Agent Blue requested to meet with Detectives Steele *and* Daggers. Right away."

Steele raised her eyebrows at me. "Well?"

"Well, what?" I said.

"Can you maintain your composure if we go back?" she asked.

I took a deep breath and let it out through my nose. "I'll manage. I promise." And I'd have to, unless I wanted to risk alienating Shay again. I could do better than I had yesterday. I knew I could. "Besides, I'm curious to know what Blue has to say. I'm having a hard time believing his summons and Burly's presence here are coincidental."

Before we left, I engaged myself in a stern chat with Peabody and Carter. I made doubly sure they knew to deliver the fresh corpse directly to Cairny at the station, and to make sure she accepted the body before they left, otherwise they'd learn the origins of the phrase 'holding one's feet to the fire.'

I'd already lost one dead hobo. I didn't plan on having it become a habit.

21

I repeated a mantra to myself as we walked to the army base. *Stay calm. Be polite. He's not a threat.* And after some thought and reflection, both overnight and during the walk, I'd come to the realization that Agent Blue, in all honesty, probably wasn't the monster I'd made him out to be.

Shay was right. He'd acted professionally in all our interactions, even if he had lavished my partner with a little more attention and good cheer than she otherwise deserved. While he *had* interfered in our investigation, he'd done so as a duty of his profession, and he hadn't insulted me or belittled me or looked at me the way businessmen eye gum on the soles of their shoes. I, on the other hand, had behaved like a petulant child whose favorite toy had been taken away, screaming and crying and kicking my feet in the direction of anyone dumb enough to get within striking distance—even the people I cared about. That must've been what set Shay off...

I was a bigger man than that, even if I didn't always show it. So what if Agent Blue had a fancy college degree and multiple commendations? So what if he wore a crisp uniform that accentuated the best portions of his lithe frame instead of a worn leather jacket that made him look like a walking sack of potatoes? So what if his elven ancestry had blessed him with immaculate features, a full crop of dark hair, and a smile that could make panties suddenly lose their elastic properties? Neither Shay nor the Captain had said I had to *like* the guy. I merely had to behave myself in a civil manner, and I could do that...so long as his advances toward Shay didn't progress beyond the cordial.

He met us at the door to the MP building and ushered us into his office, his face more drawn than I remembered it. He pointed us toward his guest chairs as he took his own.

"Detectives," he said. "Thank you for coming over on such short notice."

A couple beads of sweat dotted his temples, which I initially took as a sign of anxiety but soon realized might've been environmental in origin. His office was *hot*. Whichever janitor or maintenance engineer whose job it was to stoke the building's central fires must've fallen asleep on the bellows.

Shay took note of the unseasonable warmth, as well. She loosened and removed her scarf, setting it on the army sleuth's desk as she took a seat. "Not a problem, Agent Blue. Detective Daggers was both awake and alert when we received your missive, which is a rarity at this time of morning."

"And I'm on my best behavior." I splayed open my jacket, hoping the extra air would help, as I showed the agent my crossed fingers. "Scout's honor."

Blue nodded, a *slight* amount of the tension draining from his face. But only a little. "I'm glad to hear that."

"We would've arrived sooner," continued Steele, "but another matter drew our attention. So what is it you wished to discuss, Agent Blue?"

The elf took a deep breath and sighed. "No point in beating around the bush, detectives. Privates Chavez and Delvesdeep are gone."

I leaned forward in my chair reflexively. "*What?*"

"They deserted?" asked Steele.

"How did that happen?" I asked. "Didn't you have them locked up?"

Blue held up his hands to stem the tide of questions. "The pair were under supervision, but not under lock and key. Somehow they slipped their guard detail, or perhaps convinced them to look the other way for a few minutes."

I opened my mouth to speak, but Blue stopped me before I could. "Trust me. I'm as upset about this as you are. More, in all likelihood. Not only is it a poor reflection on me as the lead investigator in this inquiry, but it now adds a whole new pile of unsavory work onto my plate. I'll have to examine if there was a breach in conduct that allowed the two privates to escape and determine who precisely was involved. And I can assure you, there *will* be consequences, regardless of whether my new investigation unearths any actual malice or merely rote incompetence. The important piece of information for you is that they're gone. We suspect they deserted around an hour before dawn, give or take thirty minutes. And while such an action is far from a tacit admission of guilt in yesterday's murder, it doesn't look good."

Shay turned to face me, tilting her head and lifting her eyebrows. Based on the blank look I responded with, I think she realized I had no clue what she meant.

"I think we should tell him," she said.

"Tell me what?" asked Blue.

Part of me rebelled against relating anything of use to the ACIC agent—the part of me that ruled the roost yesterday—but in the spirit of renewed cooperation, I agreed. "Might as well. In the light of what he told us, I'd say it's relevant."

Blue's eyebrows furrowed.

"There was another murder this morning," said Steele. "Another transient in the Delta district. Same modus operandi as yesterday's slaying. No obvious witnesses to the murder, although it's possible we'll find some. We came straight here from the crime scene."

Blue's eyebrows drew together even further. He cupped a hand and pressed it over his mouth and chin. "I...don't understand. Why would Privates Chavez and Delvesdeep murder another vagrant?"

I leaned back in my chair and suppressed a smile. Agent Blue's use of the word 'another' indicated he'd suspected the pair, and perhaps Sergeant Timothy as well, of culpability in Lanky's murder, which was more than he'd revealed on the matter during our time with him yesterday. I enjoyed his slip of the tongue, but that wasn't what made me want to smile. It was his immediate conclusion to our news. The *obvious* conclusion. A conclusion that made me feel somewhat better about his possibly undeserved degrees and commendations.

Meanwhile, my mind raced forward at a mile a minute, cranking through the implications of our own murder discovery combined with the details of Kelly and Drake's escape. But I didn't share my thoughts, and not because I wanted to stymie Agent Blue for my own personal enjoyment. Mostly, I needed time for my theories to coalesce...although one additional thought came to mind that helped seal my lips.

Blue and Steele both sat in thought. I broke the ice with a conservative reply. "It doesn't make sense, does it? But I'm sure there's a logical explanation to their actions and that we'll be able to ferret out said explanation. Assuming we can *find* Drake and Kelly."

Blue removed his hand from his chin. "You're right. Our first order of business should be tracking down and apprehending the two privates. Unfortunately, while the army takes desertion seriously, it's not something we devote a lot of resources to outside of the occasional hearing and court-martial. You, on the other hand, do this sort of thing on a regular basis. If we could start a city-wide manhunt—"

"Not going to happen," I said. "The death of a couple hobos, while concerning, doesn't boil the public's blood enough to justify that expense. And even if it did, we'd need solid evidence that Kelly and Drake are the killers. Right now all we have is speculation and hearsay."

"So how do you propose we find them?" he asked.

"Steele and I will head back to the precinct," I said. "Gather a few of our fellow detectives. Maybe a few beat cops. I doubt we'll be able to convince our captain to spare more resources than that, but it's a start. I'm not entirely sure what your chain of command is like, but if you could do the same thing, it would help. Our side would begin by canvassing the privates' haunts, which I'm hoping you could provide us with, after your team talks to the other members of their squad or division or whatever it is you call it."

Blue nodded. "We can certainly do that. I'd already planned much the same thing. What else?"

"Stay in touch," I said. "And stay nimble. On your toes. Speaking of which..." I glanced at Steele. "We should do the same, but in the literal sense. The clock is ticking."

22

As we stepped from the stifling heat of the office into the cool air outside, the hamster manning the wheel in my brain slowed from a full on sprint to a steady jog, and though I hadn't been completely forthcoming with Agent Blue, I had told the full truth about one thing: our need for speed.

I hailed a rickshaw as we exited the army base, and one manned by a skinny youth with a shock of yellowy-orange hair slid to a halt in front of us. Shay climbed in first, and I followed.

"5th Street Precinct," said Shay to the driver.

"Scratch that," I said. "Take us to the DEITA immigration station."

"What?" said Steele. "The DEITA station?"

The driver gave us a confused glance.

"Ignore her," I said. "The DEITA station. Now. Chop-chop."

I flicked my hand for him to go, and we lurched forward as the young man put his wiry muscles to work.

"Hold on," said Steele over the clatter of the rickshaw's wheels on the cobblestones. "Did I black out for a minute back there? You *did* say we were going back to the office, to get backup for a search, right?"

"I did."

"So...you lied to Agent Blue." She rolled her eyes. "So much for being on your best behavior."

"It wasn't so much a lie as an omission of truth," I said. "And besides—I hadn't organized all the key points in my mind yet. I'm still not sure I have. Let's just say some of them are in a state of flux."

"And what key points are these?"

"Well," I said. "You remember our original theory regarding Tim, Kelly, Drake, and Lanky?"

"The beating gone wrong?" said Steele. "Of course I do."

"Then you'll also remember something that didn't fit our narrative. Lanky's presence in the street. If Tim and Drake attacked Lanky after his unsuccessful sexual assault on Kelly, why move him out of the alley?"

"We already went over this," said Steele. "Maybe the fight spilled out that way."

"Possibly," I said. "But that's a stretch given how deep in the alley the brawl started. It's a weak explanation for our observations."

"So what are you saying?"

"Take the evidence we've gathered today," I said. "Kelly and Drake skip the army base, and shortly thereafter Burly shows up dead, which is extremely suspicious. But let's consider the more important question. *Why?*"

"Why, what?" said Steele.

"Why kill another hobo?" I asked. "What's their motive?"

Shay settled into the cushions of her seat and moistened her lips with her tongue. After a moment of silence, she shook her head. "I don't know. I can't think of anything."

"Exactly," I said. "They don't have one."

My partner narrowed an eye. "So are you saying you *don't* think they killed anyone? Neither Burly *nor* Lanky?"

"What if they were telling the truth?" I offered. "Not about everything, mind you. Just about Lanky. Maybe he did run at them, bleeding and screaming bloody murder."

"But that's ignoring the testimony we got about the argument and the woman's voice," said Steele. "Not to mention Sergeant Holmes and Private Delvesdeep's injuries."

"I have a theory about that," I said. "Did you read the personnel files we took from the army archives yesterday?"

"I glanced at them this morning, but I didn't go over them with a fine-toothed comb."

"Good," I said. "Then I think it'll all make sense."

Steele lifted her eyebrows at me, silently urging me to divulge more of my secrets.

"You'll find out soon enough," I said. "At least, I hope you will. If I'm wrong about Kelly and Drake, then I'll spill the beans and ask you for your help. Besides, we're almost there."

And we were. Our driver, thanks to his long, lean legs and the energy of youth, was flying down the streets of New Welwic. Up ahead, I could see a gap in the skyline—the intersection of the city with the western banks of the Earl. The DEITA building wouldn't be far from there.

A few minutes later, after some furious huffing and puffing on behalf of our ginger-haired driver, we skidded to a halt in front of the DEITA station's majestic exterior. Three stories high, with spires at each corner and constructed out of alternating dull red and cream bricks, the square building took up a solid city block—or it would if half of it weren't balanced over pylons driven into the shallow banks of the Earl. Originally, the station had been constructed entirely of timber, but despite the presence of the river, the entire thing had burned down a mere three years after its christening. The newly refurbished version—new being a relative term in a city bursting with buildings who'd celebrated their bicentennial birthday—looked great from the outside, but I knew the inside would make a county fair look like a deserted street corner at four in the morning. At least I'd be able to put my bulk and surly demeanor to good use pushing through the crowds.

I gave the driver a generous tip and leaped to the ground. Shay followed me.

"Stay close," I told her. "It's a jungle in there, and I don't want you getting lost."

"I'm not a puppy, Daggers," she said.

I frowned. "That's not what I meant. It's busy. We could easily be separated."

Shay regarded me with a warm glance and a thin smile. "Yes. I know what you meant. Don't worry. I'll stay close. Now, what are we looking for?"

"Kelly and Drake," I said as I approached the central doors.

"No kidding," said Shay. "I meant, where should we look for them? As you've pointed out, this place is a zoo."

"Keep an eye out for ships headed north along the Earl," I said. "Anything leaving within the next hour."

Shay grabbed onto my jacket, and I pushed through the front doors and into the maelstrom of warm bodies, angry shouts, and stale sweat odor within. With my partner clinging to me for dear life, I shouldered my way through the seething masses at the foot of the immigration lines and in the direction of the boat terminals. I had to fight against a tide of immigrants unloading from a nearby barge, but after surviving the swell, I made it to an island of relative safety between the arrivals and departures.

I took a deep breath—regrettable, once the body odor reached my nostrils—and looked around. Humanoids of every size, shape, and skin color swirled around us in a blur of activity.

"See anything?" I asked.

"Not yet." Steele pointed further into the building, toward the docks. "Should be that way, though. I see ships through the windows."

I ventured further into the abyss, feeling like a ping pong ball as I bounced between groups of backpack-clad goblins, dwarves dragging carts piled with family heirlooms and legacy mining gear, and half-breed ogres lugging enormous trunks under their arms. Tall, stately elves blended with packs of fair-skinned fey, all of them clad in the muted blacks and browns and navy blues of winter.

My eyes glossed over, and I began to despair that even if I'd guessed correctly, I'd never find Kelly and Drake in such a madhouse. That's when I felt a yank on my coat.

"Over there!" said Shay, pointing into a crowded section of benches.

I had to search for a second before I noticed them, sandwiched between a guy who looked like Quinto's younger, fatter cousin and a pair of twittering gnomes. I wouldn't have recognized them—both Drake and Kelly wore uninspired civilian gear—but thankfully Shay's eyes were better than mine. Perhaps she'd also noticed the chalkboard above them, listing a departure for *The Laughing Jenny* a half hour from now.

"Nicely done," I told my partner.

I made it to within about twenty feet of them before they spotted me.

"Oh, shit!" said Drake. He grabbed Kelly by the arm and darted down the aisle, knocking the poor gnomes to the floor and setting off a series of distraught yells.

I whipped my badge out in a flash, wielding it before me as if it were a torch in a cave. "Police! Stop! Out of our way!"

My proclamation didn't have the desired effect. A full third of the people around us did exactly the opposite of what I asked, standing and flailing about and getting in the way. Thankfully, they did the same to Drake and Kelly, who collided with a pack of old ladies dressed in yachting attire.

I pushed past faux-Quinto and caught a glimpse of Drake's face as he scrambled to his feet. His eyes stretched wide, his nose flared, and his jaw muscles bulged—the look of a frightened wild animal.

Even though I felt confident in my ability to run down and apprehend the pair, I knew fear, crowds, and confined spaces could make for trouble, as evidenced by the gaggle of grousing grandmothers on the ground. An extended chase in the middle of the DEITA station could result in a full-blown panic, not to mention a few people getting sent to the hospital. I needed a quicker, more elegant solution.

"Wait," I called as Kelly rose to her feet. "Don't run! I know you didn't kill anyone!"

That made the pair pause, which was all the time Shay and I needed to close the gap.

Kelly's face looked much the same as Drake's as I reached them. "Oh, damnit, Drake," she said. "Damnit! I knew we wouldn't get away before they found us. I told you I could deal with it. Now, look. We'll get tossed into military prison, for sure!"

"No one at the army knows you're here," I said. "Now calm down. Nobody's getting thrown into prison."

My patented old lady charm was apparently in re-mission, as the pack of old crones started to badger me over Drake and Kelly's reckless behavior. I threw around some reassuring platitudes before shooing Shay and the former soldiers in the direction of the most secluded corner of the DEITA station I could find.

After clearing the area of rubberneckers, I turned my eyes to the privates. They stood against the wall, their eyes on their shoes and their arms crossed, like teenagers who'd been busted on misdemeanor drug charges. Each wore a tightly packed rucksack on their backside, likely filled with all their earthly possessions.

"What do you want?" asked Kelly, without lifting her eyes.

"I want to know what really happened," I said. "Partially to satisfy my curiosity, but mostly because uncovering the truth is my job. And because it might help us solve the murder."

Kelly continued to look at the floor, and I noticed a hint of something wet at the corner of her eye. "You said you knew we didn't kill that homeless man. What does the rest matter?"

"It matters because sexual assault is still a serious crime," I said.

Drake and Kelly both looked at me, their eyes widening.

"That's right," I said. "I knew right off the bat. It was obvious, and my partner Steele saw the same thing I did. Isn't that right?"

Shay nodded.

"At first I thought the homeless man attacked you—" I gestured at Drake. "—and that you and Tim killed him in retaliation. But that's not what happened, is it?"

The wetness around Kelly's eye reached critical capacity, trickling down her cheek in a thin streak.

Drake responded through a clenched jaw. "No. It's not."

Steele gasped. "Oh my gosh... I see it now. It was Sergeant Holmes."

"Exactly," I said to Kelly. "The homeless man didn't assault you. Holmes did, after he'd had enough drinks to let his inner asshole shine through. You resisted. Screamed. That brought Drake running. And seeing Holmes doing that to Kelly...well it threw you into a rage, didn't it, Drake? You attacked Holmes. Thrashed him good, and probably would've kept right on going if not for the appearance of that homeless man, who showed up just as you told us, bloody and screaming."

Drake gave a small, resigned nod as Kelly wiped away the tear.

I was on a mental roll, my faculties clicking. "The hobo's appearance shocked you all into a state of alertness. You couldn't sweep his death under the rug, which meant you needed a cover story for each other. Sergeant Holmes agreed to overlook Drake's assault on him, a commanding officer, assuming the two of you forgot about his sexual assault. And you decided to keep your mouth shut, Kelly, because even though it goes against every grain in your body, you couldn't stand to see Drake punished for coming to your aid."

I left out the last part, the underlying reasoning for Drake and Kelly's actions. From the personnel files, I knew they came from the same town and had enlisted together. It was how I suspected I'd find them at the DEITA station, looking for passage home. But their mutual enlistment, and Kelly's silence on the assault, hinted at something more. Maybe Kelly had followed Drake to the army, enlisted alongside him because she fancied him, but perhaps Drake didn't know. Or perhaps it was precisely the opposite. Perhaps Drake had followed Kelly, and only following Drake's thrashing of

Sergeant Timmy had she realized her hometown friend had feelings for her. Either way, I wasn't about to stick my nose in the middle of their relationship when they might not know the status of it themselves.

Kelly ground her teeth, her fear and embarrassment quickly fading back to the anger I'd noticed yesterday morning. "Good job, Detective. You satisfied your curiosity and uncovered the truth. Now if you don't mind answering my original question, what the hell do you want?"

"Exactly what I said I wanted. I need to know everything you can tell me about the vagrant who died."

Drake shook his head. "Look, we didn't lie about that part. I swear. He'd already been attacked when he came at us in that alley. He collapsed in the street right where you found him, and he died probably fifteen or twenty minutes after he first showed his face."

"And you didn't hear anything out of the ordinary beforehand?" I asked. "Or see anyone suspicious?"

"Are you kidding?" said Kelly. "I'd just been *assaulted*. Drake and that bastard Tim were busy killing each other, and I was screaming at them at the top of my lungs to stop. Nobody noticed that bloody hobo until he was practically on top of us."

"Really? Nothing?" I asked. "Not even after the fact?"

I felt a light touch on my arm. Shay met my eyes and gave her head a taut shake. "Daggers...they're telling the truth."

I sighed. While having my curiosity sated was nice, it wouldn't help me apprehend whoever was roaming the Delta district killing homeless people.

Drake stuffed his hands in his pockets. "So what now? If you're going to drag me back to the army base, then do it, but let Kelly go. She didn't do anything wrong. She didn't even want to desert. I'm the one who convinced her."

"That's noble of you," I said. "But I don't think that's quite how the army brass would see it. And as much as I'd love to see Sergeant Timmy get his ass handed to himself over his assault on Private Chavez here, the ACIC investigators would need Kelly's testimony to make the charges stick. And since you've both deserted, there's no way to keep your noses clean, even if the judicial committee found your actions warranted, Drake. Which means I only see one way out of this mess..."

"Being?" said Drake.

I gave my partner a sideways look. "Well, assuming Detective Steele here agrees with me...then as far as I'm concerned, this meeting never happened. We never saw you. Heck, we never travelled to the DEITA station in the first place. And if I were you two—which I'm not— I'd make sure to get my ass on that ship that's headed north in about fifteen minutes or so. I'd change my name, never mention my army service to anyone ever again, and never look back. But hey, as I said. That's me."

I glanced at Steele. She didn't say a thing, but her face softened and her lips curled upward in a warm smile, so I assume she agreed.

Kelly studied me through narrowed eyes. "Really? You're letting us go?"

"Sometimes those boats leave early," I said. "Better get a move on."

Drake and Kelly took one look at each other and skedaddled, disappearing into the roving crowds. Meanwhile, Steele kept observing me with that goofy, closed-lip smile of hers.

"What?" I asked.

"Nothing," she said, the grin finally fading. "But I can't help but wonder...if Drake and Kelly—or Sergeant Holmes for that matter—didn't kill Lanky, then who did?"

"No idea," I said with a sigh. "Unfortunately, it puts us back at square one."

"Not quite square one," said Shay. "At least now we have another body, with the same M.O. as the first. And as long as Officers Peabody and Carter followed your directions, we should have a subject for Cairny to analyze."

"Good point," I said. "And speaking of which—we should get back to the precinct before that one disappears, too."

23

As we walked down the steps to the morgue, the chill, subterranean air—far colder than that outside—hit me, and I shivered. Shay reacted much the same way, except after her shiver, her hands went to her throat, and she paused.

"Oh, no..."

"What?" I asked.

"My scarf," she said. "I left it at Agent Blue's office."

Shay's long brown curls hid a fair amount, including the top of her blazer and the majority of its lapel, but when I looked at her from the front, nothing blocked the delicate length of her neck from my eyes.

"Huh," I said. "I didn't even notice. Too focused on trying to catch Drake and Kelly, I guess."

"Yeah, me too," said Shay. "Bummer."

"It's not lost forever," I said. "You can always go pick it up."

"I know. But now I'll be cold while we talk to Cairny."

I lifted an eyebrow as we rounded the corner into the examination room. "Don't you have a saying for times like this? What is it? If you're going to be dumb, you'd better be tough?"

"Don't throw that in my face," said Steele.

"Why not?" I said. "I get the impression your dad always did."

My partner silenced me with a reproachful glare.

Cairny stood over an exam table, wearing a lab coat over a black turtleneck that hugged her chin. Burly lay prone on the table, stripped to the waist and with a clean, white sheet thankfully obscuring everything south of the border.

Cairny looked up at the sound of our voices and tucked a few strands of loose, black as midnight hair behind her ear. "Oh. Hey, guys."

I breathed a sigh of relief at the sight of Burly's corpse. I'd been explicit with my instructions to Peabody and Carter, but the conspiracy theorist within me still harbored some doubts. Even now I had half a mind to put a security detail on the morgue's entrance, but that might be letting my crazy a little too far out of its cage.

In addition to the sigh of relief, Burly's corpse also induced in a me a less favorable reaction. He did *not* look good. The discolorations I'd noticed on his face were far more severe on the rest of his body, painting his skin in various shades of grey and purple and green. I couldn't tell if he'd been badly beaten before the eventual death blow had been delivered to his skull or if perhaps he suffered from a severe fungal infection.

I grimaced as I came to stand by the table.

Shay's nose wrinkled in response to the dead guy's odor, but apart from that, she managed her facial tics better than I did. "Well. At least he's here."

Apparently I wasn't the only one worried about the security of our charnel house.

"Don't worry," said Cairny. "I'm taking good care of him. Or at least as good as I can. He's in rough shape."

"No kidding," I said. "He seems to be going south fast."

Cairny consulted a clipboard on the table and made a note with a pencil tucked off to the side of it. "Speaking of which...can you fill me in on how you found this man? Those cops who dropped him off—Peabody and, what was it? Caruthers?—gave me a spiel, but I want to make sure I heard it straight."

"Sure," I said. "Early this morning, in the fog, a couple of drunk yahoos barreled into this poor bum—"

"Or he bumped into them," said Shay. "They provided conflicting stories."

"Right," I said. "Anyway, however it happened, the guy got knocked over. The male half of the pair knelt down to help him and noticed the blood on the back of his head. Realized he'd been attacked. And they went to find help."

"For what it's worth, neither Daggers nor I think they had anything to do with the murder," said Shay. "They were far too stupid for that."

Cairny frowned and pulled her eyebrows together. "Ok... And you're sure it was this guy?"

My conspiracy theory siren started to howl again. "Huh? What do you mean?"

I leaned in close to get a good look at Burly's face. He sported the same beard, matted hair, and facial features I remembered from earlier this morning. Unless he had an identical twin brother who was also a down-on-his-luck transient with bad skin who'd *also* been violently murdered by a blow to the back of his head, then this was our guy.

"Yeah," I said, stretching out to my full height. "This is him. Why do you ask?"

Cairny gave Steele a suspicious look, as if she didn't believe me.

"What is it, Cairny?" asked Shay.

"Guys, I don't know how to tell you this," she said. "But this man's been dead for about four days."

I blinked. "Come again?"

"All the caveats apply about me not having performed a thorough examination yet," said Cairny. "The beat cops dropped him off less than an hour ago. But it doesn't take long to come to that conclusion. I mean...really. He's not fresh."

I wanted to argue with the coroner, but apart from the fact that she'd never led me astray, her assessment of his time of death would explain his lovely complexion and unique aroma.

I turned to Steele. "Alright. Things have *officially* started to get weird."

"Agreed," she said. "But on the bright side, at least this sheds some light on that couple's testimony. Apparently, Norma knew what she was talking about, and Gary was full of hot air."

"Yes, clearly he stumbled into Burly and not vice versa," I said. "But that doesn't help us answer the more

pressing question, which is: why the hell would someone violently murder a hobo, and then four days later,
prop the stiff up against the side of an embroidery shop
in the middle of a midnight fog storm?"

Shay took a breath and held her hands up. "Yeah. I'm
at a loss."

"Not to mention," I said, "that Norma said the guy
grunted when Gary hit him. How does a corpse do
that?"

Shay shook her head. "No. You've got it mixed up.
Norma said Burly went down like a log, which thanks to
rigor mortis, he more or less is at this point. It was Gary
who said he grunted."

Cairny's ears perked up. "What's this about a grunt?"

"One of our witnesses claimed the dead guy grunted
during the collision," said Steele. "The other one—the
reliable one, apparently—said he didn't."

"Not necessarily," said Cairny, holding up a finger.
"It's possible this man—you're calling him Burly?"

I nodded. "It seemed to fit as well as anything else.
And it's a nickname that's not deprecating of his chosen, cash-light lifestyle."

"Right," said Cairny. "Anyway, it's possible he had air
trapped in his lungs, and when this man, Gary, hit him,
the air could've escaped through his windpipe. I've
heard of it happening before, even with corpses that are
a few days old like this one. In fact, the reports I've read
of such incidents describe the sound as eerie and unset-
tling." Cairny steepled her fingers and tapped them together. "Oh, I wish I could've heard it. That would've
been exciting."

I gave the raven-haired coroner the fisheye. "You're disturbed, you know that?"

"You say disturbed," said Cairny. "I say geeked out. This is my hobby as well as my profession, you know."

I didn't ask. Given the oaths I'd taken to uphold the law, I'd rather not know if Cairny spent off nights dissecting bodies in her own basement.

"Well, you learn something new every day," I said. "But unfortunately, that rather unique piece of mortuary wisdom doesn't explain Burly's presence in the street last night. I don't suppose you have any *other* insights?"

Cairny smiled. "Remember that caveat about me not having performed a thorough examination yet?"

"Let me guess," I said. "You need more time."

She gave me the old snap and point. "Bingo. Good thing you've got such a sharp knife in your drawer, Shay."

My partner snickered. "He has his moments."

"Alright," I said. "Well, we'll let you get back to work, Cairny. We have enough to do as it is."

"Such as?" said Steele.

"Looking for the thread that ties Lanky's and Burly's murders together," I said.

Which meant, for the most part, that we had a whole lot of legwork staring us in the face. I sighed. Have I ever mentioned how much I love my job?

24

I lied to Cairny.

My first order of business was to track down Boatreng, who I then escorted to the morgue so he could produce a drawing of Burly. I told the sketch artist to use an artistic license in his interpretation of the man's original complexion, otherwise no one would recognize him when I showed the drawing around the Delta district in search of clues.

Cairny complained the entire time we were there, grousing about how she couldn't effectively complete her analyses with us hovering over her, but Boatreng worked efficiently. With the subject right in front of him, he produced a sketch in about ten minutes. Once I'd relieved him of the drawing, Shay and I headed upstairs, stopping by my desk for the sketch of Lanky before heading out into the late fall chill.

Our first stop was to an apartment building east of the precinct in a swanky, recently gentrified neighborhood referred to as Tullytown. Before our departure from the morning's crime scene, Shay had been smart enough to extract a home address out of our inebriated, jazz-loving couple, which was a better way of finding them than my proposal of using bloodhounds. Once we located their base of operations, we headed up the stairs to the fourth floor, and I unleashed the full force of my fist onto their door.

It took three rounds of furious pounding before Gary answered. His mop of hair had transformed into a broom, sticking out to the side in a decidedly unhip fashion. He mumbled questions and rubbed his eyes as I invited myself in, whereupon I nearly collided with Norma, dressed in a nightgown even more translucent than her questionable yellow dress from earlier.

I tried to keep my leering to a minimum as I questioned them again, grilling them over the series of events that led to the discovery of Burly's rotting corpse, but infuriatingly enough, the pair stuck to their respective stories, including the parts they disagreed upon. Neither offered even the slightest trace of new information, although I did pick up on several not-so-subtle hints from Norma to get the hell out of her apartment. Eventually, I let slip the fact that Burly had been dead for four days, hoping the news might unlock some revealing facial features from the pair, but both looked at me blankly. Norma asked me straight up if they could go back to bed.

I gave up. They were a dead end.

With that candle snuffed, Shay and I tromped back to the Delta district and began the real work. We started at the embroidery store and worked our way out, canvassing every shop, boutique, bar, club, restaurant, and sock hop joint we could find. We slithered like a snake,

moving over and up and back and up and over again
through the streets, showing our sketches of Lanky and
Burly and asking the same questions over and over
again.

We managed a few hits scattered between an otherwise dizzying mountain of blank looks and disappointment. The proprietor of a sausage-on-a-stick cart
recalled shooing Lanky away from his tubular meat
products a few days ago. A boulangerie owner recalled
doing the same thing to Burly when he wandered in
unannounced a week prior. Three separate bar owners
thought either Burly, Lanky, or both looked familiar, but
none of them could provide us with their habits or
haunts, much less a name or other identifying information.

The best piece of information we gleaned—the *best*,
mind you—came from another homeless man who
stopped us upon seeing us show off the sketches. He
claimed Lanky had stolen his coat a month back and
demanded we return it. After lying and telling him I'd
look into the matter, I asked where the theft occurred,
and he pointed us toward an alley a couple blocks from
where we'd found him dead yesterday morning.

That provided me the impetus to return to the scene
of the original crime, but by the time we finally arrived,
I needed a break. I settled myself upon the stoop of the
shuttered Lucky Baldwin's and rubbed my feet through
my shoes.

"You doing ok?" asked Shay.

"You know me," I said. "I can't get enough low-
intensity aerobic exercise."

Shay shook her head. "And to think you give me crap for being too skinny. Not such a disadvantage when it comes to endurance activities, is it?"

"Hey, I'm working on it," I said. "Just you watch. I'll be down to a svelte two-oh-five by the new year."

"No fair leaving Daisy at home on the day of the weigh in, though." Steele glanced into the alley between the bar and the back of the Church of the Divine Rebirth. "So what do you make of that derelict's testimony?"

"The guy who claimed Lanky stole his jacket?" I asked. "I don't know. I guess it means Lanky had sticky fingers, and that he spent most of his time in this general vicinity. Which makes sense why he was murdered here. If I was a deranged hobo killer, I'd go where the transients live to find new victims."

Shay hummed. "Right. Which makes me think we're canvassing this district with the wrong sketches in hand. I mean, let's be honest. Nobody cares what happens to the homeless population. These business owners we've been visiting? They'd rather all the vagrants went away. So they ignore them. Tune them out. I'm surprised we've had as many successful hits as we've had, to tell the truth. Whoever killed them, on the other hand, might be far more remarkable."

"Problem is," I said, "other than the fact that we have no idea who we're looking for—who really qualifies as suspicious in this neighborhood? There are bars galore here, and they're busiest at night, filled with all manner of New Welwic's best and worst. While that gives us more potential witnesses, it also gives us more potential suspects, and makes the locals immune to the presence of suspicious outsiders."

Shay shook her head and sighed. "I guess." She nodded in my direction. "Your feet ready to keep moving?"

I leveraged myself into a standing position using the lip of the doorway. "As ready as they'll ever be. Unless you want to give them a nice little massage..."

"Dream on."

"Hey, can't blame a guy for trying," I said. "Why don't we revisit this church and that brew pub we stopped at yesterday morning? We've got sketches this time, so perhaps that'll help ring more bells. And then? Lunch. I'm *starving*."

25

We scooted around to the front and pushed our way back into the Church of the Divine Rebirth. I shivered as the damp, chill air touched my skin, protected as it was from the sun's rays by the trees. I imagined the dense interior foliage worked wonders in the summer months, but in the winter it left something to be desired—which, I suspected, explained the church's barrenness. I couldn't spot a single patron in the building's cavernous main room, homeless or otherwise. Likely they'd all swarmed the nearest house of worship that chose to use its tithe money on firewood.

"Hello?" I called. "Anyone home?"

My voice echoed off the walls a couple times before dying amidst the bark and remaining leaves of the trees.

I snorted. "Wonderful. How these religious nuts convert walk-ins off the street if they're not Johnny on the spot with the theological mumbo jumbo is beyond me."

Shay glanced at the empty recessed common areas set into the earth between the tall oaks and maples. "Maybe they already gave up for the day."

"A workday that's over before lunch?" I asked. "Sounds like a good gig if you can get it."

I made a beeline for the back of the establishment, where the building's wooden benches clustered around an open area and where doorways into the back of the house beckoned.

"You're not going to take the scenic route?" asked Shay as she followed me. She nodded in the direction of the walking path meandering drunkenly through the trees.

"I don't have time for that," I said. "My stomach is getting closer to rebellion by the minute. Besides, I figured that thing was more for the church's faithful, and last I checked I hadn't signed on to become a Rebirther, or Rebirthian, or whatever it is these whack jobs call themselves."

"I don't know," said Steele. "In the grand scheme of things, their religion sounded pretty tame. I got the impression it was mostly about a closeness with nature. Lots of faiths emphasize that."

"While true," I said, "those other religions don't plant trees in their cathedrals in lieu of roofs."

As we reached the benches, the creak of a door drew my attention. An impossibly tall, gangly youth with a bowl cut ducked and stepped out from underneath the frame, carrying with him a metal ball suspended from a trio of fine chains. Smoke poured out through small holes in the ball, carrying with it scents of dried flowers and herbs.

I flagged the kid down with a wave. "Hey, Slim. What's new?"

Shay elbowed me in the ribs. "Call him by his name. Just because he's mute doesn't mean he likes your disparaging nicknames."

Chester walked over to meet us, swinging the metal ball back and forth, spreading smoke and incense as he did so. The chains seemed like threads in his skillet-like hands, and I imagined he could crush the fragrant ball like a grape should he choose to do so. He nodded in greeting.

"Slow day, huh?" I asked.

He nodded as he continued to swing the ball back and forth.

I gestured in the contraption's direction. "Are you going to keep that...*thing* in motion the entire time we talk?"

Chester dipped his head, and Shay tapped me on the arm. "I think it's called a thurible."

I gave my partner the fisheye. "I thought that was one of those metal things you put on your index finger while stitching."

"That's a thimble."

Chester pointed at Steele and nodded again. Apparently, my highly-prided vocabulary didn't extend to religious paraphernalia or sewing equipment.

My stomach growled at me, and I figured I'd get to the point. I dug the two sketches out of my pocket—both of which already showed wear along the creases—unfolded them, and showed them to Chester.

"Alright, tall guy," I said. "If you'll recall, we stopped by yesterday to investigate a murder. This fellow on the left is the one who got axed. This one on the right is another vagrant who we found dead this morning. We're trying to find any information we can on the pair. Either of them look familiar?"

Chester's eyes narrowed as he looked at the sketches. With his free hand he rubbed his smooth chin, and he kept the thurible swinging rhythmically with the other. I got the impression he'd had lots of practice. Eventually, he pointed at Lanky's sketch and nodded.

Perfect. Now we'd reached the interesting part of the interview. "And I don't suppose you could, you know...tell us anything about him?"

Chester shrugged and shook his head, but then he extended a finger before beckoning with it and pointing in the direction of the open doorway.

Shay and I deftly interpreted the gesture. We followed him through the entryway, into a barren corridor, and up to the second floor, where we stopped before a closed door. A faint, monotone chanting drifted over from the other side.

Chester knocked, making the wooden barrier clatter in its frame.

The chanting stopped. "Come in," came a gentle voice.

Chester opened the door, revealing a small, well-lit room heavily populated by plush, colorful pillows, a pair of low coffee tables, and a wide variety of houseplants. More smoke and incense infested the air, enough to make the thurible's meager emissions seem like a gnat's flatulence. I gagged as the thick combination forced its way down my throat.

Inside the room, Pastor Bellamy sat on a pile of pillows on the floor. He rose awkwardly as we approached, using the wall for support—probably because of his bum knee. "Ah, detectives. Please, please, come in. What brings you back into our warm embrace?"

Shay snorted and made a sound reminiscent of a dog preparing to vomit. While she struggled to contain her overactive olfactory senses, Chester moved to the far side of the room and hung the thurible from a long, metal stand with a hook at the end. Then he joined Julian Bellamy at his side.

"Well, we were hoping to, ah, ask you about some... arhem! That is, some... hurhurm!" I waved my hand in front of my face as I coughed. "Sorry... Could we open a window? Or move into the hallway?"

"Absolutely," said Bellamy. "My apologies. Chester?"

The assistant moved to the side of the room and threw open the windows before grasping a long handled fan that stood at their side. With a few powerful back and forth strokes of his arms, the air began to clear.

I glanced at Shay to see if she was doing any better. She performed some facial aerobics and paired them with a weird blowing air out the side of her nose thing, but she nodded her approval.

"Thanks," I said as I gave Chester a nod. "Pastor, if you'll recall, yesterday we told you about the murder that occurred in the alley behind your church. We've hit a snag with regards to our suspects, but on the bright side—for us anyway—we've had another murder. Not too far from here. Another transient. Given that you said many of them cycle through your church, we were hoping you might've seen one, or both, before."

I dug the sketches back out of my pocket and showed them to Bellamy. As he looked at them, Chester tapped him on the shoulder and pointed at the drawing of Lanky.

Bellamy nodded sagely. "Ah, yes. Good eye, Chester. This other one, I've never seen. But this man—" He tapped Lanky's drawing. "—I remember quite well. He'd drop by every couple weeks. Help himself to our generosity, or take advantage of the shelter the boughs of our trees provide. Kept to himself, mostly. From the few times I tried to engage him, I got the impression his mental faculties were somewhat suspect."

"In what way?" I asked.

The pastor brushed his salt-and-pepper hair back as he shrugged. "The usual. I think he suffered from paranoia. Perhaps even delusions. Such things aren't uncommon in the homeless population."

Shay coughed and cleared her throat. When she spoke, her voice sounded raspy. "Do you know any specifics about him? His name. Hometown. If he had any friends. That sort of thing."

Bellamy tapped his chin and stared at the ceiling. "His name. Yes. What was it... Chuck? No... *Buck*. That's it!"

"Is that a first or a last name?" I asked.

"I don't know," said Bellamy.

"And I don't suppose he shared any other information with you?" I asked.

"Not really," said Bellamy.

"Right. Because that would make our lives *far* too easy." I sighed and cast my eyes out the window, where they were treated to all the majesty and splendor of the shuttered bar's roof, and beyond that, another brick wall.

"Is there...anything else I can do for you?" asked the pastor.

I nodded in the direction of the windows as I tucked the sketches back into my pocket. "We had another report from a homeless man placing Lanky—err, I mean, Buck—in this general location. What do you suppose drew him here?"

"Other than us?" asked Bellamy.

I didn't have the heart to tell the pastor that street people probably *didn't* flock from miles around to gander at their wacky roof-less church. "Um...yes. Other than you."

He shrugged again. "I don't know. Perhaps he frequented the trash cans behind that restaurant next door. They always seem to do good business, especially throughout the day. I imagine they must throw away some leftovers."

"Don't you feed the homeless?" I asked.

"Yes," said Bellamy, "but we are of meager means. Limited donations of late have meant fewer meals for us to distribute."

My stomach growled again at the mention of food. "Alright. Well, I appreciate your help. If you think of anything else, any information that might help us identify the victim or lead us in the direction of his killer, please drop by the 5th Street Precinct. Steele?"

I jerked my thumb toward the door, but Steele gave me a narrow-eyed nod first. "Daggers...why don't you show them that token?"

I blinked. I'd forgotten about the thing, but Shay had a point. The strange imagery on the token's face held a bit of a cultish aura about it, so why not ask the whackos to see if it rang any bells for them?

I dug the coin facsimile out of my pocket and handed it to Bellamy. "We found this on the body of the second vagrant. I don't suppose you know what it means?"

The pastor's brows furrowed. His lips pressed together, and after a moment, he shook his head. "No. I'm sorry. I don't recognize this symbol."

He held the token back out to me, but I didn't take it.

"Chester," I said. "What about you? Anything?"

The tall young man stood to Bellamy's side, hands clasped in front of him. He'd remained motionless during our back and forth. Now his eyes darted from me to the token to Bellamy and back to me. I swore I caught a hint of motion in the youth's jaw, but he merely shook his head.

26

I spent the majority of our minute long jaunt over to the Delta Deli & Brew Pub mulling over whether the facial tic I'd seen on Chester had been real or a figment of my imagination, but the deli's shopkeeper bell brought me back to attention.

Shay held the door open for me. "After you."

"Thanks," I said.

Despite Pastor Bellamy's claims about the deli's popularity during daylight hours, the place stubbornly remained as barren as I remembered it. Like the previous morning, a single customer sat at one of the booths by the windows, tapping his fingers on the table and eyeing us with distrust.

At least this time someone manned the hostess station, though not the same greasy-haired orc as before. A rust haired man with freckles dotting his high cheekbones, perhaps in his mid thirties, stood there, hunched over the lectern with his mouth half open. I wondered if he was drugged or merely tired.

I approached him. "Hi. Uh...is Wayne here?"

"Who?" The word came out slurred, and I placed my bets on drugged.

I wracked my brain. "Oh, how did he pronounce it? *Way-ee-anne?*"

"Wheyiane," said Shay.

"Right," I said. "That guy."

"He'th indithpothed today."

As the redhead spoke, I realized the entire left side of his face refused to move alongside the rest. Perhaps I'd been wrong, and his dumbfounded appearance was due to a medical condition rather than sloth or dope.

I tried to ignore the man's lisp. "What happened to him?"

"Intethtinal dithtreth."

I grimaced. "Say no more. Who's in charge, then?"

The guy gave himself the pointy thumb treatment. "That'th me. Mark Andrewth. I'm uthually the nightthift manager."

"Nightshift?" said Steele. "That could be beneficial."

Mark's eyebrows crumpled together. "What'th thith about?"

"We're detectives," I said. "We're investigating a murder of a homeless man that occurred in the alley a couple nights ago, as well as another similar homicide we found out about this morning."

Mark's eyes widened in response to my initial declaration of fact, but they quickly returned to normal size. I pulled out the sketches.

"These are the two vagrants," I said. "One of them may have gone by the name of Buck. Do either of them look familiar?"

Mark took a quick glance at the sketches—perhaps a little *too* quick. "Nah. Thorry."

"You sure?" asked Steele, perhaps picking up on the same speed of reply I had. "Take a closer look. One of them in particular was known to frequent this area."

Steele's appeal didn't change Mark's mind. He frowned—or at least tried. Half his mouth didn't cooperate. "I'm telling you, I've never theen thethe guyth."

"Alright. No need to get testy." I swapped the drawings for the token that also resided in my pocket. "What about this? We found it on one of the dead guys. Do you have any idea what it is?"

"Lookth like a token of thome thort."

I wanted to press my forehead into my palm, but I somehow managed to keep my composure. "Yes, we know that. I meant if you had some idea of what it represents, or where it came from."

Mark stared at me blankly.

"Wonderful," I said as I returned the metal disk to my jacket.

"Anything elthe you need?"

I tried to engage my brain in further lines of possible questioning, but my stomach kept poking its head in and screaming at me. If I didn't cram something in my maw soon, I might collapse in on myself like one of those inflatable kid's dolls under the weight of a Quinto belly flop.

I turned to Steele. "You want to do lunch?"

My partner suffered an eye tic. "Here? Are you serious?"

"Yeah, why not?" I said. "You remember our chat about hidden culinary gems, right?"

"Well, yes, but—" She grabbed me and pulled me close, lowering her voice as she did so. "Daggers, there's no one here. I mean *nobody*. And did you forget what Mark here told us. Wheyiane is out due to *intestinal distress*. I wonder where he could've contracted such a thing..."

My stomach made its unhappiness known with a vicious, abdominal wall-shaking rumble. "Look, Shay," I said. "I don't know how much longer I can go. Besides, how bad can it be?"

She sighed and frowned. "Fine. But don't blame me if this experience goes south. And I do mean that quite metaphorically."

I gave Mark the nod. "Alright then. Table for two please."

I think Rusty looked displeased by our decision to extend our stay, but given his half-paralyzed face, he was extremely hard to read.

He gestured toward the tables. "Have a theat."

I picked a table that gave Shay and me a fair berth from the sourpuss in the corner. Mark followed us to the table.

"Tho... what can I get you?" he asked once we'd sat.

Shay gave me a dubious glare before turning it upon the man with the palsy. "Um...menus?"

"Oh. Right," he said. "Jutht a thec."

He wandered back to the hostess stand and returned with a pair of sheets which he distributed among us. I took a quick glance at the contents, which didn't take long. The menu listed only five options, each of them with sterling descriptions accompanying the item names. The first one read: *Turkey and Cheddar Sandwich: Turkey and cheddar cheese, on a sandwich. Cheese optional.*

"So...what's good here?" I asked Mark.

The man took a peek at the menu, as if he couldn't remember everything on the page. "Um...the ham and cheethe?"

I could feel the heat from Shay's cheeks radiating toward me. I made some quick executive decisions before her clothes caught fire.

"Two ham and cheeses, then," I said. "I'll take a brew. Whatever it is you've got fresh and on tap. And my partner will take a hot tea."

I shooed him away before Shay bit him. He disappeared behind the bead curtain separating the front from the kitchen. I tried to engage Shay in conversation while we waited for our meals, but she still hadn't cooled to a reasonable temperature. After a few minutes, I began to despair we might never see the droopy-jawed night manager again. Then the shopkeeper's bell rang.

An orc—not Wayne, but similar in appearance—walked in and took a look around the restaurant. A moment later, Mark poked his head through the bead curtain, made eye contact with the new arrival, and motioned him back.

I rubbed my chin, wondering if perhaps the new arrival was a chef, when Mark reappeared with a serving tray. He placed a steaming mug of tea in front of Shay before providing me with a sudsy, yellow beverage, and finished the table service with the delivery of our sandwiches.

The latter had all the visual appeal of a stripper in her fifties, so I turned my attention to the beer. I took a careful sip, and surprisingly enough, it wasn't half bad. In fact, it was light and crisp. Refreshing.

I picked up my hoagie—which, unless appearances deceived me, was constructed in the most minimalistic way a ham and cheese sandwich could be—and took a bite.

I chewed, set it down, and glanced at Shay. She'd just finished her own first morsel.

"I don't want to say I told you so," she said. "But..."

"I know," I said. "It's awful."

Shay flashed me a forced, knowing smile. "How's the beer?"

"Fair," I said. "Your tea?"

"It's tea," she replied. "Which is a step up from the warm dish water I half expected."

I picked up my ham and cheese and took another bite, but try as I might, I couldn't convince my tongue of its worth. My stomach, on the other hand, wasn't quite so picky, so I forged a compromise and kept eating.

Two more parties came in through the front door while we ate, a group of three goblins and a pair of elves. Both picked up take out orders, delivered to them by Mark in brown paper bags with the tops folded over, just as the dwarves' breakfasts had been yesterday morning.

After they'd both left, the suspicious man at the back table rose, joined Mark at the hostess station, and engaged him in a short, hushed conversation. Then he left, but not before shooting a dubious glance in Shay's and my direction.

I leaned into my sandwich for another bite and almost took off the tips of my fingers. I'd consumed the whole thing, and I'd drained my mug of ale. When I checked Shay's plate, I found she'd even eaten some of hers.

Say what you would about the quality of the food, but at least the Delta Deli's entertainment was top notch.

27

I gave my weary feet a break and treated Shay and myself to a rickshaw ride back to the precinct—and by treated, I mean used the department's coffers—but I didn't think the trip from the relatively nearby Delta district would cause too much commotion. The Captain, despite his gruff exterior, never put up much of a stink when the transportation budget disproportionately benefited his sole female detective.

I thought we'd make it all the way back to our desks in silence, but as we transferred from the wheeled cart's confines to the hard ground in front of the station, Shay deviated from the norm. "You've been abnormally quiet the whole trip back."

It wasn't a question. More of a statement of fact. I responded in kind. "Conversation is a two way street, you know."

"Oh, no," said Shay, wagging a finger. "I'm smarter than that. I knew I should wait."

I held the front door open for her and peered at her quizzically. "What do you mean?"

"I've seen that look on your face before," she said with a smile. "The one you donned as we left the Deli. You wore it right up until now. It's your 'I'm concocting a crazy theory' face."

"See, now," I said, "I take exception to that word. *Crazy.* It implies my theories aren't grounded in facts, when more often than not, they are."

"*More often than not?*" If Shay wore glasses, she would've looked at me over their brims. "You realize that's an objectively verifiable statement."

"Whatever," I said. "I'm often right."

"Like that time you thought your favorite mystery writer was a shapeshifter?"

"Hey, I wasn't *that* far off."

Shay settled into her chair, and I followed her lead.

"So," she said. "Lay it on me. What's your newest hypothesis, based on the best bits of conjecture and guesswork your mind has to offer?"

I smiled and leaned forward in my chair, thankful for the opening. Truth was, despite my defensive nature regarding them, I didn't require a lot of prodding to divulge my theories. Usually I forced them on people whether they liked it or not.

"Well, you don't have to ask me twice." I intertwined my fingers and lifted a provocative eyebrow. "I've been thinking about the Delta Deli. There's clearly something fishy going on there. Pastor Bellamy said they did good business—and they'd have to if they wanted to stay open. But the place was barren, both today and yesterday morning. And not surprisingly. The sandwiches were terrible. But there *was* a clientele. Takeout business didn't seem too shabby. But why? That food wasn't like a bottle of fine wine, expected to improve with age. And no one in their right mind would go back for seconds. So what are they peddling?"

"I'm completely on board with you so far," said Shay, "but I've got to admit, I'm disappointed. This isn't a crazy theory. These are observations. Obvious ones, if I say so myself."

"Well, then buckle in, tenderfoot," I said, "because I've got three words for you that'll bring Lanky's and Burly's murders and the Delta Deli into a horrifying new focus."

Shay lifted a dubious eyebrow.

"Black...market...beef."

Shay blinked. "Come again?"

"Think about it," I said. "The deli is clearly selling *something*, delivered via those brown paper bags. Nobody is dining in because they're too afraid of other people realizing what they're eating. And if you'll recall, not a single human came by for a pickup order. Admittedly, I've never heard of elves dining on human flesh before, but at least for them, it's not cannibalism. *And* it explains Lanky's disappearance from the morgue."

"His name was Buck, remember?" said Steele.

"Whatever. I'm going to keep calling him Lanky. The point is, he's a prized piece of flesh. Given the high price beef fetches, a big guy like Lanky must've been a tempting target."

"Daggers, are you listening to yourself right now?"

"You bet I am," I said. "And I'm hearing nothing but sense. Even Burly's death and reappearance fits. Burly, like Lanky, was a big guy. A huge hunk of meat just waiting to be harvested. But he had a problem. You saw his skin. Before we learned about the timing of his murder, I was sure he suffered from a degenerative disease. So what if I'm right? Maybe the folks over at the deli realized they couldn't serve him to their customers. That he was a health hazard. It even explains Wayne's disappearance with 'intestinal distress.' He must've sampled Burly, gotten sick, and so they dumped him in the street."

Shay regarded me with a mouth half open, squinty-eyed look.

"If I'm interpreting that facial expression correctly," I said, "then, yeah, I feel the same way. Good thing I ordered us the ham sandwiches, huh?"

"That's...not what was on my mind," said Shay. "Rather I was thinking I shouldn't ever encourage you again."

"Oh, come on," I said. "If you think it's a flawed theory, then poke some holes in it."

"Well, for one thing, Cairny said Burly died about four days ago. Why would the deli owners kill Burly, let him sit around in their kitchen ripening for three days, and *then* decide he wasn't worth serving? Oh, and there's the part where you seem to think a business that specializes in selling *human hobo flesh* would be concerned with proper sanitation and health practices."

"Hey, a business's reputation is its livelihood," I said. "If word got out about some bad beef, it could be the end of the line for Wayne and his slack-jawed buddy Mark. But, hey, I'm all ears if you have a better theory."

Shay shook her head. "Daggers, you know that's not what I do."

"But maybe it should be," I said. "You pick up on far more details than I do when we visit crime scenes, stuff you don't even realize, I'll bet. All those details swirl around in your mind like butterflies during a storm, until you go in there with a net and try to make them behave—at least, that's how it works with me. The point is, you have to put work in. Stretch those creative muscles. It's the only way they'll grow."

Shay sighed and gave me a sideways look. "I don't know, Daggers..."

"Nope. You're not wriggling your way out this time." I tapped a finger on the desk. "I want to hear one crazy theory from you, right now, that ties everything together."

"I don't have one," said Shay. "What am I supposed to—"

"Don't worry about it," I said. "Say whatever comes to mind. It doesn't have to make sense at first. Think of it as an exercise. A way to pull unformed thoughts out of your subconscious and refine them into something meaningful."

Shay looked at me with an odd expression on her lips, then nodded. "Ok. Fine. I'll try it."

Her body language indicated she wanted to take the conversation in a different direction, but she didn't fight me. "Let's see...where to start. Well, for me anyway, this case hinges on the mysteries of Lanky's and Burly's bodies. If we can explain their circumstances, I think the rest will fall into place. The most important part is why anyone would bother stealing Lanky's corpse?" She stuck a finger in the air. "And something you mentioned in your theory actually makes sense. What if...Lanky's body *is* valuable? But why?"

"This is good," I said, encouraging her. "Keep it coming."

"What if Lanky's body was valuable for medical reasons. Somebody needed him for an experiment, or to harvest his organs? No, that's too crazy. That's almost on *your* level of hypothesizing." Shay gave me a look before her eyes widened. She snapped her fingers. "I've got it! Perhaps it wasn't Lanky's body per se that was valuable. It's what was on it!"

"But we searched him," I said. "He didn't have anything on him."

Shay wagged her finger, her smile spreading. "Not so fast. We gave his pockets a cursory search, but we were looking for the usual sorts of things. Cash, personal items, anything that could identify him. Who knows what else he might've been carrying? Perhaps something small. Something easily hidden. It could've even been *in* his body."

"Are you suggesting Lanky might've been a drug mule?" I asked. "If so, you've just volunteered to tell Cairny she needs to give Burly a rectal exam."

"Maybe. Or maybe not... It depends on what Lanky could've been carrying. But lucky for us we still have Burly in our care."

Shay sat there, index finger on her chin and her eyes boring holes into the ceiling. As I watched her, I felt a burst somewhere around the middle of my chest. Not a heart attack, thankfully. Something more ethereal. Pride, I think. Seeing my partner test the limits of her own creative prowess, all thanks to some cajoling on my part, made my day. With a little luck, it might make hers, too.

I stood. "You're doing great. Sit here and keep at it. I'm going to grab something to keep the creative juices flowing, something brimming with caffeine. You want me to brew you a tea while I'm at it?"

"Sure," said Shay distractedly, and then, with a glance and a smile, "Thanks, Daggers."

I made my way to the break room, the pride within me expanding to encompass a few other emotions I'd been sorely lacking in recently: joy and hope.

28

A s I wandered into the break room, I couldn't help but notice a large, grey mass, swathed in chinos and a tweed jacket, draped across the couch.

"Quinto," I said. "Good gods, man...what happened to you? You look like you got trampled by a herd of elephants."

"I did it," he said, barely moving as he glanced in my direction. "I prevailed. Almost got the best of me, but I'm made of stern stuff."

"That sounds like my line," I said. "Except I'd add a witty quip to the end. Something along the lines of, 'I'm made of stern stuff—red meat, whiskey, and the soul of a fifty-five year old barroom arm wrestling champion, to name a few.'"

Quinto ignored me and pointed to a side table at the head of the couch. "Mind handing me my mug?"

A cup of tea steamed merrily from the table's face, thankfully free of the odd licorice smells of yesterday's version. I grabbed it and passed it to the big guy. "So...what exactly did you conquer?"

"The Captain's paperwork," he said as he took a sip from his beverage. "I finished it."

"Get out of town."

"No, really," he said. "I handed the mountain off to the old man about fifteen minutes ago. Been laying here ever since."

My brow furrowed. "What time did you get in this morning?"

Quinto shrugged. "I don't know. Four, maybe?"

"FOUR AM?" I cried. "What the hell is wrong with you?"

"It's called a sense of pride, my friend," said Quinto. "Helps me get things done. Although, I have to admit, I'm regretting it at the moment. And that regret will only worsen the later it gets in the day."

"Don't worry about it," I said as I approached the coffee pot. "Pretty much everything people do at four in the morning they end up regretting."

I poured myself a tall cup of joe before delving into the wild unknown that was the tea box. I flicked through the packets as I poured hot water into a fresh mug.

"You're a tea drinker, Quinto," I said. "What do you recommend?"

That made the big guy sit up. "You're switching sides? Are you feeling ok?"

"Did you not notice the coffee in my first cup?" I asked. "I'm getting something for Shay."

"Oh," he said, slumping back into the couch. "Well, that cardamom tea is pretty nice. Has a festive flavor, if that makes any sense. Or you could do the regular black stuff. That's what I normally get."

"Cardamom it is, then." I popped a bag of the former into the hot water and took a seat across from Quinto as I let it steep.

"So," said Quinto. "Seeing as I've been locked in a vault for the past, oh, I don't know, ten hours, why don't you fill me in on the case? Since I finished his paperwork, Captain agreed to let me tag along with you and Steele for the remainder of the day."

"Aren't you a lucky guy?" I said. "Not much to relate, though. Oh, except for the fact that we found another formerly living homeless dude dead by the same M.O. as Lanky. And that we ruled out the GIs as murderers. Oh, and that the second dead hobo was murdered about four days ago and may have been dumped in the street because his corpse didn't meet the quality standards of this city's black market meat providers."

"Say *what?*" asked Quinto.

"Well, that last part is speculation, but the rest is true. Weird, huh?"

"That's putting it mildly," said Quinto.

"Yeah," I said. "We're trying not to drown in the evidence, but I'm sure we'll pull the threads together into a life jacket soon enough. Depends on what else Cairny can tell us about our second body. Speaking of which...how was your date last night?"

"Oh, it was great," said Quinto. "Flimflame was top notch, though I thought the food preparation theatrics were a bit over the top."

"Come again?" I said. "Was this a dinner or a show?"

"A little of both," said Quinto. "Flimflame is one of those iron plate griddle restaurants. You know, the ones where they juggle utensils and light onions on fire?"

I had no idea what he was talking about, and I thought flaming onions sounded more like chemical warfare than dinner, but I figured Shay would be more than happy to explain the fad to me if I so desired.

"So everything between you and Cairny is still hunky-dory, then?" I asked.

Quinto nodded. "You bet. We pair really nicely with each other. Play off each other's strengths and weaknesses."

"I was more interested in the salacious details, myself."

Quinto rolled his eyes. "You would be. I don't kiss and tell, but I'll say that it's all good. It's a slow burn."

I snorted.

"What?" asked Quinto.

"Nothing," I said. "I *really* wanted to make a venereal disease joke, but luckily for you, I restrained myself."

"Yeah, given how this day is going, I must be walking about with a four leaf clover in my pocket," said Quinto. "So how about yourself. I, uh...noticed you and Steele weren't on the best of terms yesterday."

"What?" I waved it off. "That was nothing. A misunderstanding. A bump in the road."

"You sure about that?" asked Quinto.

I'm not sure if he expected an honest response or if he simply intended to force the analytical part of my mind into a state of reflection. Either way, the fact of the matter was I still had no idea what set Shay on the war path yesterday. I assumed it was a combination of me waking up on the wrong side of the bed, acting in an unusually boorish fashion, and Shay suffering from a cyclical hormone imbalance, but what if the incident had been set off by something *specific* I'd said or done?

I shrugged. Since our relationship had risen back into positive territory, I was loathe to spend too much mental energy analyzing the matter. Better to put my brain to use thinking about the case and figuring out what objects passing clouds resembled.

"I'm telling you, we're fine," I said as I rose and collected the beverages. "Now are you going to loaf in here all afternoon, or do you want to join Steele and me in some brainstorming? She's on a tear. Give me more time to mentor her, and I think she can give me a run for my money in the wild and crazy ideas department."

"Yeah, yeah," said Quinto with a lazy wave of his hand. "I'll come. Give me a few minutes. I still haven't fully recovered from my ascent up paperwork mountain."

"Suit yourself," I said. "We'll be at our desks when you catch your second wind."

I headed back into the thick of the pit, eager to see if Shay had loosened any more creative bits from the inside of her skull, but as I reached our workstations, I discovered they were empty.

I set our respective mugs down and scratched my head. I didn't think I'd let Quinto distract me for *that* long, had I? And Shay's smile and sparkling eyes had indicated her newfound love for my innovative methods. She wouldn't skip out on that, not in mid thought. Perhaps she'd simply embarked on a trip to the ladies room.

I heard her laugh, and I turned to see if she'd stopped to swap jokes with one of our mutual office acquaintances. Sure enough, I spotted her inside the heavy double doors with a guest—but not a mutual friend.

Agent Blue.

29

My stomach churned as I watched the smartly dressed elf investigator, standing there in the heart of *my* precinct, smiling and laughing it up with *my* partner and *my*...well, not girlfriend, but hopefully that would change in the not too distant future, flashing his perfect grin and leaning in too far and acting interested in everything Shay had to say.

My mind offered up the morning's mantra on a silver platter, and every rational instinct within me screamed at me to sit down, grab my coffee, and nurse it with the zeal of a mother whose milk had just come in. To ignore the laughs and smiles and relegate them to my mental dustbin. To treat Agent Blue with all the care of a stallion swatting at flies with his tail.

But what can I say? I'm an idiot.

I stuffed my hands in my pockets, donned my best sneer, and made my way to the precinct's entrance.

Blue noticed me first, though he only spared me a glance before turning his attention back to Shay. "Ah, Detective. There you are."

Steele faced me, and in her hands she held a length of cream-colored wool. "Look, Daggers. He brought my scarf back. Isn't that sweet? Really, Agent Blue, you didn't have to do that."

Sweet? Was she kidding? I suppressed a snort, meaning the burst of air firing through my nose sounded more like a gag than anything else. "Yes. What a kind, un-doubtedly motivation-free gesture on the part of the Agent, here."

Shay narrowed her eyes at that, but Blue waved it off, as if he hadn't even heard me. Apparently, he was too smitten to bother deciphering my thinly-veiled slights.

"It wasn't about the scarf," he said. "You've been to my office multiple times already. It was only fair I re-turn the favor. And if I was coming, then why wouldn't I return your misplaced property?"

How magnanimous of him. I felt my scowl deepen. "That's great, Blue. Now what do you want?"

This time, the elf agent finally paid me some mind, his smile melting as I forced him to interact with me. "Well, I came by for the reasons we discussed this morning. I was able to liberate some meager resources through my chain of command, and we're in the process of interviewing those individuals in charge of watching over Privates Chavez and Delvesdeep. But I was hoping you and your fellow officers would've had more luck tracking down the pair. There's only so much we can do on that front."

I glanced at Shay, who looked back at me with pursed lips. We hadn't discussed how we'd officially deal with Kelly and Drake's departure, but at least we'd both agreed our encounter with them was strictly off the books.

As I thought about how to respond to him, Shay stepped in to save the day. "Unfortunately, Agent Blue, our investigation has shifted in a different direction. Between what we discovered this morning at our second crime scene and a few details that have surfaced since then, Privates Chavez and Delvesdeep aren't our chief priority anymore. We simply can't spare any resources to track them down at the moment."

Blue lifted a brow. "Wait...what new details? What have you learned?"

I shouldn't have opened my fat mouth, but I did anyway. Sometimes it works faster than my brain. "I think what Detective Steele is trying to say is that you should *butt the hell out.*"

Blue straightened and drew down his brows. "Excuse me?"

My machismo began to take over. "Did I stutter?"

"Look, Detective Daggers," said Blue from between thin lips. "I thought we'd reached an understanding. We can achieve more together than we can individually. And as much as you might like for this case to be entirely within your jurisdiction, it isn't. So until you've brought charges against someone for the murders of the two homeless men you've found, and those charges *aren't* brought against one of my military charges, then you're simply going to have to deal with my butt in your business."

"Oh, I bet you like to put your butt on a lot of things. And other body parts, too."

It wasn't a particularly snappy comeback, but it was the best I could do under duress, especially considering I couldn't get the mental image of Blue seducing my partner out of my mind, no matter how hard I tried.

"Daggers, what the—" Shay grabbed me none too gently by the arm. "Agent Blue, I'm sorry to cut things short, but I need to talk to my partner *in private*. We'll be in touch."

Shay dragged me down a side corridor until we arrived at one of our interrogation rooms, at which point she threw open the door, shoved me inside, and slammed the door behind her. Her eyes blazed with a fiery anger that I hadn't seen since her first day on the job when I'd needled her mercilessly over the slightest minutiae. With her scarf dangling from one hand, she planted her fists on her hips and splayed her legs, and somewhere inside me, my logical self muttered, *I told you so.*

"Daggers, what the *hell* is wrong with you?" cried Steele.

I reacted instinctively. "I'll tell you what's wrong. It's that Agent Blue. Butting into our investigation. Thinking he owns the place. Why—"

"Stop it," she said as she held her palm toward my face. "I don't want to hear that bullshit any more. This is not about him and the case. This is about *you.* So I'm going to ask you again. *What is your problem with him?*"

I felt my heart beat faster and my chest constrict. I didn't want this to be how Shay and I broached the subject. Not here in an interrogation room, and not with her breathing fire and snarling demands. But she knew how I felt. She absolutely *knew*. There was no doubt in my mind. And she'd accept no less than the truth.

I took a deep breath and tried to calm my nerves. "Well, I... I mean, he was, you know...making advances. Putting the moves on you."

"What?" said Shay. "No he wasn't."

"Are you *kidding*?" I said. "With the smiling and the laughing and the googly eyes. *He brought you your scarf.*"

"I don't know what you think that means, Daggers," said Shay, "but even if you're right, who cares? What does it matter?"

"It matters because... Because..." Good gods, she was really going to make me say it, wasn't she? "Because I like you. Because I thought we were building something special together."

Shay dropped her arms to her sides and sighed, and as she did so, some of the heat left the air. "Look, Daggers. I've never said it before, but...I admit it. I like you, too."

Birds sang and morning glories opened as the sky burst from behind a thick bank of clouds—or so it felt for a fraction of a second before Shay continued.

"But, liking someone isn't an end-all, be-all condition. There's reasoning behind the emotion, and qualifiers attached to it. Be honest with me, Daggers. Do you even know *why* I like you?"

I gave the question the thought it deserved. "I assumed it was because of my rakish wit and undeniable charm."

"Come on, be serious."

I blinked and tried to figure out how my jaw worked, and based on the dispirited look Shay replied with, she knew I was telling the truth.

"Oh," she said.

"Um...yeah."

With her free hand, she reached up and rubbed her neck. "Well, maybe that's something you should think about before we progress any further with this...*whatever it is* between us."

I tried to come up with a worthy answer, but I needed more than a few seconds in which to do it. Heck, it might require geologic timescales. Regardless, a knock at the door interrupted my attempt.

Shay pulled the door open. "Yes? What? Oh...hey Quinto."

The big guy stood outside the door. He averted his gaze to his feet as he took note of the expressions on our faces.

"Uh, hey guys," he said. "I'm...sorry to interrupt. But Cairny found me in the break room. Said she wanted to share some things with you. I'd seen you walk this way, and so I started looking, and, well...you know..."

I knew the interrogation rooms had been constructed with silence in mind, but I also knew from experience the padding in the walls didn't kill *all* the sound. How much had Quinto heard?

I swallowed back a lump in my throat and forced my mind to the task at hand. "It's alright, Quinto. Lead the way."

30

Even though I'd journeyed down to the morgue a half dozen times over the last day and a half, this trip felt different. The chill air hit me like a ton of bricks, the darkness enveloped me, creeping in at the corners of my vision, and my feet clattered off the stairwell steps like a bell tolling out a death knell. I interpreted the sensory bonanza as a metaphor for the direction of Shay's and my relationship. Never mind she'd said she liked me—she *actually* liked me, for real if unstated reasons—but my life had been filled with enough whiffs, near misses, and outright, crushing disappointments that depression came to me as second nature.

I could battle against it. I'd turned the tide before, both through divine intervention and through copious consumption of hard liquor, but I'd yet to win the war. I sometimes wondered if I ever would.

Cairny stood in front of Burly's corpse, now with the white sheet pulled to his neck, a clipboard held in one hand. She looked up at the sound of our feet and waved with her free hand.

"Steele. Daggers," she said. "What fortunate timing."

I didn't think she meant it as a joke—despite progress in that area, I could count on one hand the number of zingers I'd heard from Cairny's lips over the years—but she couldn't honestly have forgotten she sent Quinto to find us minutes prior, could she? While her quirks sometimes irked me, I wouldn't resent Cairny's mooncalfish nature this time—especially if it kept her from asking too many questions about why Shay and I looked like jilted lovers and Quinto had miraculously reduced his opacity by a solid eighty percent.

I stepped to the far side of the examination table. Shay and Quinto took up battle positions at my arms, though based on their body language, the only bouts they might have a chance of winning were silence and awkwardness competitions.

I wasn't in the mood for idle chatter either, so I cut straight to the point. "What have you got for us, Cairny?"

"Well, a couple points as a matter of accounting." She held up a finger. "First, you'll recall I mentioned I thought this man—Burly, I think you called him—died about four days ago. I'd like to revise that to place his death anywhere between ninety-two and one hundred and four hours ago. I'm not sure if that'll be of any help to you or not, but more information is always beneficial, I always say."

I couldn't recall Cairny ever uttering such an adage, but again, I wasn't in the mood to argue—or do much of anything for that matter.

"What else?" I asked.

"I also think this man suffered from something colloquially known as spotted fever," said Cairny. "But don't worry. It's not contagious. It's a zoonosis, transmitted via vector."

I checked a box in my mind. So...I *had* been right. The hobo *did* suffer from a disease. Of some sort, anyway. "A zoo nose what?"

"Zoonosis," said Cairny as she placed her clipboard on the edge of the exam table. "A disease transmitted to humans via animal contact. In this case—" She picked up a covered cell-culture dish and held it out. "—these little guys."

I shuddered as I lay eyes on the beady, black bloodsuckers. "Ugh! Gross. Ticks."

Shay grimaced, her lips sagging in disgust. "Well, I'll be taking a thorough shower later."

"A prudent choice," said Cairny as she replaced the dish on the table. "But I doubt any of them jumped ship to you guys. In fact, contrary to popular belief, ticks are physically incapable of jumping. Rather, they transfer to suitable hosts by a process known as 'questing,' where they hang onto leaves or blades of grass, or human extremities, and wait for a new host to brush past."

"Thanks for the biology lesson," I said. "Now I feel much better about the possibility of small insects crawling all over me and hiding in my nether regions."

"You're welcome," said Cairny, oblivious to my sarcasm. "You know, while I spent most of my time in college studying anatomy and histology, I did always harbor a soft spot for entomology. Which, if you're wondering, means the study of bugs."

"I got that one," I said. "But thanks for the vote of confidence."

"This is all fine and dandy," said Shay, "but I don't see how it's going to help us identify the man or figure out who murdered him."

"Well then, why don't we move on to something more relevant?" offered Cairny. "Like the manner of his death."

Quinto walked to the top of the table and squatted, staring at Burly's skull. "Let me guess...he died by blunt force trauma to the back of the head?"

"Oh, Folton," said Cairny. "I expect that kind of cheek from Daggers, but you?"

"Wait," said Shay. "Are you saying he *didn't* die from blunt force trauma?"

"Well, he was hit in the back of the skull with a blunt instrument, to be sure," said Cairny. "But he didn't die from the blow. He was smothered."

Interesting. Clearly Lanky had eventually died from the blow to *his* head, but if Burly had died via asphyxiation, it indicated a further key point to the killer's M.O., one that hadn't been implemented with Lanky—perhaps because he escaped.

"How can you be sure, Cairny?" I asked.

Cairny brandished her finger again. "Good question. Smothering is extremely difficult to prove, you know. Sometimes you'll find evidence of cyanosis, or bluing, around the nose and mouth, but given the age of this cadaver and the man's spotted fever, anything I told you in regards to that line of thought would be guesswork. The most obvious telltale signs of smothering are bloodshot eyes and the presence of a bloody, frothy fluid in the air passages, and of those I found evidence of both. And besides—the blow to his skull missed his occipital artery. He shouldn't have bled out from the wound. Not unless the impact knocked him unconscious for a longer period of time than I expect it would've."

Shay joined Quinto at the top of the exam table and knelt to look at Burly's skull. It wasn't an angle that gave the best possible view of his wound, but given Cairny's revelations about the man's parasite problems, I wasn't too eager to reposition his head, either.

Shay pursed her lips. "What can you tell us about the...well, I want to say murder weapon, but that may not be accurate, so I'll just say weapon."

"I didn't find any evidence of wood fibers in his brain or muscle tissue," said Cairny, "so I'm guessing it was something made of metal. Something strong, and with enough heft to it to fracture his skull."

"What exactly are we talking about here?" I asked.

Cairny retrieved the clipboard from the table and flipped over a couple pages to a crude but effective sketch, which she handed to me. It showed a weapon somewhat smaller than I'd originally anticipated based on visual inspections of Lanky and Burly.

"I thought you might ask that, so I drew you a diagram," said Cairny. "I'm guessing a rod, perhaps three quarters of an inch in diameter. It could be anything, really. My guess would be a pipe or structural support rod or—"

"A honing steel?" I offered.

The jet-haired coroner considered that before ultimately nodding. "Why...yes. Proper weight. Proper strength. That could work quite well."

Shay rose and eyed me suspiciously. "Daggers...where are you going with this?"

I smiled, the melancholy induced by Shay's revelations about her feelings for me momentarily relegated to my emotional 'To-Do' pile. "I'm thinking we need to get a warrant for the Delta Deli."

31

After extracting a warrant from the folds in the Captain's jowls, Quinto, Shay, and I headed back to the Delta district. We elected to walk—or rather, Shay did, despite the overabundance of rickshaws hanging around outside the station. I'd assumed she'd want to save her feet any possible undue stress, but maybe she opted for the walk for ulterior motives. Perhaps she hoped for a bit of quiet solace outside the forced intimacy of a rickshaw bench, or perhaps she wished for exactly what I most feared—the time and environment in which to brood.

During our jaunt at the precinct, clouds had rolled in, obscuring the sun and hiding its warm rays from view, which had prompted Shay to return her cream-colored scarf to its rightful position around her neck. The donning of said woolen article, however, had been a joyless affair, lacking the sensuality and grace of the morning's effort—or at least, it had been to my eyes, made dull by Shay's sharp tongue. Even now, as she led the way down the streets of New Welwic, with tight pants hugging her lower half and begging to be ogled, I couldn't bear to look at her.

What was wrong with me? Why was it every time I exposed something to the general vicinity of my heart it withered and died like a flower under a steady stream of potent dog urine? I thought my relationship with Shay had been progressing naturally, and positively, if a little slowly. We'd shared laughs and smiles and tender moments, bites from meals and still life portraits of our personal histories. We'd grown and matured and bettered ourselves thanks to each other—or at least I had. I'd even lost weight and started treating random people with kindness and respect, for Pete's sake! And yet all that growth and change and hard work had fallen to pieces in the last twenty-four hours. All because of that stupid, dapper, well-spoken Agent Blue.

I clenched my teeth and shook my head. No. That wasn't true. *He* wasn't the problem. I was. Shay had made that abundantly clear. And even though she hadn't gone into detail regarding which of my qualities were the problem, she didn't have to.

I knew. Insecurity. Jealousy. Depression. Doubt. I was a psychiatrist's dream patient, except without the spare change needed to buy weekly doses of mood-altering drugs. It just so happened Agent Blue pushed several of my emotional buttons at the same time, all while also interfering with my investigation in a knee-to-the-groin-like tour de force. His appearance had merely been the inevitable needle to my balloon, proving my recent joy in Shay's company as nothing more than a mirage.

But then again...Shay *had* said she liked me. With qualifiers and exceptions, of course, but there was *something* about me she didn't find repugnant. And that, at least, was a start. I just had to figure out what it was—and then cultivate it into something worthy of her attention.

Quinto's heavy hand clapped me on the shoulder. "I think we've made it, pal."

I looked up and realized we'd arrived at the Delta Deli. Shay stood outside its front door, her arms crossed as she looked at the sign. Like me, I don't think she'd uttered a word during the entire walk.

She sighed. "Daggers, I..."

I waited on her with baited breath. "Yes?"

"I know the Captain granted the warrant, but I don't understand this at all. Why in the world would anyone at this Deli kill Lanky or Burly?"

My shoulders slumped. I thought perhaps her silence had been an indicator of her own emotional turmoil, but apparently she'd spent the return trip to the deli thinking about the case.

"Look," I said. "I'm not completely sure either. Maybe they really *are* killing hobos and selling them for parts. If so, we should steel ourselves—no pun intended—to what we might see in that kitchen. But regardless of the reason, I'm sure you agree *something* out of the ordinary is going on in there, and given Cairny's diagnosis, we have enough evidence to merit a look-see."

"Or so you managed to convince the Captain," said Steele. "To be honest, he must've been feeling extremely generous given the spread you laid out before him."

"Please," I said. "The words 'Captain' and 'feeling' are incongruous. The man has the emotional capacity of a hunk of granite, and he's roughly as easily persuaded. Now, let's not waste any more time. Quinto, bring up the rear. Make sure nobody sneaks out, or takes a pot shot at our exposed backsides with a metal rod."

Quinto snorted. "One of these days you'll have to stop giving me the easy jobs and force me to do the hard work of looking around and poking stuff."

"Very funny."

I pulled open the door and let myself in, taking a quick look around the establishment as I did so. The deli's population had dwindled from two down to one. Only slack-jawed Mark remained. I found him sitting behind the hostess stand on a stool he must've liberated from somewhere in the back.

He tried to engage me in witty conversation. "Uh...hey."

I flashed him the signed and sealed warrant as I walked past him. "Police investigation, Marky. Out of the way."

"Hey, wait," he said. "You can't go back there. That'th a private thpace."

I plunged through the bead curtain before the guy's feet even hit the ground and found myself in the middle of an entirely unspectacular room—a commercial kitchen with four walls, a ceiling, the bead curtain behind me and a door to a pantry, adorned with pots, pans, knives, rolling pins, butcher's blocks, and assorted piles of plates, silverware, and glasses. A wide, cast iron stove took up the majority of one wall, though based on the temperature in the kitchen, a fire didn't burn in its belly. Crates had been stacked next to it—a fire hazard if ever I'd seen one—most of them staring at me from the pits of their planks with empty, knotted eyes.

The one thing I'd expected to see and didn't—other than dismembered burly men—was salable product. Only a few of the crates held any loaves of bread, and while the menu hadn't exactly featured a vast array of choices, I did think I'd find at least *one* example of a fresh fruit or vegetable somewhere on the racks or prep stations. I knelt over a wide chest I assumed was an ice box and flipped open its lid, holding my breath as I did so.

I exhaled. Again, no hobo body parts. Just cold cuts.

A bead cascade made me turn. Shay stood inside the curtain, scanning the room. Manager Mark and Quinto followed her shortly, the former visibly agitated.

"You're not thuppothed to be in here," he said, his mouth flapping awkwardly. "Thith ith thtrictly for employeeth only. There'th thanitary conthernth related to your prethenth."

I glanced at Quinto and he shrugged. "I don't think he understands the legal system very well. Namely that police warrants trump the health department."

I stood and frowned. I'd been sure something unseemly was taking place back here, but the evidence indicated the restaurant was entirely on the up and up. Heck, the kitchen was even *clean*. Apparently my fears about joining in a fierce struggle with the porcelain god as a result of my lunch choice were overblown. However, I *did* find it odd the kitchen was so underpopulated. Where was yesterday's goblin chef, or the orc guy who came in earlier? And what about the beer? I didn't spot any brew kettles or barrels that looked as if they might contain that most delectable of fermented creations.

I walked over to a wooden knife block containing an assortment of thirteen different knives. I selected the one with the largest handle and pulled it out. A chef's knife, probably about eight inches long. It would be illegal if carried on the street, but luckily for restaurateurs everywhere, the city's lawmakers hadn't extended the ban on sharp, pointy things to commercial kitchens. I angled the blade in the light, admiring its clean edge. I didn't think the thing had ever been used.

"Thtop it," said Mark. "That'th private property. Handth off."

"Shut it," said Quinto.

His tone, and perhaps his massive size, had the desired effect. Mark clamped his yapper.

Shay joined me as I gingerly reached for the honing steel in the block, lifting it out by the ring on its end. If someone had gripped it recently, there might still be prints on it. Unfortunately, as I glanced at the finely-grooved steel rod, I couldn't find any more evidence of wear on it than on the chef's knife. Either the attacker thoroughly cleaned it to hide any evidence of malfeasance, or the thing was brand spanking new.

"Are you seeing anything I'm not, Steele?" I asked.

I trusted my partner's observational prowess more than my own, although she may have been distracted by our emotionally-charged exchange in the interrogation room. Then again, so was I.

Shay shook her head. "Can't say I am. Everything seems clean, organized, and *grossly* underutilized—

which is suspicious in and of itself. But I'm not seeing any dents or scratches or other signs of struggle. No scuff marks on the floor, and no blood splatters on the surfaces. Although it's possible they could've been wiped down..."

Mark made his presence known again. "Wait...blood thplatterth? What are you guyth talking about?"

Normally I disapproved of letting sensitive information loose within earshot of potential suspects, but with the less mentally adept, it could be an effective strategy. I don't think Mark had a whole lot going on upstairs, and based off his reaction, he truly was clueless as to the motives behind our search. Either he was a stooge, or I'd let my suspicions lead me into another judicially-unfounded blunder.

Shay tilted her head and narrowed her eyes. "Did you hear that?"

"Hear what?" I asked.

"It was sort of a screeching sound." Shay held up a finger. "There is was again."

This time I heard it, too. A screeching sound, indeed, but one not human in origin. More like metal scraping on metal, or the grinding of a rusty piece of machinery. Another sound followed it—an angry voice, if I wasn't mistaken.

I glanced at my feet. The noises came from underground.

Mark bolted for the exit, but Quinto clotheslined him, knocking him to the ground with a painful thud.

I heard another voice, and I shifted my eyes to the pantry door. Nightmare scenarios from the worst sorts of slasher novels flashed through my head, everything from torture dungeons to human rendering plants.

I ripped Daisy from the interior of my coat, gripping her with white knuckles as I approached the pantry. I gulped, took a deep breath, and threw open the door.

32

I plunged into a dark space and blinked as I oriented myself. Walls encroached upon me in front and to my right, but a glimmer flickered below me to the left, so I descended the steps I found there toward the pale light. The wooden planks groaned underneath my weight, announcing my presence to whatever band of ruffians, deviants, and homicidal maniacs might be present within.

In a bare twelve steps, I'd made it to the bottom. I paused as I gaped at the contents.

Before me, a half-dozen pure bloods and half-breeds sat on a wide bench, twiddling their thumbs and looking bored—except for those who'd already turned their eyes onto me. Across from them, a diminutive goblin—the so-called 'chef' we'd met yesterday morning—sat behind a stately desk, elevated on a giant stool so he could see. At the moment, he leaned over the desk, helping a tall orc with a ruddy braid cascading down his back press his thumb into a square slip of paper. Beside the slip stood a number of rubber stamps and next to that, an open ink pad situated over a thick piece of blotting paper.

Behind the desk, a hulking cast iron contraption full of wheels and clamps and heavy plates screeched as another goblin cranked on a lever at its side. Next to it, I spotted stacks of the square paper slips, all blank, as well as gold leaf, jars of multi-colored inks, and a compartmented box full of movable type.

I blinked. A printing press? And fingerprints and stamps and gold embossed seals? What was going on?

I suddenly noticed every eye in the place had shifted onto me, except for that of the far goblin, who'd gone from cranking on the lever to cursing up a storm as he furiously yanked on a strip of paper jammed between the rollers.

The hairs on the back of my neck rose, and I turned to find Shay standing behind me.

She took in the sights quicker than I did. "A forging operation? For...immigration permits?"

Perhaps my partner should've exercised more discretion, because as she expressed her suspicions, all hell broke loose. The two nearest bench warmers, an orc with a handlebar moustache and a wild-eyed dwarf, bolted toward us. Shay shrieked and jumped to the side as the former barreled into me. The orc knocked me to the side as I lashed out with Daisy, catching the guy across the back as the dwarf slipped into the stairwell.

I stumbled and caught myself against the wall as the space erupted in a chorus of shouts and curses, most of them in languages I didn't understand. The remainder of the bench mob took a step toward the stairs, but paused as the orc and his sidekick the angst-ridden dwarf flew back into the room as if they'd bounced off an invisible wall. Thankfully, the wall wasn't invisible, and it had a name. Quinto moved in to block the stairwell exit, manager Mark gripped in a headlock under his left arm.

The mustachioed orc snarled, showing his teeth as he balled his hands into fists. Sensing Daisy yearned for sexual liberation, I let her engage in a little three-way action with the floor-bound orc and his little brother from another mother. After a few lustful whacks, she satisfied their cravings, leaving them sprawled across the floor in a post-ménage state of unconscious bliss. After that, the rest of the unruly crowd settled down, not wanting to be subjected to Daisy's sadistic tendencies.

I took charge of the situation, using Daisy as a pointer as I issued demands. "All of you—back on the bench. Orc breath, with the red braid—you, too. Goblins—up against the wall. Steele, go get backup. ASAP. As many bluecoats as you can find. And tell someone we're going to need a wagon."

Steele slipped past Quinto and disappeared up the stairs, which prompted the big guy to toss Mark to the ground and gesture for him to join the bench mob. Despite their compliance with my demands, the foreigners and half-breeds didn't stop their yammering, asking questions and begging me for mercy—or so I assumed. Again, I didn't understand half of what most of them were saying.

"Quiet! All of you!" I waved my nightstick around in a threatening manner, hoping the whistle of steel cutting through the air would supplant their voices.

It more or less worked. The shouts and cries degenerated into concerned mumbles and angry glares shot in my direction. I walked to the desk and grabbed the slip of paper with the orc's fresh thumbprint on it. Shay's eyes hadn't deceived her. It *was* an immigration permit—or would be once it went through a few more printing and embossing steps.

I'd never heard of anyone forging them, but it made sense. Even though the government didn't charge to hand them to immigrants, it did, on occasion, refuse to issue them to those with mental health concerns or obvious criminal backgrounds. In addition, issuance of an immigration permit alerted the tax collectors to one's presence, and I could see the allure of remaining off the books in that regard.

I snapped a mental finger and shot a glance at the printing press. Once I knew what to look for, I spotted it right away. Behind the placards. A big stack of folded brown paper bags. Well, that explained the takeout orders.

I squinted into the furthest reaches of the basement. Something I hadn't noticed at first twinkled in the lantern light. Something rusty and metallic. A copper brew kettle. Three of them, to be precise.

Imagine that. Apparently, the deli wasn't *purely* a front for illegal activity. If only the sandwiches had lived up to the level of the beer, perhaps my overactive imagination wouldn't have led me here on an unfounded witch-hunt—of which, clearly, this had been, unless I miraculously found a tertiary hobo butchering business in another secret basement located underneath this one.

216 ALEX P. BERG

My charges didn't allow me much time to indulge in my disappointment, constantly testing the limits of my watchfulness and trying to wander off. If only I could've traded my nightstick for a crook and a border collie...

Eventually, Shay returned with a cluster of beat cops, and we began the slog of tagging and processing everyone, loading them onto a paddy wagon, sweeping the deli for evidence that might help us locate previously issued forged permits, impounding equipment, and the myriad other mundane tasks that made me remember why I loved my job in homicide so much.

After an hour or two of work, Steele, Quinto, and I trudged our way back to the precinct, no richer in knowledge regarding our case than when we'd left. I half expected Shay to razz me over my ridiculous black market beef theory as we walked, but instead she stayed silent. Perhaps she thought I'd suffered enough throughout the day already, or she simply didn't want to engage me in idle chitchat unless absolutely necessary.

As we pushed into the station's interior, I eyed my desk and well worn chair with longing, but the Captain harbored no sympathy for my back or feet. He intercepted us before we'd made it even halfway through the pit.

"Daggers. Steele. Quinto. What are you doing here?" he asked.

"What do you mean, sir?" asked Steele. "We just finished a raid at—"

"Yeah, yeah. I know," he barked. "I heard. But I sent a runner after you three about ten minutes ago. Didn't he find you?"

We shared blank looks among our detective triumvirate.

"Figures," said the Captain. "I don't even know why I pay those urchins."

"He probably just missed us," said Shay.

He eyed her warily. "You're too trusting, but maybe that's a good quality. Anyway, don't stand here wasting space. Go on. Get back up there."

"Where?" I asked. "The Deli?"

"The Delta district," said the bulldog. "There's been another incident. No, don't ask. I don't have the details. Just get your butts to 37th and Fairweather. And get me some damn answers! There are only so many transients that can get axed in one district before someone starts breathing down my neck."

What my butt really wanted was a nice long break in my preferred resting spot at my desk, but I didn't think the Captain would appreciate me putting the needs of my posterior before that of the department, so with a resigned sigh, I performed an about face and headed back out.

33

Our feet carried us toward the Captain's prescribed destination, an intersection farther northeast than either of our previous crime scenes but still within a stone's throw of the DEITA station. Though Shay continued her vow of silence, Quinto apparently decided I'd been handled with kid gloves for long enough. He peppered me with questions the entire walk up, mostly regarding the circumstances of Burly's discovery, seeing as he'd missed out on that. Despite my initial reticence, it felt good to talk. If nothing else, Quinto's barrage prevented my psyche from crawling back into one of the dark holes inside me.

As we reached the intersection in question, I realized the Captain hadn't explicitly told us where we were heading, or for that matter, what we should look for. As luck would have it, however, we weren't the first members of the city's finest at the scene. I spotted Phillips nodding and mumbling to himself under a black striped awning at the front of a long, narrow building, one with arched windows and a subdued gothic feel.

"Phillips!" I called.

The young beat cop spotted us and waved us over. "Hey, Detective Daggers. Good to see you. You, too, Steele and Quinto."

I think the young guy meant it, despite my harsher than necessary treatment of him yesterday morning. One of the best parts of youth was the body's speed of recovery, both mentally as well as physically.

"So," I asked. "What's the deal here? We didn't get a whole lot of details before the Captain ran us out the door with a switch."

"Not sure," said Phillips. "I arrived a couple minutes ago myself. I've been trying to get a statement out of the bystander who alerted the runner."

"Oh. Great." I took a look around. "And, uh...where is this witness?"

I heard a high-pitched, piqued voice. "Over here, dimwit."

I tracked the source of the sass to a windowsill in front of me, upon which perched a ten-inch tall homunculus with translucent wings roughly as wide as it was tall.

A pixie. Wonderful.

I'd harbored a high level of distaste for the diminutive, winged prats ever since a childhood taunting incident involving a pack of them, a beehive, my hair, and about a cup's worth of refined sugar, but even if didn't suffer childhood nightmares because of them, I'd probably have disliked them anyway. The buzzing of their wings made them sound like enormous flies, and as a species, they tended to be brash, loquacious, and cheeky. I sometimes wondered if their abrasive personalities were a result of extreme short man syndrome, but then again, they could fly, which I'd be pretty jazzed about if I were one.

The pixie who'd spoken sat cross-legged on the stone sill, eyeing me with disdain. It—I couldn't determine its gender right off the bat—wore a billowing black shirt over matching pants. Its shoes, also black, sparkled as if with glitter, and fingerless gloves of a predictable color partially concealed its hands. Surprisingly, however, the creature sported a bright shock of blue hair.

I found my voice after scowling at the miniature winged person for a few seconds. "And...you are?"

"Meriwether Angelsdust," it said, which didn't particularly help me in the gender determination department. "Now are you going to stand and gawk or are you going to help?"

"What seems to be the problem?" asked Steele, stepping forward.

Meriwether finally noticed my partner. "Hey, hey, hot stuff. Who died and sent me to heaven?"

It flipped its hair to the side and smiled—or, rather, *he* did. I think my gender question had been answered.

"I'm, uh...flattered by your interest," said Shay, "but in case you missed it, I'm a detective, too. I'm here in a professional role."

"Hey, that's cool, baby," said Meriwether. "I love *roleplay*."

Quinto eyed Phillips and jerked a thumb at Meriwether. "Is this guy for real? Where'd you find him?"

"Hey, I live here, asshole," said the pixie.

"Alright," I said, holding my hands up. "I know I'm the most unlikely source of reason among the lot of us, but why don't we calm down and start over fresh. Meriwether—you sent a runner for help, right? So what's the problem?"

The pixie rolled his eyes and snorted. "Fine. I was inside, snoozing, when I heard this loud thumping and—"

"Hold on," I said. "You live here? What is this place?"

"This?" said Meriwether, pointing at the building. "Church of the Holy Oblivion."

"Church of the...?" I stopped myself before I completed the statement. I remembered the last time I inadvertently let my tongue flap over at the place with the trees for a ceiling, and I didn't want to get the same sort of rambling religious spiel from a woebegone pixie. "You live in a church? Don't tell me you're a pastor."

"Me?" said Meriwether. "Nah. I just live and work here."

We all gave him looks with varying degrees of confusion.

"Hey, it's different, ok?" he said. "I pick up trash and dust in the hard to reach portions of the rafters. In return, they let me stay here rent free."

"So what happened?" asked Steele.

"Well," said Meriwether, "as I was saying before Inspector Peabrain over here interrupted, I was sleeping inside when crashes and screams woke me. Coming from the direction of the reflection rooms and sleeping quarters—you know, for the humans. Again, I sleep in the rafters."

"You were sleeping during the day?" asked Quinto.

222 ALEX P. BERG

"Hello?" said the pixie, showing off his garb. "Church of the Holy *Oblivion*? We get most of our patrons at night. And it's not like I give the sermons, anyway."

"So, was there a fight?" I asked. "Is anyone hurt? Did someone murder a hobo?"

"*Murder a hobo?*" Meriwether gave me the fisheye. "Is that what gets you off?"

My patience wore thin. "It's been a thing, lately. Now, out with it. What happened? In fact, why are we standing out here? Why don't you show us?"

"Help yourself," said Meriwether. "I'm staying right here where it's safe."

I felt a rush of adrenaline. "Wait...is there still someone in there?"

Meriwether shrugged. "How would I know?"

"Are you saying you didn't go investigate?" said Quinto. "That you don't even know what happened?"

Meriwether scoffed. "What a stupid, big guy thing to say. Of course not. One errant footstep or flailing slap and I'm dog food. Look, I heard noises and screams. I got the hell out. End of story."

I sighed and pressed a hand to my forehead. Despite my aching feet, I'd been somewhat eager at the prospect of another murder—not because I relished in the slaying of vagrants, but because it might help shed light on an otherwise murky case. But the more Meriwether flapped his gums, the more convinced I became his experiences were likely as not the product of a wayward alley cat knocking over some trash cans.

"Let's get this over with," I said. "Meriwether, you're coming with us—and don't give me any guff. It's so you can show us where you *thought* you heard the commotion. If you somehow get ground under a boot heel in the few short moments it takes to do that, then I'm sure the police department will deliver a kind letter to your next of kin."

Meriwether grumbled, but I think he realized if he didn't help us, we wouldn't secure the building that served as his home, so he acquiesced.

Together, we pushed into the chapel, which was as austere and depressing as you might expect from a church with the name of the Holy Oblivion. Lacquered pine benches lined a thin aisle, culminating at a narrow pulpit painted in black, but it was the emblem behind the pulpit that caught my eye.

"Um, Daggers..." said Steele.

"I see it." I dug the token out of my pocket and held it at arms length in front of my face to could compare it to the wall design. The two mirrored each other perfectly—geometrically-designed vortices swirling around central circles.

"Hey," said Meriwether. "You've got one of our oblivion mementos. And here I thought you weren't familiar with our religion."

"Where did you hear these noises and screams from, again?" I asked.

"In back," said Meriwether. "Upstairs, I think. From the direction of Deacon Vo's office."

"Show us," I said.

The pixie led us past the pulpit, up a flight of stairs, and down a corridor, but as an open doorway pulled within view, he zipped past to hide behind us.

"That's Vo's office," he said. "His door's usually locked."

If any screams and thumps had echoed down the hall earlier in the day, they'd long since disappeared. All I heard now was the buzzing of Meriwether's wings and the beating of my own heart. Nonetheless, I pulled Daisy from my coat and gripped her tightly before stepping into the open doorway.

My jaw nearly hit the floor. What *the hell* was going on?

34

The office was a mess. Papers littered the surface of a wide, unembellished oaken desk, and ink from an overturned bottle ran across its surface, soaking the pages and dripping onto the floor like the blood of the damned. An overturned bookshelf vomited tomes of varying shapes and sizes onto the floor, the latter of which languished alongside shards of glass from broken windows that gleamed in the light of the late afternoon sun. Pieces of what might've once been a chair peeked out like gophers from between the carnage, but it was the centerpiece of the room that drew my attention.

Two bodies sprawled on the polished wood underfoot, not more than three or four feet from each other. The first belonged to a man in his late forties or early fifties, short in stature, with close-cropped black hair and almond eyed.

"Aww, crap," I heard Meriwether mutter over the buzz of his wings. "That's Vo. This isn't good."

What an understatement. I'd get to him, but first I walked over to the other body. I planted my hands on my hips and stared.

Shay joined me at my side. "Well...we found Lanky."

I knelt down to get a closer look. He wore the same moth-eaten pants and threadbare coat I remembered. Same long, matted hair. Same bushy beard. It was Lanky, no question about it. But to suggest he was completely unchanged from when I saw him last would be incorrect. There appeared to be new abrasions on the skin of his arms and on his palms, as if someone had scraped it with sandpaper. In addition to that, his clothes had deteriorated. Numerous new tears graced his ensemble, including a number of what appeared to be punctures in his coat and underlying shirt. There must've been at least twenty of them.

I plucked at the shirt and stuck the tip of my pinky into one of the holes. It barely fit. Grimacing, I lifted the shirt from Lanky's waist, revealing a goodly portion of his torso. As expected, small, bloodless incisions covered it.

"Daggers," said Steele. "Come take a look at this."

My partner knelt over a miniature claymore about the length of my outstretched hand. At first I thought the thing had been dropped by a heavily armed relative of Meriwether's, but as I noted its dull edge and cheap construction, I realized it was a letter opener. The width of its blade matched the size of the holes in Lanky's shirt.

"Don't touch it," I said. "Maybe we can get prints off it."

Shay nodded, and I returned to Vo's body. Quinto squatted next to it, his face looking much as I imagine mine did, with his brows so furrowed I feared they might knit themselves together. Phillips, meanwhile, stood at the entrance to the room with his arms crossed, no doubt trying to stay out of the way.

Meriwether alighted on the edge of the desk. He cupped his chin in one of his tiny hands and shook his head. "Not good, man. Not good. He didn't deserve this. He never hurt anybody."

I squatted next to the body, across from Quinto. "You said his name was Deacon Vo?"

"No," said Meriwether. "His name was *Cornelius* Vo. Deacon was his title. He was the grand master of our church. At least the local branch."

I passed my eyes over Vo's body. He wore an unmonklike pair of black trousers that he'd matched with a checkered grey dress shirt with double cuffs. A few ink splatters dotted the grey cloth, but I didn't notice any red ones, nor did any blood pool on the floor. I did, however, notice some distinct, uneven bruising around his throat, with the worst spots to either side of his windpipe and farther around the sides. His eyes bulged, and his mouth, which hung half open, contained a swollen tongue.

"Looks like he was strangled to death," said Quinto.

I nodded as a gleam of something metallic from around his neck caught my eye. I dug a pencil out of my coat pocket and snaked it under the man's collar, the top button of which was unbuttoned, and used it to draw upon a fine silver chain. Attached to the end was a medallion, perhaps twice as large as the token we'd

found on Burly, featuring the now familiar vortex symbol of his church.

I stood, interlacing my hands and wrapping them
around the back of my neck, as I stared at the body. "Ok,
Meriwether. Walk me through this one more time.
When did you hear the commotion?"

"I don't know," he said. "Maybe half an hour ago, or
a little more."

"And you didn't hear anything before that, right?"

Meriwether shook his head. "Nope. Told you, I was
sleeping."

"How heavy of a sleeper are you?" I asked. "Would
you have heard if someone came in through the front
door?"

"Probably," he said. "But there's another entrance in
back. It's usually locked, but..."

But maybe it hadn't been this time. Or maybe someone had a key. "We'll check it out," I said. "Does anyone
else live here?"

"Nah," said Meriwether. "Vo had a couple under-
studies, but they're volunteers. They hang out a lot, but
they don't live here."

"And none of them are here now?" I asked.

Meri shook his head.

"Of course not." I jerked a thumb in Lanky's direction. "I don't suppose you recognize that guy?"

"Me?" said the pixie. "You're the one with the dead
hobo fetish."

Shay joined me at my side.

"See anything I missed?" I asked.

"Well, I can't really answer that, seeing as I don't
know what's in that thick head of yours," she said. "But

other than the letter opener and the puncture wounds and the state of Mr. Vo here? Did you notice Lanky's lower quarter?"

"Huh?" I glanced in the body's direction. "What about it?"

"His shoes and pants are dirtier than I remember," said Steele. "As if someone dragged him through a back alley or a muddy lot."

Someone—emphasis on one. I made a mental note as I sighed and dropped my hands to my sides.

"Please tell me you have a theory, Daggers," said Quinto.

I shrugged. "Honestly, big guy? I'm at a total loss."

"Come on," said Shay. "That doesn't sound like the Daggers I know. What ever happened to concocting crazy theories on the fly, regardless of whether or not they make sense? It's just an exercise, right?"

I wanted to smile. If nothing else, she did pay attention to my investigative advice.

"Ok," I said. "Maybe...Vo hired Lanky and Burly to do something for him. Something illegal. Perhaps they blackmailed him after the fact. Asked for more money to keep their mouths shut. Vo didn't like that so he killed them, except Lanky got away. And he had something on his person that would connect him to Vo. Something like that token. So Vo broke into the morgue, stole Lanky's body, and returned it here. Except..."

I growled and threw my hands in the air. "Damn it, this doesn't make any sense! It was Burly who had the token on him, not Lanky. Lanky didn't carry anything connecting him to Vo—not that we know of, anyway.

And none of this would explain why Burly's body was in that street several days after his death, or why someone, likely Vo, mutilated Lanky's corpse with a letter opener, or why someone strangled Vo to death."

"Maybe it was a weird form of autoerotic asphyxiation," said Quinto.

"Please," I said. "I love creepy, kinky theories as much as the next guy, but he didn't do this to himself."

"Maybe someone found out Vo killed the homeless men and came to exact revenge," said Steele.

Phillips piped up from the doorway. "Yeah. Could've been a relative. Or an ex-lover."

I held up my hands. "Stop it. Just stop it, all of you. We all know my theory has more holes in it than Lanky's mangled shirt, so stop trying to buttress it up with logic."

Shay and Quinto exchanged glances and shrugged.

I pressed a hand to my forehead. "Alright. We'll knock some sense into this, one way or another. Quinto, why don't you hit Taxation and Revenue and Public Records before they close? Dig up whatever you can on Vo and meet us back at the precinct. Phillips— alert CSU. Get them to go over this office with a fine-toothed comb. In the meantime, Steele and I will check out the rest of the church. See if we can find any additional evidence, and we'll personally transport the bodies to the morgue. Hopefully Cairny will still be around by the time we get there. Sound good?"

I received a bunch of nods in response. Part of me wanted to gather everyone into a huddle and clap as we dispersed, but I felt that would've been a little disrespectful to the dead.

35

The day's light faded rapidly as we approached the precinct, and whatever god controlled the weather apparently decided we mortals deserved another dose. Wispy strands of mist crept lower and lower through the sky, befriending gargoyles and working their way into the gutters of the taller buildings, and the morning chill which had been banished returned with a vengeance. If not for the fog, I suspected we might suffer the first truly cold night of the season.

I parted ways with Shay at the front of the station. Though we'd found some additional clues on our survey of the Church of the Holy Oblivion—namely that someone had forced open the back door en route to Vo's office—we hadn't uncovered anything groundbreaking that exposed the innards of the case for all to see. While she took on the unenviable task of interviewing our sassy, oversexed pixie friend, Meriwether, on anything he might've overlooked, I helped move Lanky's and Vo's bodies to the morgue.

Luckily, Cairny hadn't yet vanished. I found her sitting at a desk at the far end of the examination room, filling out forms.

She looked up as I and the herd of bluecoats under my wing entered, all of us stamping our feet and depositing debris over the clean floor.

She stood and shook her head. "Oh, no."

"Hey, don't give me that," I said as I crossed the room to meet her. "You signed on for this. Don't act frustrated because we brought in more work for you right around closing time."

"I was more concerned about the fact that people keep dying," said Cairny.

"Oh," I said. "Well, on the bright side, one of them isn't new. We found Lanky, our corpse from yesterday morning."

The beat cops deposited Lanky and Vo onto a pair of adjacent exam tables, removing them from the heavy, black leather bags we used to transport them as they did so.

Phillips lingered among the bluecoat crew. As he left, I called out to him. "Phillips! Don't forget to record the drop off on the clipboard by the door."

The young guy shot me a familiar hand sign—his index finger and thumb pressed together into a circle and the rest of the fingers splayed out. It was either the universal sign for 'You got it' or a crude representation of a sphincter. I hoped he meant it as the former.

I clapped my hands and rubbed them together as I approached Vo's body. "Alright, Cairny. Let's do this."

"*Let's?*" she said.

"You know what I mean," I said. "I need answers, and the sooner I get them the better. So...chop-chop."

Cairny glided to a brushed steel cabinet on the side of the room, drawing open one of the drawers and extracting a pair of delicate white gloves. She slid them onto her hands before joining me.

"First of all, Daggers," she said, "and don't take this the wrong way, but I'm getting rather sick of seeing your face in my morgue. Don't you have other avenues to pursue?"

"Do you really want me to answer that?" I asked.

Cairny proceeded as if I hadn't spoken. "And second of all, you know it takes me time to perform my examinations. There's no way I'll be able to give you a report on both of the bodies before I head home for the evening. I'd need to put in serious overtime hours to finish *one* of them."

"I know," I said. "Just because I put in long hours doesn't mean I expect everyone else to make the same sacrifice."

Cairny peered at me with a narrowed eye and a raised brow. "That's a joke, right?"

"More of a white lie," I said. "I prefer to seed the work environment with rumors of my herculean efforts and productivity. Who knows? Maybe word of it will reach the Captain's ears and he'll buck the trend of handing me single digit salary increases at year's end. The point is, I don't expect you to stay here all night carving up bodies in the name of justice—although, let's be honest, you'd probably enjoy it. I just need a few hints. Some clues to help me piece this thing together.

You can do that right? Should be a breeze for someone as sophisticated and experienced as you."

Cairny raised her other eyebrow. "So, since lying didn't work, you're trying flattery?"

She'd picked up on it. Apparently, dating Quinto had improved her social skills. "Hey, whatever works, right?"

"What do you need, Daggers?" she asked.

"Alright. First. This guy. His name's Cornelius Vo." I pointed at him. "We think he was strangled. Can you confirm?"

Cairny pressed a hand to Vo's chin, tilting his head to the side so she could better gaze upon his neck. "I'd say choked, but yes. Whether or not it killed him is another matter."

"Choked?" I asked. "Is there a difference?"

"From a semantic perspective, no," said Cairny, still looking at the bruising. "But to me, strangulation implies the use of a cord or wire or other object, whereas choking is most often performed with the hands, as was clearly the case here."

"I suppose that makes sense," I said. "So what can you tell me about it?"

"Whoever strangled him had large, strong hands."

"Come on," I said. "Don't be snide."

"I'm not," said Cairny. "Daggers, you seem to think I'm a miracle worker, but that's not how I operate. Are you even familiar with the scientific method?"

Not wanting to be lectured, I ignored her and plowed forth. "Do you think you could pull prints off his neck?"

Cairny scrunched her lips. "Doubtful, but I can try. Body heat, moisture, and excreted oils all tend to dete-

riorate the quality of a fingerprint, making it exceptionally hard to pull one from skin. Your only saving grace
may be the age of the print. I'm guessing this man
didn't die more than, what...a couple hours ago?"

"Something like that," I said.

"Right. So with luck, I might get something." Cairny
cleared her throat. "Assuming, of course, that I get some
peace and quiet in which to work."

"Hey, I can take a hint," I said. "Just answer me one
quick question about Lanky before I go."

I moved over to the exam table on which the tall guy
lay and rummaged underneath it for the evidence bags
I'd seen the bluecoats deposit. I found the one I wanted
and slid the contents out on the table beside Lanky's
corpse.

"This is a letter opener we found at the scene," I
said. "It looks as if it was used to stab Lanky's corpse at
least two dozen times."

Cairny eyed it as she stepped to the side of the table.
"And?"

"Well, can you confirm the wounds were inflicted by
this letter opener? And that they're post mortem?" I
don't even know why I added that last part. I hadn't
peeked under Lanky clothes yesterday, but I think I
would've noticed the holes in his shirt.

Cairny took a glance under Lanky's vestments. "Yes.
Due to blood coagulation, the wounds are clearly post
mortem."

Cairny looked at me as if that answered everything—
which, to be fair, it did. At least what I'd specifically
asked.

I stared back. "So...why would anyone stab a corpse? Is there such a thing as necrosadism, where people get pleasure out of defacing the dead?"

Cairny tilted her head and stared at me. "Daggers, this is the part where I tell you to go do *your* job and leave me alone to do mine."

I snorted. "Fine. But no screwing around with Quinto tonight. I want full reports on these two by to-morrow morning, because if we don't solve this thing soon, I think we're all going to get a crash course in sa-dism thanks to the Captain."

Cairny didn't seem moved by my appeal, probably because she was the precinct's only coroner and the Captain never applied the coals to her feet. Nonetheless, I knew she'd have the reports for me on time, for in-scrutable reasons. Professional pride or some other nonsense, probably.

I made myself scarce and let her get to work.

36

As I reached the top of the stairwell, I spotted Shay back at her desk, sipping on a cup of tea. I headed in her direction, but a shadow flitted across my field of vision, followed closely by a snap like that of a snare drum. I turned my head toward the lounge room, where I caught the aftermath of Meriwether ricocheting off the glass. He seemed not to notice, as he kept buzzing around the room pell-mell in wide circles.

I kept my eyes on the pixie as I settled into my desk chair. "What in the world's gotten into him?"

Shay shrugged sheepishly. "He, uh...found the coffee."

"Don't tell me he's never had any before?" I said.

"Apparently, pixies brew it differently. Like, without the beans."

"I can see why."

I shifted my gaze to Shay as she took another sip of her leaf juice. The steam drifted lazily into the folds of her scarf, which she'd neglected to remove following her arrival at the precinct.

I let my eyes linger on her for a moment as I wondered what to do. We hadn't had a moment alone since the interrogation room incident, and I felt as if I should say something. Apologize, perhaps, but for what exactly? Or should I try to convince her of my worth, as a friend, as a partner, as something more? My stomach clenched, paralyzed by my indecision.

I took the easy route out and skirted the problem altogether. "So...did you get anything useful out of Meri before he whacked himself out on caffeine?"

"Surprisingly, yes." Shay spoke effortlessly, as if she had no inkling of my inner struggle. Then again, she probably didn't. Why would she? "Once I got past his perfunctory come-ons, I found him reasonably agreeable. And boy, does he like to talk. I get the feeling he was acting tough in front of you and Quinto, because after I got him alone, he really opened up about Vo. I think he's pretty bent out of shape about his death."

"Did you ask him about Vo?" I asked.

Shay smirked and lifted an eyebrow at me.

"Let me rephrase that," I said. "Surely you asked him about Vo. What did he have to say?"

"Well, he said he was very quiet. Very reserved. A kind person, and staunchly devout."

"And what does that entail in their religion?" I asked.

"We didn't go into too many details—thankfully," said Steele, "but I got the impression their theology centers mostly around reason, logic, and a sense of fatalism. The idea that life is final and solitary and whatever we do during our time on this earth is the grand sum of our accomplishments."

I snorted. "That doesn't sound like much of a religion. Rather, it sounds like the exact *opposite*. I think
most of us would call that life and death."

"Well, you can go talk to Meriwether if you want,"
said Shay, "but I gathered what distinguishes their religion from atheism is they feel there's a driving force
that acts to nullify existence, and it can't be avoided.
That's the Holy Oblivion."

"I'll pass on the one-on-one pixie time, thanks," I
said as I watched him continue to zip around the lounge
room ceiling. "What else did you get out of him,
though? Did he say if Vo had any odd habits, or if he
was up to his gills in misdeeds? Maybe he hung around
in bad circles?"

"Not really," said Shay. "According to Meriwether,
Vo didn't spend almost any time away from the church,
and was practically a recluse. At least, he was following
the passing of his wife."

"I could imagine that would be pretty rough for
someone who espouses fatalism as a religion," I said.
"When did she die?"

"About a year ago."

"And how long has Meri been living at the church
rent free?"

"I think about two years, give or take a few months,"
said Steele.

Another shadow crossed over me, but unless our
coffee-addled pixie friend had grown about six feet and
added three hundred pounds to his frame, it wasn't him.
I looked up to find Quinto standing nearby, a chair in
one hand and a couple folders in the other.

"Hey, bud," I said. "Did you have a fruitful trip?"

"You could say that." He parked his chair at the intersection of Shay's and my desks and sat. "I heard you mention Vo's wife. According to the documents I picked up at Public Records, her name was Tabitha Vo."

"Hold on," I said. "You already read through that stuff?"

"I took a rickshaw back here so that I could, yes," said Quinto.

"You're married to this job, you know that?" I said.

"Don't act like you're not curious about what's in here," he said. "And also...shut up. I have important information to share."

I ran my fingers across my lips and flicked the invisible key into the air.

"As I was trying to say, " said Quinto, "Vo's wife Tabitha, who he married roughly three years ago, did die recently. But not *about* a year ago. She died *exactly* one year ago. To the day."

"What?" I said. "Let me see that."

Quinto passed me her death certificate. I scanned my eyes to the appropriate box, which listed today's date one year prior. Then I found the cause of death.

My eyes widened. "Hold on. She committed *suicide?*"

"That's what it says," said Quinto.

"Hand that my way," said Steele, as if my and Quinto's two sets of eyes couldn't be trusted.

I obliged her as I turned back to Quinto. "What else did you uncover?"

"That's the only juicy bit," said the big guy. "Apparently, Vo lived at the church. Didn't pay taxes, but that's some sort of religious loophole, I think. Other than that,

nothing popped out at me. No mental illness or anything like that."

Shay put the death certificate down. "So, let me get
this straight. Someone kills Vo on the one year anniver-
sary of his wife's suicide? I find that one *hell* of a coinci-
dence."

"No kidding," I said. "And what a way to go, too.
Maybe the Holy Oblivion does exist, and it has its
sights set on its most fervent followers."

"Don't be silly," said Steele.

My old, grey-skinned detective friend sat there, tapping his enormous fingers against his chin.

"What's on your mind, Quinto?" I asked.

He flicked his hand. "I don't know. It's just that, ever
since I read through these files on the rickshaw ride
back here, I've had this nagging feeling. Like I've heard
that name before."

"Who?" I asked. "Tabitha Vo?"

"Yeah," he said.

I leaned back in my chair. Now that he mentioned it,
the name *did* sound a mite familiar. Where had I come
across it?

Shay eyed me curiously. "What...you, too?"

I nodded. "Yeah."

She smiled. "Maybe the two of you tried to pick her
up at a bar."

"A staunchly devout married woman?" I asked. "*Right*.
Because that's my type."

I closed my eyes and tried to focus. At first all I saw
was the back of my eyelids, but then my mind gave me
some line. I saw a flash—a fraction of a memory. Me,
standing in the halls of the precinct, with a cup of cof-

fee in my hands. I was talking to someone. Detective Elmswood.

My eyes snapped open. "Elmswood."

"What's that?" said Quinto.

"Elmswood, from upstairs," I said. "I remember him mentioning her in passing. I think he was investigating her death."

Shay tapped the certificate in front of her. "Are you saying perhaps her death *wasn't* a suicide?"

"Well, clearly he ruled it that way," I said. "But I'm thinking it's something we should ask him about."

37

We stampeded up the stairs to the second floor and descended upon Elmswood's desk, but as luck would have it, we found it empty. His partner Drake's desk was similarly unoccupied.

I spotted Boatreng shrugging into his coat and flagged him down. "Boatreng! Hey, hold on."

He sighed and dumped his satchel into his chair. "What now? You finally locate a witness to one of your murders? Give me an address. Hopefully it's on my way home."

I eyed the man's brown leather bag. *Of course* he wore a satchel. What else would an artist carry? "No, it's not that. Have you seen Elmswood?"

"I think he left about ten minutes ago," he said. "Why?"

I snapped my fingers. "Dang."

"Let's try the records room," said Quinto. "We can find his old case file there."

We bid speedy adieus to Boatreng and trampled our way back down the stairs, past the end of the pit, and into the station's bowels. After fighting our way through walls of cobwebs and skirting past the desiccated remains of long-forgotten interns, we arrived at a locked gate. To the side of it stood a narrow kiosk, and inside that sat an overweight old man with a drooping white moustache that gave him the appearance of a walrus.

I skidded to a halt in front of his stall. "Goodman. Boy am I glad you're still here."

In some ways, I envied him. His gout and subsequent weight gain had made it impossible for him to continue his service as a beat cop, but he'd served the department so well for twenty odd years that they'd stuck him down here guarding the records room, where he could read in peace to his heart's content, assuming the oil in his lantern didn't run dry. Like me, he enjoyed mystery novels, and thanks to the distinct freeness of the public library system, he churned through about one a day. If only my duties allowed me the same luxury...

Then again, he was a fat sixty-some-year-old man with no friends to speak of and a leg that was twice its normal size, so I didn't envy him *that* much.

He lifted his head from a book, one entitled *The Hurly Boys: Stuck on Witch's Hill.* I was surprised he could read in his lantern's flickering light. "*Still here?* Where else would I be? Dead?"

"I don't think that poorly of you, Goodman," I said. "I meant it's getting late. We thought you might've already headed home."

The fat old man glanced at his watch. "Come to think of it, it has been three thirty-five for some time now." He jiggled his wrist, sending the loose flesh on his underarm bouncing along for the ride. "Damn it. Must've forgotten to wind the thing."

Quinto snickered. "That *Hurly Boys* novel must be pretty engaging."

The series, which had about four hundred iterations, was aimed at teenagers, so it was mildly amusing to see someone of Goodman's caliber reading one.

"Can it, Gaptooth," said the guardsman. "For your information, I ran out of quality reading material ages ago, so I've been relegated to this fluff to keep my brain from melting. If only more mystery writers cranked books out on a more predictable schedule..."

"Amen to that," I said. "But on a more important note, we need to get into the vault."

"No problem." Goodman reached under the lip of his desk and produced a key. "I'm headed out, though, so you know the drill. Lock the key in the safe when you're done."

"You got it."

I took the key, slid it into the record vault gate's lock, and cranked on it. The metal contraption responded with a clunk, and I slid it to the side.

Shay stepped through the portal, took a deep breath, and exhaled. "So. This is the famed records vault. Smells...musty."

"Don't tell me you've never been here before," I said.

"Oh, I've come down," said Shay. "I had to introduce myself to Goodman—"

"Of course you did," I said.

"—but I've never been in the vault proper," continued Shay. "Never had a need to until now."

I shook my head. "See? This is how I know this place is going to pot. Back in my day, we didn't *have* interns whose jobs it was ferry files back and forth to the vault. We did it ourselves. In the snow. Uphill. Both ways."

"Daggers, you still work here," said Steele. "And I don't even know how to respond to the rest of that."

"Are you two coming or not?" Quinto's voice echoed off the makeshift walls of cardboard boxes and steel shelving that filled the vault. A flickering light created a halo around his massive frame as he descended into the depths, and I felt a twinge of sympathy for Goodman. Hopefully the old guy would be able to limp his way out without his trusty lantern.

I rushed after Quinto, past stacks and stacks of dull brown file boxes, each marked with a department and a range of dates. By the time I made it to the homicide files, Quinto had already pulled out the box with the date range encompassing Tabitha's investigation. He'd set it on the floor, and he thumbed through the contents with his sausage-like fingers.

"Here it is." He yanked a manila folder from its entourage, one with 'T. Vo' and the date on the tab. He flipped it open and held its contents up to the flickering lantern light.

Because of the big guy's positioning, I couldn't see what the file contained. "So? What does it say?"

"Give me a sec," said Quinto. "I'm not a speed reader. Ok, let's see... Elmswood did, in fact, rule Tabitha's death a suicide."

"And how'd she die?" I asked.

Quinto flipped a page. "Well, uh..." He grimaced. "*Ooh.* She jumped out a window. At the Church of the

Holy Oblivion. And unless I'm mistaken, she jumped out *the* window in Cornelius Vo's office. The same one we saw today that had been busted up."

"Was Vo a suspect in her death?" asked Shay.

Quinto's eyes scanned across the page. "Yes. But...Elmswood couldn't place him at the scene."

"And no one suspected any foul play?" I asked.

"Well, I wouldn't say *that*," said Quinto. "But from what's recorded here, it does seem likely she killed herself. Elmswood and company did some thorough digging into her past. Interviewed Vo as well as a number of her friends and acquaintances. They all said pretty much the same thing—that she'd been extremely depressed and distant leading up to her death. 'Conflicted' is a word that pops up multiple times in the report. Apparently, Elmswood thought her conversion to the Church of the Holy Oblivion was the nail in her coffin, so to speak. Given how few cheery, upbeat individuals convert to the religion, that action helped prop up the story of her depression."

"Really?" I asked. "There wasn't any evidence indicating this wasn't a suicide? No stray prints, or anomalous injuries, or suspicious depositions?"

Quinto flipped a few more pages. "Doesn't look like it."

"Were there any other suspects in her death?" asked Shay.

Quinto flipped back to the second page. "One. Her ex-husband, another minister by the name of Julian Bellamy."

Shay and I nearly bowled each other over with the strength of our exclamations.

"What?"

"You're kidding!"

"Quinto," I said. "Why didn't you mention that sooner?"

The big guy stared at me blankly, and I realized he'd never tagged along on our trips to the temple of the leafy green trees.

"We need to get to the Church of the Divine Rebirth," I said.

"Hold on," said Quinto. "I'm not entirely sure what I've missed here, but according to this report, Julian Bellamy couldn't have killed Tabitha Vo. He had a rock solid alibi. Apparently he was delivering a sermon to twenty or so people at the time of her death."

Quinto pressed a needle against the bubble of ideas in my mind, and I thought it might pop, but at the moment of critical pressure, I recalled a seemingly flippant statement Cairny had made in the morgue. Something about Deacon Vo's killer.

"Bellamy," I said. "Was he alone? During the sermon?"

"Huh?" Quinto glanced at the case file. "I don't know. It doesn't say. Why?"

I smiled. "Because I know who killed Cornelius Vo. And Tabitha Vo, for that matter. Now come on. We need to get back to the Church of the Divine Rebirth right away."

38

Quinto, Shay, and I pushed open the doors at the front of the Church of the Divine Rebirth and stepped into the darkened interior. The last vestiges of day had long since bid their farewells, and upon the sun's departure, the creeping fog had pounced on its opportunity. Outside, the mist swirled, ominous and thick, but inside the church, it dripped from the sagging boughs of the trees like dew-soaked spider webs and wrapped itself around their trunks in chill, heartless embraces. A half-dozen lanterns set at the structure's sides cast a hazy glow, not so much illuminating the interior as providing glimpses into its gloomy depths.

Quinto cast his gaze into the darkness. "Names be damned—this church is far more terrifying than that Holy Oblivion place."

"It's much less so in the day," I said. "Now, come on. We have warm bodies to find. And keep your ears peeled, Steele. I don't want anyone creeping up on us in this fog."

I led the way, meandering through the church interior more than I wanted to thanks to the fog. After I'd convinced myself no one hid among the place's numerous recessed stone pits or between the wooden benches at the far end, I ventured into the living quarters beyond. I stepped through the dimly lit corridor in back slowly, intending to check off each room one by one, when Shay stopped me with a hand to my shoulder.

"I heard a creak. That-a-way." She gestured up, in the direction of Bellamy's office.

I mounted the stairs, liberating Daisy from the interior of my jacket as I did so. As we reached the door to Bellamy's office, I stretched my ears, but I couldn't detect anything other than my own breathing. Nonetheless, I gave Quinto a nod. He nodded back. I pressed my hand to the door knob and turned.

A heavy hint of the day's incense lingered in the room, tickling my nose but thankfully without the same gag-inducing force as before. A lantern burned bright against the far wall, shining light onto the colorful piles of pillows and the into the houseplants' dense underbrush.

In the middle of the pillows knelt Chester, clad in the same ankle-length grey robe I assumed was his only choice of attire. One of the thuribles—empty, based off the lack of smoke trailing from the openings in the metalwork—lay on the ground near his knees, but in his huge hands, he held something tangentially related.

A long piece of metal—steel, if I wasn't mistaken—perhaps three quarters of an inch across, with a hook at the end. The thurible stand.

"Drop it, Slim," I said as I walked into the room, "and put your hands behind your head."

The gangly youth did partly as I asked, dropping the thurible stand to the ground where it bounced harmlessly off the cushions, but he leapt to his feet and stared at us with frightened eyes. He glanced at me and then Quinto, who hunched over, coiled and ready to pounce, before moving his eyes to the window, which stood open by the barest of cracks.

"Don't even think about it, Chester," I said as I held Daisy out in a threatening manner. "We're faster than we look, I promise you. And don't think you can talk your way out of this." The irony of the statement hit me as soon as I'd said it. "We know everything. We found Vo's body at the Church of the Holy Oblivion. I don't know if our coroner will be able to pull your prints off his neck, but I'm certain once we take a closer look at those massive hands of yours, we'll find your prints *somewhere* in his office."

Chester's brow furrowed as his eyes darted back and forth. He worked his mouth, but no sound came out.

"Curious how we knew it was you, are you?" I asked. "Come on, young man. Did you think we wouldn't make the connection between Vo's late wife and Pastor Bellamy? He had an alibi—a concrete one, I might add—but you? Where were you that day, one year ago tonight?"

As expected, Chester didn't respond, but he wet his lips and rubbed them together.

"Cat got your tongue?" I asked. "Figures. So, tell me. Why did you do it? Did Bellamy order you to? Or did you do it on your own? Was Bellamy still in love with his former wife? Did it irk you that he cared more about her than you, his faithful apprentice? Or was this a murder of religious zeal? Perhaps Tabitha was unfaithful to your beloved Bellamy, and so you thought her soul would be better put to use somewhere else, birthed anew as a caterpillar or a pine tree."

Chester's mouth opened, and he croaked out a response in a stereotypically squeaky teenager voice, though one several octaves lower than the norm thanks to the size of his larynx. "I... I..."

"Oh, you're talking now?" I said. "Good. Because I'd like for you to explain the murders of the two homeless men. Why did you kill them? And why bother smothering one of them with one of the countless pillows at your feet when you clearly get a kick out of strangling people with your bare hands?"

"I...I didn't kill anyone," squawked Chester, his voice sounding like the illegitimate child of a bass drum and a piece of rusty farm equipment. "You've...made a mistake. This isn't what it looks like."

"Really?" I said. "Because it looks like you delicately caressing the various household implements you've used to murder people."

Chester pressed his elephantine hands against his temples and shook his head. "No. No. I just started to piece it all together myself. The missing transients. The events of yesterday morning. My master's response upon seeing that token from the Church of the Holy Oblivion."

"Aha," I said. "So you lied. You *did* know what it was."

"Well, yes," said Chester. "But only because Master Bellamy claimed not to. I knew he was familiar with that church, because of his ex-wife's conversion. I couldn't figure out why he'd lie about that."

I recalled Chester's reaction to the sight of the token, the way he'd glanced from me to the token to Bellamy and back to me and the way his mouth had twitched. I *hadn't* imagined it. His indecision as to whether or not to contradict his master could've explained his actions, which meant he *might* be telling the truth—or at least part of it.

"Keep talking," I said.

"I first noticed it yesterday morning," said Chester as he wrung his hands together. "It was after you came and asked Master Bellamy about the disturbance outside. Master Bellamy said he heard a man and a woman shouting at each other, followed by fighting, and that's all true. I heard it as well. But I thought it started before that. I awoke to a scream, perhaps two or three minutes before I noticed the shouting outside, and I could've sworn it came from *inside* the church. My thoughts were for Master Bellamy's safety, so I hurried first to his office and then to his quarters to see if he was ok, but I couldn't find him. It was only later, after the shouting began, that I found him back here."

"Why didn't you mention this before?" asked Shay.

I jumped at the sound of her voice. In my hawklike focus on Chester Skillethands, I'd almost forgotten about her and Quinto.

"I thought perhaps I'd imagined it," said Chester. "Master Bellamy was unharmed, and no one other than the two of us lives at the church. No one would've been here at such an early hour."

"Where's Bellamy now?" I asked.

"I don't know," said Chester. "He left around night-fall, or at least that's when I noticed him gone. He's been doing that for a couple weeks now—leaving unannounced I mean. Always at night. I think he didn't know I'd noticed, but I wake easily."

I glanced at Steele. "What do you think?"

She seemed to catch my drift. "He could be telling the truth. If Bellamy somehow cut out a bit earlier than Chester thinks, he might've been able to make it to the Church of the Holy Oblivion within our murder window."

Quinto grunted. "Let me remind you that, according to the eye witness accounts in Elmswood's file, Bellamy couldn't have killed Tabitha Vo."

"No," I said. "But that doesn't mean he didn't blame Cornelius Vo for her death, whether justly or not."

I glanced at the seven foot tall youth again. "Chester, if you think you're going to have any chance of convincing us of your lack of involvement in this, you'll to need to help us locate Bellamy. So I'll ask again. Where is he?"

"I'm telling you, I don't know," he said. "And I swear I had nothing to do with his wife's death. Honest to the souls of rebirth, I thought she committed suicide. But..."

"But what?" asked Steele.

"Well, if Master Bellamy *is* indeed involved in something heinous," said Chester. "If he *did* have clandestine affairs with those homeless men, or if he attacked them, he must've done it somewhere nearby. Somewhere in this church, if I'm not imagining the scream I heard."

"And you think you know where?" I asked.

Chester gave me a small nod. "Follow me."

39

Quinto followed Chester closely—*very* closely, practically breathing on his neck—as he led us down two flights of stairs to the church's basement. We snaked along a narrow passageway, past a cold pantry and a couple of densely-packed storage rooms, before eventually stopping at a door at the far end of the corridor.

A chill radiated off the basement's stone walls. I shivered as I nodded toward the door. "Well?"

Chester knocked, then when no one answered, he tried the doorknob. He turned and shrugged. "It's locked."

"Well, Captain Obvious," I said. "Do you have a *key?*"

Chester shook his head. "Only Master Bellamy does. These are his private chambers. I've never been down here myself. In fact, it's the only place in the church I haven't been, which is why I brought you here."

I still clutched Daisy in my right hand, so it was a hand and a fist that I rubbed together in glee. "Alright, then. Step back everyone, and let me do what I do best."

Quinto frowned and grunted. "Why is it every time an application of force is required, you make me do it—except on the rare occasions a door needs to be kicked in?"

"The perks of seniority, my friend," I said. "Now stand back."

I slammed Daisy's tip against the face of the door three times. "Police! Open up!"

I didn't actually think there'd be anyone inside, but yelling before I sprang into action gave me a heady thrill, and it protected me in case of liability should someone be standing on the other side, looking through a peephole. I sent the heel of my boot crashing into the door above the lock. Wood splintered, cracked, and gave way, and I surged into the great unknown beyond.

I blinked, expecting a yawning void of darkness or perhaps a janitorial closet, but I found neither. Instead, three or four dozen votive candles spread their light throughout a wide room, from nightstands and wall sconces and even from the floor. All of them flickered, their wicks lit, indicating someone—most likely Pastor Bellamy—had recently left. Much like Bellamy's upstairs quarters, pillows of varying shapes, colors, and sizes littered the floor, and a metallic gleam from the far side of the room caught my eye. Another thurible stand, with the thurible itself on the ground at its feet.

Despite the lack of smoke coming from the metal censer, the room smelled of incense almost as strongly as Bellamy's quarters had earlier today—perhaps due to the collective output of the candles—but lying underneath the aromatic oils and whiffs of potpourri was something altogether different. A putrid collection of scents. Blood. Rot. Decay. I couldn't put my finger on what, but I suspected if I could, I'd want to wash my finger thoroughly afterwards.

I entered the room, dodging pillows as I walked. Shay skirted around me, headed in the direction of the thurible stand, while Quinto escorted Chester in. In the center of the floor, in a space clear of cushions and clutter and haphazardly ringed by candles, a collection of branches and sticks and bleached wood mingled with grayish-white beams—bones?—to form an oval with a perimeter roughly large enough to contain a man. A dark stain marred the oval's center. Blood, I assumed.

"What in the world is this?" I said.

I hadn't expected an answer, but Chester gave me one regardless. "A psychitaph."

"Psychopath?" I asked.

"Psychitaph," repeated Chester. "I've never seen one myself, but I've read of them in some of the ancient texts on our religion. According to lore, they were crafted by those in sects with proximity to the sea and fashioned out of driftwood and whale bone."

I knelt at the side of the conglomeration, eyeing the non-plant based parts. While I wasn't particularly well-versed in marine biology, I was pretty sure those *weren't* whale bones. They looked far too small and femur-y for that.

"And what is it, exactly?" I asked.

"Again, I can only relate what I've read," said Chester. "But the lore says they're ceremonial sites. People built them to celebrate the passing of a soul and its inevitable rebirth as a new being. Hence their construction from bones and wood—reminders, plant and animal, of life's erections."

I thought of a joke, but it wasn't the time for it. "This doesn't creep you out at all? I'm pretty sure these remains are human."

"That...*is* a little disturbing," said Chester. "But not so much to me as it is to you, I imagine. You must understand, to me, a person is defined by the soul that inhabits it. Once gone, that soul is reincarnated as a different being. A person's remains are something neither to be feared nor celebrated. They're merely the remnants of a soul's current incarnation."

"You might want to rethink your legal strategy," said Quinto. "Normally, claiming to be unfazed by ritualistic bone altars doesn't bode well for defendants."

Chester opened his mouth to argue, but Steele hopped in before he had a chance. "Daggers. Quinto. Look at this."

She approached, holding the thurible stand with a handkerchief. She tilted the steel pole, letting the candlelight play over it, and I noticed a spot near the tip that didn't reflect light well.

"Is that blood?" I asked.

Steele nodded. "And the pole is dented. This has to be the murder weapon."

"Ok," I said as I passed a hand through my hair. "Let's try to figure this out. Bellamy lures people here, transients who've visited the church in search of food or shelter, then conks them on the head with that metal stand. He did it to Burly and smothered him with one of the pillows. He tried to do it with Lanky, but maybe he hit him with a glancing blow and couldn't finish the job. Lanky escapes and crashes the party between Tim, Kelly, and Drake—which fleshes out the story of *what* happened but doesn't even come close to shedding any light on the why."

"But that only gets us through yesterday morning," said Shay. "Who stole Lanky's body? Was it Vo? If so, why? And who dumped Burly in the alley? Did Bellamy murder Cornelius Vo?"

"And," added Quinto, "who, if anyone, murdered Tabitha Vo?"

"Exactly," said Steele. "And *what in the world* ties all this stuff together?"

I turned to Chester with a questioning look in my eye. I hated relying on a suspect for critical information, especially a suspect who might be lying to me through his teeth and waiting for an opportune moment to envelop my neck in the tender embrace of his paddle hands, but he was the only one who might have some idea of what any of this meant.

"Come on, Chester," I said. "Surely Bellamy mentioned something about what he was up to. Or let it slip accidentally. With your self-imposed mutism, I'll bet he didn't worry about you giving his plans away."

Chester shook his head. "No. He was eminently pious. Spoke and cared only about the Divine Rebirth."

"So you have no idea where he could be?" I asked.

"No."

"Then what about this thing?" I indicated the jumbled mass of sticks and bones. "And don't tell me it's a ceremonial altar. No way was sweet, innocent Pastor Bellamy just helping hobos speed along their path to the spirit realm for no other reason than to restock the well of souls, or whatever similar crackpot idea you all believe in. So what is it?"

"I...I don't know," stammered Chester. "I've told you what I know."

"Damnit, man!" I slammed Daisy into a nightstand, sending splinters flying and knocking candles to the ground. I wanted nothing so much as to trample the pile of bones and bleached wood into dust under my boots, but I thought the CSU teams might have some choice words for me if I did that.

Chester sank to his bottom and pressed his hands to his face. I heard sobs as he shook his head. "I...I don't...I'm sorry, I just don't..."

"Now look what you've done," said Steele.

I held up a hand for silence. I knew very well what she'd say. That he was only a teenager, and that I didn't need to lose control of my emotions like that. But I'd met boys younger than him who'd committed murder, and he could still be involved. And besides, if now wasn't the time to get frustrated and emotional about the state of the case, then when was it? We'd finally managed to inject some facts into the investigation only to have our prime suspect disappear into the vast unknown, and unless an angel lounging on the surface of the sun decided to cast a few rays of brilliance our way, we'd be stuck with our thumbs up our butts as we tried to explain to the DA what Bellamy's murder of the hobos had to do with Vo's death.

It had to come back to Tabitha. It had to. She was the only link between Bellamy and Cornelius Vo, and her murder/death/suicide/whatever had to somehow explain the rest of the pastor's actions. But how? I could understand Bellamy's desire to kill Deacon Vo and extract some measure of vengeance in the process, but how did Lanky and Burly fit in? And what was Vo's interest in the two vagrants? Why did Vo steal Lanky's body?

I stared at Chester, sobbing into his gigantic hands, and I couldn't help but think about Vo, how he'd died, and Cairny's analysis.

I rubbed my chin. Then I rubbed it some more. Then I squinted and chewed on my lip.

Shay noticed my routine. "Are you doing ok, Daggers?"

"Do you remember our talk earlier about crazy theories?" I asked.

"You're working on one?" asked Quinto.

"Yeah," I said. "One that's crazy and creepy and disturbing—and did I mention crazy? But it makes some sense."

"And let me guess," said Steele. "You're about to dazzle us with its brilliance."

I shook my head. "Not yet. This particular idea is too crazy to share, the type of idea that might get me sent home by the Captain for a much needed rest. But I'll share it soon, if the evidence supports it. In the meantime, Chester?"

The traumatized youth looked at me.

"I need to know something," I said. "Where is Julian's ex-wife buried?"

40

I stood in front of the entrance to Lowgate Cemetery, the worn stone and crumbling mortar of its pillars contrasting starkly against the finely wrought iron of the gate. A wall, five feet high and covered in leafy creeper vines, stretched out to the sides, disappearing into fog that had thickened since our departure from the Church of the Divine Rebirth. Heavy trees stretched their boughs over the edges of the wall, shadowing us with their gangly limbs—or they would've if there'd been even a scrap of moonlight to speak of. Enveloped as we were by the heavy mist, our sole source of light was a flickering lantern liberated from the halls of the church. It hung from one of Chester's hands, the fire within thrashing desperately as it fought a losing battle against the encroaching gloom.

"This is it," said Chester. "Master Bellamy's ex-wife's grave is inside, down the path, to the left of the pond, and up the hillock."

"We're following you," I said.

The youth reached out with his free hand and pushed against the wrought iron gate. It screeched in protest as it gave way, emitting a rusted metallic wail piercing enough to wake the souls of the damned.

I followed Chester along the dirt path, bringing Shay with me as Quinto brought up the rear. Dry leaves crunched underfoot as I walked, and somewhere in the distance, a bird called out with a warbling, undulating cry. Barren branches formed an arch overhead, their leafless tendrils looking like hands of bone. At my sides, gravestones peeked through the gloom, their faces covered with dark green moss and pale lichens and smooth, ropy protrusions that I couldn't identify as either vines or roots. Monoliths, obelisks, and mausoleums peppered the more traditional gravestones, each of them similarly attired as the smaller arched slabs of limestone and granite.

Goose bumps crept up my arm, and for once I didn't think it was the chill.

I tried to tear my mind from its thoughts of all the horrible things that go bump in the night by engaging my companions in conversation. "I've got to admit, Chester, this seems like the perfect place to bury one of your own."

"Yes," said Steele. "The dichotomy of death and nature is very *unique*. It might be nice to wander around this place, just for the experience. You know...in the daylight."

"You could bring Cairny," said Quinto. "I bet she'd love it. On second thought, though, she might never come back to work."

"Please," I said. "You can take the morgue out of the girl, but you can't take the girl out of the morgue."

Quinto shot me a quizzical look. "I don't think that's how the saying goes. It's not even in the right order."

Chester ignored our banter, seemingly focused only on my initial statement. "You must remember, Detective, Master Bellamy's wife was not one of our own. She converted. To my knowledge, however, she did list in her will the desire to be buried here. Perhaps, in her heart, she didn't fully abandon the teachings of the Divine Rebirth."

"Or, she never bothered updating her will," I said.

Shay stepped on an acorn, cracking it with a pop, as we rounded the edge of the pond Chester had mentioned. "So, Daggers. When do you plan on filling Quinto and me in on our reasons for being here?"

"I told you," I said. "I want to see if I'm right first. No point setting you atwitter with my theories if they're unfounded." Although I didn't think that would be the response I'd generate. Incredulity and horror were much more plausible.

"We've talked about your irrational fear of criticism and ridicule before," said Steele, "but this isn't about that. This is about the rest of us walking into a situation blind, without any idea of what to expect. If you have a credible theory for who and what we'll find when we reach Tabitha Vo's grave then tell us. And trust us to act appropriately with the information you provide."

Her words sunk in slowly, especially that last part. Trust her. I *did* trust her, just as I also cared for her, although...perhaps I didn't show it often enough. Was that why she'd gotten so frustrated with me earlier? I always thought she'd enjoyed my witty banter and gruff charm, and while those things undoubtedly brought a smile to her lips, apparently those weren't the qualities of mine she found most attractive. Maybe she wanted to see more of what I harbored on the inside—the icky, complicated stuff under my layers of skin and muscle and bone. But why would she have any interest in that? Most of the things I nurtured there were dark and lonely and broken. Then again, sometimes the most tender shoots sprouted from the bleakest places. The graveyard was a testament to that.

I stored that bit of cud to chew on later. In the meantime, Shay's first talking point had been the most pertinent. If I was right in my suspicions, things could get hairy, and she and Quinto had a right to know.

"Fair enough," I said. "Back in Bellamy's private basement, I got to thinking. Through what we found at his church, Bellamy is implicated in, if not outright responsible for, Lanky's and Burly's murders. Burly is connected to Vo via the token we found in his coat pocket, as is Lanky by the fact that we found his body at the scene of Vo's death. So there's an indirect connection between those two. But Tabitha is the key. She's the only direct connection between Bellamy and Vo. She's Bellamy's motivation. The rest is noise."

"I'm not sure where you're going with this," said Steele. "Are you saying you think Tabitha introduced Bellamy to Vo, and they were working together in some capacity? And that Bellamy betrayed Vo, and now he's come to confess his actions to Tabitha's grave?"

I felt the ground at my feet slope up. "No, no. That's not what I'm getting at."

"So what *are* you getting at?" asked Steele with a raise of her eyebrow.

"How do I say this without sounding completely insane?" I sighed and passed a hand through my hair. "Ok, ignore Tabitha for a moment. Let's consider Lanky and Burly. I know you cut out from work early yesterday for, well...reasons. But while we were separated, I spent the majority of my time interviewing everyone I could over Lanky's disappearance. He's a big guy. To move his body would've taken at least two people. Two outsiders carrying a stiff would be a sight hard to miss, and yet nobody—Cairny, Phillips, the beat cops outside, even the station's janitor—saw a thing. How is that possible? Unless it wasn't two people. Unless the only person who snuck in and out was the kind of person who's used to being ignored and shoed away.

"And then there's Burly. How did he get outside that embroidery shop? What possible reason could someone have for depositing his corpse there, of all places? And remember Gary's testimony, about Burly's grunt? Yes, I know Norma contradicted him, and I recall Cairny's theory, but still."

Shay narrowed her eyes. "Again I'll ask...*what are you getting at?*"

"What if nobody moved either of their bodies?" I said.

"Wait...*what?*" said Quinto.

"Think about it," I said. "Julian Bellamy is the head pastor at the Church of the *Divine Rebirth.*"

Shay's mouth opened and closed a couple times before any sound came out. "You're not suggesting—"

"Yes," I said, catching the look in her eyes. "What if Lanky and Burly moved *themselves?*"

41

Steele hadn't yet formulated her response as we crested the hillock, and because I'd kept my eyes trained on her to see how she'd react to my theory, I ran straight into Chester's back.

I grunted as the tall youth stumbled forward. "Chester, what are you—"

I stopped in mid sentence as I lay eyes on what had frozen Chester's feet. Off to the left of the path, a soft, orange glow radiated from within the fog, reminiscent of the light emitted from between a jack-o-lantern's teeth.

Chester recovered himself—at least physically—as he pointed toward the glow. "That's where the grave... Master Bellamy's ex-wife..."

I pieced together the rest as I retrieved Daisy from my coat interior. Though she'd felt the fresh, late autumn air on her face more than once today, she hadn't seen much action, and for once, I hoped it stayed that way.

"Come on," I said in a hushed voice to Steele and Quinto. "Stay close. You too, Chester. Don't get any ideas."

The fog at my feet thinned as I approached the glow, and after a few more steps around wayward graves and over thick patches of underbrush, the mist fully lifted to reveal the scene underneath.

Julian Bellamy stood at the side of a gravestone that rose to his hip, one free of vines and moss and with a certain roughness to it that spoke of its recent construction. He held his hands in the air, his eyes shut tight as he chanted in a low voice. I couldn't tell if he spoke in a different language or merely without the intent to be heard. At his feet, a hole six or seven feet long plunged into the earth, and next to it, a trio of shovels stuck out from a pile of fresh soil teetering dangerously at the excavation's edge.

The orange glow radiated out of the newly opened grave. The color fluctuated between a pale red and a bold yellow, but unlike the lashing tongue of a flame, the glow produced no traces of smoke. I did, however, smell something of an earthy, sulfurous quality—a cross between bad eggs and a wet dog's coat—and underneath that, a familiar scent of rot and decay.

Around the grave, Bellamy had erected a perimeter of scrap wood and bones, as he had in the basement of his church. The eerie light played off the remains of the living, giving them a horrifying, bloodied appearance, and while the construction appeared rushed and in-complete—especially the portions planted into the loose pile of earth at the grave's side—it appeared to be serv-ing its purpose...whatever that might be.

A snap of a branch, probably from Quinto's heavy foot, jolted me to alertness. I took a measured step toward Bellamy and called out to him. "Step away from the grave, Bellamy. It's over."

The salt-and-pepper haired pastor ignored me, continuing his barely audible chant that he paired with a delicate dance of his hands.

I thought perhaps the man hadn't heard me, so I reasserted myself, louder this time. "Bellamy! Step away from the grave!"

Bellamy's eyelids cracked, though he didn't bother to look at me. When he spoke, his voice lacked any of the warmth and congeniality I remembered. "Leave, Detective."

"What?" I said. I wasn't accustomed to murder suspects speaking to me in such a brazen manner.

"I said *leave*," repeated Bellamy. "You might think you know what's going on here, but trust me you don't. You don't have even the slightest inkling of what you've stepped into. There are powers at work here beyond your comprehension, beyond even your desire to comprehend. Now leave, and let the will of the Divine Rebirth settle a debate whose resolution is long overdue."

I wasn't entirely sure what the pastor was talking about, but the distraction I'd caused by my presence seemed to have affected his ritual. A cold tendril of mist draped across my neck, and the grave's variegated glow dimmed as he spoke.

I took another step forward. "I'm not going to warn you again, Bellamy. Put your hands down and step away from the grave."

Bellamy's eyes snapped to me, and the earth groaned under my feet. "*You're* not going to warn *me?* Detective, it is I whose patience is reaching its end."

The groan I heard could've emanated from Quinto's lips—he was notoriously ornery as it approached his bedtime—and the shifting I'd felt under my feet could've been the hill's reaction to having Tabitha's grave dug up. Miners had found themselves trapped under mountains of fallen rock for less egregious excavations. I kept telling myself these things as the mist at the edge of my vision began to swirl, churn, and roil, and as an increasing chorus of moans and groans sounded not from behind me in Quinto's recognizable bass but from all around.

I swallowed back a lump in my throat and spoke with far more confidence than I felt. "In case you haven't noticed, Bellamy, there are four of us and only one of you, and no amount of freaky resurrection magic will change that."

Bellamy laughed a grim laugh, and I realized how stupid that last statement sounded. But despite whatever power Bellamy might possess, I didn't think he could raise an army of the dead before I introduced Daisy to his skull.

I took two quick steps in his direction. Bellamy skirted to the grave's side, over near the shovels, but thanks to his limp, he didn't move quickly. I smiled. Ending this would be easier than I'd thought.

"Ah, but Detective," said Bellamy as he inched toward the mist. "You didn't think I dug this hole myself, did you?"

Three shovels. One middle-aged man with a limp. I'd curse myself for missing that later, at a more pleasant time when there wasn't a snarling zombie lunging at me from out of the mist.

42

A big guy, shabbily dressed and cut from the same cloth as Lanky and Burly, hit me square in the chest with the force of a donkey's kick, knocking me into a thorny bush that tore at my coat as I fell. I grunted as my back hit the earth, and again as the man landed on top of me. His long matted hair fell in my face, bringing with it a strong unwashed odor and the same scents of decay I'd smelled on Burly's corpse and underneath the residual incense in Bellamy's basement quarters.

I heard Shay scream and Quinto roar, but all I could see from the confines of my bush was a collection of tiny thorns and the bearded face of my homeless attacker, staring at me with cold, dead, unmoving eyes.

Thanks to my occasional dabbling in classic horror fiction, I knew what to expect from the soulless husk. He'd moan and drool all over me, bellyache about his insatiable hunger for brains, and try to bite me in the neck. Fortunately, I'd be able to outwit him and avoid his chompers and molasses-slow blows through my superior intellect and speed.

Unfortunately for me, everything I'd ever read about zombies had been written by ignorant hacks. I cocked a shot at his face with Daisy, but he avoided it with alarming speed—the same speed as a living man's. Then instead of biting me, his hands shot to my neck, and he pressed his fingers into the soft flesh around my windpipe.

I clawed at his mitts with my free hand and whacked him in the back with my truncheon with the other, which produced not so much as a grunt. I tried again, harder this time, with the same result.

The pressure around my neck increased, so I focused my labors to dislodge the man's fingers, and I found some success. I pried a few of them off me for a split second—long enough for me to take a ragged gasp—before he slapped my hand away and redoubled his efforts. I kneed him in the groin, hoping that might have some effect where the blow to his ribs hadn't, but he didn't even flinch.

Gods, the guy was strong! Blood pounded in my temples as spots danced in front of my eyes, and I couldn't help but think of Vo. He must've lain there, thrashing as blackness enveloped him, stabbing Lanky over and over with the letter opener, hoping each subsequent puncture would break off his attack in a way the previous dozen hadn't.

I couldn't make the same mistake Vo did. My attacker wouldn't feel pain, wouldn't care if I broke his ribs and flattened his testicles into pancakes. Only the fundamentals of anatomy and physiology could save me.

With my vision blurring and my lungs burning, I reached up and hooked my elbow over my attacker's shoulder. Either because of hubris or a lack of functioning brain cells—perhaps the horror writers had been right about that part—the zombie didn't move to stop me, focused as he was on my suffocation.

I gripped my wrist with my free hand and yanked with all the might I had left. A reassuring pop greeted my ears, and the pressure from one side of the zombie's grip disappeared.

With one arm dislocated, Rotface became a more manageable assailant. I rolled, tore my neck out of his remaining grip, and shot to my feet. Blood rushed to my head and I staggered, but thankfully the zombie hadn't discovered the extent of the damage to his arm. As he tried to leverage himself up with an arm that wouldn't hold weight, I slammed Daisy into his kneecap and followed that with a hefty stomp. His leg crunched and popped in sickening fashion, but I figured he'd have a hard time following me without functioning knee ligaments.

I tried to orient myself as I turned back toward the grave, which glowed with a renewed fury. Before me, Quinto roared and bucked like a bronco as three undead vagrants of varying size clung to his arms and back and tried to choke him into submission. His bellows echoed off the trees, but they couldn't quite drown out a low-pitched sobbing off to my side—Chester, who'd curled into a ball and tucked himself between a pair of tombstones to avoid the melee. Apparently, the undead didn't view him as a threat. That, or Bellamy had or-

dered them not to attack him unless absolutely necessary.

I swung my eyes desperately around the scene.
Someone was missing.

"Shay!" I called. "SHAY!"

"Over here!" she called, followed by a shriek.

I turned toward the sound, only to be staggered by
the force of a body slamming into me from behind. An
arm wrapped itself around my neck—that of another
homeless zombie, based on the accompanying smell—
and squeezed.

I muttered "Not again," except thanks to the pressure
of the rotting flesh around my neck, it came out more
as, "Nurgurgh agah!"

My new assailant's point of attack put me in a com-
promising position, one without ready access to his
joints and sockets, so I called upon my nonexistent mar-
tial arts training to save me. I reached up, grabbed the
guy's coat collar, and pitched forward as I bent at the
waist. The zombie sailed over me, wrenching on my
neck with so much force I thought he might break it,
but at the three quarters mark of his arc I slipped free
and he collided with the ground, bouncing off it with a
thump.

"Daggers!" Shay's voice reached me through the carnage, but I couldn't tell from where. "Are you ok?"

If she was asking me, I assumed she was, too. Perhaps, as with Chester, the zombies were largely ignoring her, seeing Quinto and me as the bigger threats—
which, literally, we were. I aimed a kick at the undead
dude at the ground and opened my mouth to answer
yes when another unwashed body slammed into me.

"Do something, Steele!" I yelled as I grappled with the new interloper.

"Do what?" she said.

I tried to locate her voice. Where was she? "I don't know. You may not be psychic, but you know more about magic than any of the rest of us. Think of something!"

Something grabbed my ankle and yanked, and I fell onto my posterior with a bone-shaking thud. The newest zombie rolled on top of me as the one I'd deposited onto the ground crawled toward me. Quinto stumbled through my line of sight, bellowing and spinning as he tried to dislodge a pair of drifters clinging to his back.

I heard a swish, as if from a sword whistling through the air, and a voice I'd forgotten about. Bellamy's. "Come out, come out wherever you are you, sneaky little half-breed."

Another swish. Steele's frightened cry. I had to help her.

I slapped a zombie hand away from my throat and kicked out, trying to dislodge the guy on me, but the second of the walking—or in this case crawling—undead brought his weight down on my arm, giving the first guy a new opening. Strong hands clamped back on my throat.

Still another swish through the air. Bellamy's voice again. "Come here, you little *bitch*."

The pressure on my throat intensified. Where was Quinto? Why wasn't Chester doing anything? I tried to reach for the zombie's shoulder, but his pal lay on my arm. I could barely move.

I heard a meaty *whump,* followed by a pained "Urnghh..." Then Steele's angry voice. "Who's the bitch now, Bellamy?"

The fingers around my neck loosened. Whatever Shay had done had worked. I tried to call out for her to continue, but I still had a thumb jammed into my windpipe, so it came out as another choked warble.

Steele figured out what to do without my advice. A ringing, metallic twang filled the air, and both of my undead attackers went limp—which of course meant the one on top of me tried to smother me with his weight.

I groaned and pushed the rotting corpse off me as I stumbled to my feet. In the fading orange glow of the open grave, I spotted Steele, perched over Bellamy's still form, one of the shovels gripped in her hands and raised overhead. She looked ready to whack him again should he move.

Quinto approached the grave, dusting his tweed jacket and rubbing his neck. He looked around nervously, his face ashen. "Ugh...thanks Steele. But how'd you know taking out Bellamy would stop his minions?"

Steele took a deep breath. Her arms shook, likely from the adrenaline shooting through her veins. "Well, what Daggers said sparked something inside me. These men... These *dead* men—" She shuddered. "They're not zombies or revenants or whatever you want to call them. They can't be, despite whatever Bellamy might've believed. If they were, we would've had to invent a whole new branch of magic to explain their presence. But they *could* be golems—of a sort, anyway. And while golems can be infused with commands and weighting structures to give them a semblance of intelligence, they can't think for themselves. They require active concentration to manipulate. So..."

"So you decided to end that concentration with a hearty shovel whack to Bellamy's head," I said.

Shay nodded. "That's right. Although the initial kick to his balls didn't hurt, either. Well...it did for him. But that was the point."

I took a deep breath and rubbed my own neck, which along with my tailbone would be inordinately sore in the morning. My heart, which beat in my chest as if I'd attempted to run a marathon, finally started to slow. Chester's soft cry hovered at the edge of my hearing, and the encroaching mist, which earlier felt cold, now felt delectable on my sweat-soaked brow.

"Guys," said Quinto in a soft voice. "Can we, uh...talk about what happened here? It might help me sleep better at night if we did."

"Save it for the psychiatrist's office," I said. "Right now we have an unenviable mess to clean up. But...something tells me we should take care of Bellamy first."

Believe it or not, nobody disagreed with me.

43

I leaned against a brick wall—the side of an apartment building in the process of being remodeled. The workers refinishing and cleaning it had long since gone home, likely with the light of day still at their backs, but now a new workforce swarmed around it. At least a dozen bluecoats, manning the torches and lanterns they'd set up, shooing errant spectators, guarding the back of the paddy wagon they'd brought with them from the precinct and keeping the horses that drew the thing calm. At least another dozen lent their intermittent presence to the mix as they shuffled back and forth between our current location and the Lowgate Cemetery three blocks to the north, bagging and tagging the bodies of the murdered vagrants—after wrapping them in tight coils of rope.

I took a sip of coffee to warm my gut. Someone had been smart enough to fill my thermos and bring it with them on route from the station. Of course, we'd need about a barrelful to sate the thirst of all the bluecoats who'd come to help, which was why I'd requisitioned the thermos for my own purposes.

Shay stood at my side, staring at the paddy wagon with her arms crossed. She looked cold.

I offered her the thermos. "Coffee?"

She gave me a distracted glance. "You know I don't drink that."

"It would warm you up," I said. "I know it's not tea, but once you get over the bitterness, it's not that bad. Heck, it even grows on you after a while."

"That's called caffeine addiction, Daggers."

I shrugged. "Whatever. So long as it's cheap, readily available, and legal, I'm not sure what the problem is. Besides, the only adverse side effects from it are lack of sleep and increased cognitive ability, and the first one's never been a problem for me."

Shay gave me a subdued wave of her hand. "It's ok. But thanks."

I heard a crunch of gravel and looked up to find the Captain, clad in a heavy liver-colored trench coat, approaching. As usual, he looked happy enough to dance a jig and break into song.

"Daggers, what the world is this carnival?" he said.

"Not a carnival," I said with a shake of my finger. "I like to think of it as a mobile command center, where I'm the ring master and all these bluecoats are my faithful employees."

"You mean your carnies?" said the Captain.

I tipped back the last of my coffee and returned the thermos's cap to its rightful throne. "Yeah, come to think of it, that was a carnival analogy, wasn't it?"

"You know, Daggers," barked the bulldog, "as much as I love large, unscheduled police expenditures that you call in without prior authorization thanks to your immeasurable ability to bluster people into submission, you still haven't explained what the hell is going on or why we're standing out in the cold in the middle of the night instead of warm in our beds, or in the worst case scenario, back at the precinct."

"Well, to be honest, Captain," I said, "I decided it wasn't a good idea to bring our captive into close proximity of the station's morgue."

The old jarhead narrowed his eyes. "Say what?"

"Our murderer," I said. "We caught him. He's a necromancer. Although he doesn't think of himself as such. He calls himself an 'agent of divine rebirth.' It's...beyond creepy."

The Captain shifted his granite-like gaze to Steele. "Did he get knocked in the head?"

"Possibly, sir," said Steele. "It got hairy at times. But he's not pulling your leg."

"No," I said. "Though that did happen to me. Literally. A zombie did it. Bruised my tailbone." I pointed for emphasis.

"I'm telling you, that word isn't accurate," said Shay. "Husk or golem would be more appropriate."

The Captain blinked and shook his head. "I think you two had better back up. Preferably to a point in the story that doesn't include any shambling, mindless brain eaters."

I lifted a finger. "Actually, they don't eat brains—"

The Captain glared at me and ground his teeth.

"—but I understand what you're getting at," I finished. "The point is, we captured the man behind the homeless men's murders. A pastor by the name of Julian Bellamy. And, unfortunately, the situation was far worse than we realized. It appears he murdered at least eight transients, including the two we found over the past thirty-six hours."

"So the man's a serial killer?" asked the Captain.

"No, sir," said Steele. "Apparently most of the murders—and subsequent resurrections, if you can call them that—were for practice purposes. With the exception of the last couple. He had other plans for them."

"I'm not feeling any more enlightened than I was thirty seconds ago, detectives," said the Captain.

"Then bear with me as I give you a little backstory," I said. "Once upon a time, our murderer, Julian Bellamy, was married to a woman by the name of Tabitha. She shared the same ideals as him, including her belief in their shared religion, that of the Divine Rebirth. It's a complicated thing focused on reincarnation of souls and trees and whatnot. Don't ask. But apparently a couple of Tabitha's relatives died, one after another in close succession, and her faith weakened. What was the point of reincarnation if someone you cared for, or you yourself, came back as a tree or a sea snail? Did you retain any of the memories that made you the person you were? Or were those memories, those experiences, gone forever?

"These were the sorts of questions that eventually made her lose her faith in the Divine Rebirth entirely. She divorced Julian and promptly joined a new congregation, that of the Holy Oblivion, a religion that espouses the concepts of fatality and nothingness after death. There she met a deacon by the name of Cornelius Vo, whom she married.

"But her ex-husband Julian wouldn't leave her alone. He followed her, harassing her at every opportunity—although he doesn't see it that way. He was trying to convert her back to his religion, and in the process, he hoped to win back her love. But his efforts didn't succeed. If anything, they deepened Tabitha's depression, as did Vo's own fierce rebuttals of Julian's creed. She no longer knew what faith to believe in. So she decided to test the true path of the soul after death for herself. Following a violent argument between Bellamy and Vo, Tabitha killed herself by jumping out a window at the Church of the Holy Oblivion."

"At first," said Steele, "we thought Tabitha had been murdered, but that doesn't appear to be the case. Elmswood investigated her death a year ago and ruled it a suicide, and after revisiting what we've learned since, we haven't found anything to contradict that. And Bellamy is adamant she committed suicide, for what it's worth. Once he broke, he seemed perfectly willing to tell us the truth about everything. I don't know why he'd lie about that."

"You already interrogated him?" asked the Captain.

I nodded.

"And where is he?" asked the bulldog.

"In the paddy wagon," said Steele. "Don't worry. He's bound and gagged. And he needs to be within a reasonable distance from his, err, *victims* should we say to be able to manipulate them. At least...we think so."

"Very well," said the Captain. "Now can we pick up the pace? Why did this man murder all those hobos?"

"I'm getting to that," I said. "After Tabitha's death, Julian couldn't stop thinking about her religious quandary, but he remained as pious as ever. More so, in fact. See, he knew the Divine Rebirth was the one, true religion to be trusted in, mostly because of his unique *talent*. He'd never mentioned it to Tabitha, or even put much effort into it, but he'd seen the *divine rebirth* with his own eyes. Organisms—bugs, mostly—had come back into life in his presence—infused with new souls, or perhaps their original ones. He considered himself a conduit for his religion. He learned and experimented, first on rodents and small animals before moving on to people. So when Steele says his murders of the transients was practice, it was. Practice for the eventual resurrection of his wife—who he couldn't wait to convince of the veracity of his religion."

The Captain passed his hand through his thinning hair. "This is crazy. How did Bellamy not recognize his abilities for the black magic they are?"

"He's pretty far gone in his delusions," said Steele. "Not only did he plan to resurrect his wife's year old corpse, but he thought she'd be fine. And I don't just mean that she'd remember him and forgive him and reconvert to his religion. He thought she'd be, you know...in one piece."

"As in not a rotten mass of bones and hair," I added.

"Thanks for the visual imagery, Daggers." The Captain eyed Steele. "And as our resident expert on all things magical, do you put your stamp of approval on this?"

Shay nodded. "Yes, sir. Bellamy admitted to as much, and necromancy is the only theory that explains the quirks regarding the scenario under which we found the dead homeless man this morning, not to mention how the body of our first victim escaped the morgue and made it to Cornelius Vo's office—who, by the way, Bellamy also admitted to murdering, through Lanky. He blamed Tabitha's death in large part on him and his fatalistic religion."

"Wait a second," said the Captain. *"We lost a body from the morgue?"*

Steele eyed me sideways. "Daggers, didn't you tell the Captain?"

"Uh...I was going to," I said. "As soon as I figured out who'd stolen it. Turns out nobody did, unless you consider Bellamy dropping by and forcing it to walk out under its own power a theft. So...case closed."

The old bulldog's jaw clenched, and I could tell he wanted to chew me out, but at the same time we'd just solved a murder that had become far more complicated and disturbed than anyone could've ever predicted. Instead, he settled for a snort.

"Alright," he said. "Good work, detectives. I'll send out runners to alert the bigwigs about this one. We'll get some serious magical backup to deal with Bellamy. In the mean time, I suggest you head home. It's late, and you both deserve some sleep...assuming you're capable of getting any after this fiasco."

The Captain headed in the direction of the police wagon, and I turned to face Steele. She looked back at me with soulful eyes, her hands stuffed in her pockets for warmth, and I got the distinct impression she was waiting for me to say something, but what? The day had unfolded like a rollercoaster, with surges and dips, twists and turns. My body ached from the encounter with the undead, and my brain felt like jelly, drained by the day's mystery and Shay's outbursts and my far too early wakeup call. I wanted to please her. I wanted to say the right thing. So why couldn't she give me a clue, rather than piercing me with those beautiful, azure doe eyes of hers?

I cleared my throat. "So...hell of a day, huh?"

Shay opened her mouth to respond, then paused before closing it with a slowly exhaled breath. "Um...yeah. See you tomorrow, Daggers."

She turned and walked away, and all I could do was stare.

That wasn't how the day was supposed to end, without so much as a 'Would you mind walking me home, Daggers?' or a 'Goodnight, Daggers' or even a less welcome but still optimistic 'Why don't we talk, Daggers?' It was supposed to end with a laugh or a hug or a drink shared over a small table at a café. I'd even settle for an awkward high-five, but this? A simple 'See you tomorrow?' That was nothing. Purgatory. Indecision at the mouth of a stairwell that only went down.

But it didn't *have* to end that way. I possessed free will, and conversations could be initiated by either member of a pair. All I needed was courage and an awareness of self.

I darted after her, past the mass of bluecoats and around the corner where I'd seen her vanish. There I spotted her, twenty paces ahead of me and disappearing into the fog.

"Shay! Wait!" I called.

She paused and turned, and I closed the gap between us.

"Yes?" she said.

I took a breath to still my nerves. "I'm sorry."

44

Shay's eyes narrowed.

"Yes, you heard that right," I said. "I'm sorry. For being such an asshole."

"Did Quinto put you up to this?" asked Shay.

"*What?* No," I said, my heart racing. "Look, I'm trying to open up to you here. I'm sorry for being such a curmudgeon sometimes, but it's ingrained in me. It's like a splinter that's stuck underneath the surface of my skin and won't come out. Sometimes it pokes through and it hurts and it makes me angry and then my flesh swallows it back up again. Yesterday was one of those days where the splinter jabs me, as was much of today. When I saw you and Agent Blue, a dark part of me came out, and it's a part that's hard to control. So I'm sorry. I shouldn't have treated him the way I did. It was wrong and rude and childish, but I just...I don't know. I felt threatened. I lashed out."

Shay tilted her head, her brow slightly furrowed. "But Daggers, why would you feel threatened by him?"

"What do you mean, why?" I asked. "Because he's smart and charming and has commendations plastered across the walls of his office. Because he wears a snappy uniform and his smile could blind birds and cause them to fly into windowpanes. Because he's an elf and you're a half-elf."

"I'm also half human."

"I know that," I said. "Look, it's not rational. I felt threatened because...because I like you, ok? I *like you.* And I don't want to lose you. I mean, lose what we have. You know."

Shay tucked a strand of loose hair behind her ear and glanced at the ground furtively. "Daggers, I... Look, I like you, too. I told you as much earlier today. But we're not even a couple."

"You think that makes it easier?" I passed a hand through my hair. "Let me tell you something. I come into work each morning—late, always, because its in my nature—and do you know what the first thing I see is? Your smiling face. That's the best part of my day. That's *my* sunrise."

Steele's face softened, and the corner of her lips curled up. "Daggers..."

"I'm not kidding. It is. And when I saw Blue coming on to you...well, I went a little crazy, ok? I saw things in my mind. Changes, and not good ones. I mean, you know me. I don't deal well with change. It's why I acted like such a horrible person when you started working with me this past summer. And it's no wonder. For me, change is my mom dying. It's my brother learning to hate me. It's my wife divorcing me. It's my son growing older and not knowing who I am. Never mind the change that brought you to the 5th Street Precinct is the best thing that's happened to me in the past three years. I saw another bad change and I lashed out. And I'm fully aware I did it in a way that pushes you away from me. I know it and I did it anyway. It's that damned splinter I talked about. I'm in a masochistic feedback loop, and I want to bash my head into a wall every time I do it!"

Shay looked at me, concern in her eyes, but clearly without any idea of how to respond.

I forced myself to calm down. "I think what I'm trying to say is, I'm not perfect. I know it. I'm a work in progress, and I have things that need fixing. But thanks to you, I'm figuring out what those things are, and slowly but surely, I'm patching myself up.

"You asked me earlier if I knew what it was you liked about me. I didn't at the time, but it wasn't that hard to figure out. You like the stuff in here." I jabbed at my heart. "Not the dark stuff, the nasty I'm trying to purge. You like my heart. That's what made you pause when I told you I'd gone to check on Allison this morning and brought her food. It's what made you smile when I told Drake and Kelly to skip town and never come back. Not because it was right in the legal sense—it wasn't—but because it was the right thing to do. The right thing for *them*.

"There's a lot of good in me, Shay, and I want to let it out. For me. For you. For my son and Quinto and Rodgers and everyone in my life. I want to beat back the demons, and I know I can. I just need a little patience."

I'm not sure if I expected Shay to cry or to kiss me or to walk away, but she did none of those things. She merely stood there, looking at me, considering what I'd said. Seconds stretched into what seemed to me an interminable silence.

"For what it's worth," I said. "I'm also sorry I spoke of that ragtime musician of yours with such disdain."

Shay smiled a bit. "Apology accepted. So, what do you propose? As far as dealing with the...dark things, I guess, inside you."

"Way to serve me a slow pitch to start." I shrugged. "I don't know. I've always bottled everything up. Kept the hurt deep down inside and prayed for it not to spray out following an emotional gut punch, but I don't think that's worked out so well. I guess I need to...confront everything. Be honest. Open. Acknowledge when I have a problem, and when I need help. Take things one day at a time and work on bettering myself."

Shay's smile didn't disappear, but it didn't grow either. Eventually, she nodded. "Ok."

I lifted an eyebrow. "Ok?"

"Yeah. Not yes, or no. Just ok."

She lifted her hand and trailed her fingers along the length of my jaw to my chin, looking me in the eyes as she did so. My stomach fluttered, and she pulled her hand back.

"Goodnight, Jake." She turned and began to walk into the night.

I stood transfixed and blinked. "Wait...do you want me to walk you home?"

"Not tonight," she called over her shoulder.

Though an improvement over where we'd left things at the end of the Captain's recap, this still wasn't how I'd hoped the night would end.

"But...where does that leave us?" I asked. "You know. In our relationship."

Shay turned her head and smiled at me—a warm, genuine smile, but one that held something back. "We'll just have to take it one day at a time. But it's a start. We'll see how it goes."

It wasn't exactly a ringing endorsement of our possible future together, but I could live with it. For now.

ABOUT THE AUTHOR

Alex P. Berg is a mystery, fantasy, and science fiction author, a scientist, and a heavy metal aficionado. Connect with him at www.alexpberg.com. If you'd like to be notified when new books are released, please sign up for his mailing list on his website. You will only be contacted when new books come out, your address will never be shared, and you can unsubscribe at any time.

Word of mouth is critical to author success. If you enjoyed this novel, please consider leaving a positive review on Amazon. Even if it's only a line or two, it would be a *huge* help. Thanks!